BEAUTIFUL TORMENTS

Beautiful Torments: A Novel

Copyright © 2025 D.T. Pierce

All rights reserved.

No part of this publication may be reproduced in a retrieval system, or transmitted in any form or by any means—electronic, mechanical, photocopying, recording, or otherwise—without the prior written permission of the publisher.

While precaution has been taken in the preparation of this book, the publisher and author assume no responsibility for errors or omissions, or for damages resulting from the use of the information contained herein.

This book is set in the typeface *Athelas* designed by Veronika Burian and Jose Scaglione.

Paperback ISBN: 978-1-955546-95-9

Hardcover ISBN: 978-1-967262-00-7

A Publication of *Phyxius Books* | Warsaw
www.dtpierce.com

To reach the author, contact: dtpierce.books@gmail.com

| 1 25 25 20 16 02 |

Published in the United States of America

BEAUTIFUL TORMENTS

D.T. PIERCE

PHYXIUS
BOOKS

To my wife, who periodically reminded me of my passion to write and sternly encouraged a boldness to brave publishing my humble works. To my children, who have shown me the expanse that is life. May this work one day help you to be brave, bold, and pursue your passions.

CONTENTS

1. The Beast Without	1
2. The Hunt	9
3. Festering Wounds	19
4. A Shadow	33
5. Going Home	43
6. Manifestation	55
7. The Color of Evil	73
8. The New Kid	81
9. An Endless Echo	95
10. If Dreams Could Talk	105
11. A Faceless Name	117
12. The Hook	129
13. Thanatos	143
14. A Savior	153
15. Saints and Sinners	167
16. Bravery and Rebuke	175
17. A Winding Path	191
18. The Beast Within	207
19. The Chosen	217
20. In the Flesh	229
21. Strange Things	243
22. The Debrief	251
23. Lucius	263
24. Court	269
About the Author	279

I
THE BEAST WITHOUT

Jacoby

I'm living proof that there are worse things than death. Death, the sadistic weasel, dangles the promise of relief, mercy even, just beyond reach as I beg upon fallen knees.

Silent, I consider what haunts me, what attempts to possess me. Yellow eyes, demanding, insatiable, slowly devouring my soul with a devilish smile. There is no escape, no respite from the agony of losing myself to madness.

My torment has transformed into a sinister apparition, an unyielding spirit hell-bent on my destruction. The beast manifested, revealing itself to my eyes alone. Dream and reality becoming one. I no longer know what's real. I'm Alice, tumbling down a rabbit hole filled with nothing but nightmares.

Something is wrong with me. A once-secret fact others have come to realize. A disease, perhaps a demonic spirit, has worked its way into my essence and taken root. Mind and body under constant siege from something I don't understand.

Life as a high school student isn't easy, a difficulty that

becomes a thousand times worse when one's sanity comes into question. The question of sanity is the reason for my presence in this forsaken place. I have come to face my judge. To have a professional decide upon the status of my mind and determine the course of my future.

I peer at the man across from me—a smug psychiatrist sitting cross-legged, wearing an all-knowing smirk—while my own extremities tap rhythmically against whatever surface is within reach. My appearance mirrors what lies within, with disheveled hair and frantic, blood-shot eyes, hindering any defense plea, but I couldn't care less. Concern regarding the judgment of others ended long ago.

The open and antique-looking room is quiet, annoyingly so. Little has been said since I arrived, except an awkward introduction. I lose track of reality at some point, consumed by the quiet, unsure of how much time has passed.

It's a spacious room, and I'm thankful for that. Small spaces bother me, ever since the third encounter. I'm told the newfound fear is unexplainable, scientifically speaking, and I hate how my body, my mind, have responded. In terms of unexplainable events, however, this falls toward the bottom of the list.

I'm sitting uncomfortably on a charcoal-colored couch that's most likely comfortable, while the psychiatrist is confidently, if not arrogantly, stationed on a brown, leather tufted chair. Around the room, bookcases stand in glory, lining every wall, except where framed degrees and certifications hang in what feels like more arrogance.

An itch to finger through the titles tugs at my mind, quickly dissipating after some thought. *Probably a bunch of psychological bullshit.* I fail to shake my interest. There aren't many places left that hold such a voluminous expanse of hard-copy books. Even libraries have shifted toward hubs of shared computer banks, data pads, and conformist coffee shops rather than centers loaded with history, knowledge, and entertainment you can touch, feel, and smell.

Years ago, a bunch of assholes attributed at least a portion of deforestation to paper books, and deforestation was categorized as a primary contributor to climate change. Never mind the mega-factories or the death of electric vehicles—apparently the world is short on graduate degrees that explore how batteries fail to run in the cold, or that a installing rapid chargers across rural American was financially impossible—and the increased consumption of fossil fuels as a result. No, it was surely the production of paper books that brought us to the brink. Such an ignorant group-think exercise was the result of the ultra-rich arriving at a climate summit via their private planes and yachts to decide the fate of what I had come to love: a paper book in hand.

Stealing a look around the room, I admit a touch of envy for something I'd hoped to have for myself one day. As a closet nerd, a mahogany styled study would certainly satisfy the classier side of that hidden and treasured personality. The purpose of my presence sours the thought.

In all fairness, John—the psychiatrist—is probably a nice man and likely unworthy of the skeptical and harsh perception. Today is our first session, after all, and per the school's order, one of many to come. The man probably deserves a chance, but experience shapes a strong worldview, especially negative experiences. I have a lot of those. By effect, I'm sure, no matter how decent John's nature, the psychiatrist's analysis of what has become my torment will be the same as all the others: that I've lost my damn mind.

Everything is too formal, too serious, which only supports the belief I'm alone, that no one believes the story. My story. It's proof that everyone thinks I'm crazy. Oddly enough, the formality of the process of coming here makes the horror of my life seem less truthful, less important. Perhaps it's all by design.

The contrast is more the situation than the atmosphere. It's a realization of the dichotomy between what I've seen and what others have not.

An old grandfather clock stands in the corner to my left. I haven't seen one of those since I was a small child. I marvel at its sophistication. The slow, methodical annunciation of seconds passing away is the only indication time hasn't stopped. Within both rage and madness, I find the tick-tock of the clock's hands soothing, reassuring somehow that life will continue, no matter what's happened or is yet to take place.

"What have people told you...regarding your *events*?" the pen wielding mind-reader asks.

The question comes as I ponder the inner workings of the clock. The gentle voice pulls me from a small and rare peace. Unfortunate. It's the happiest I've been in quite a while.

I say nothing in return, hesitant to answer, considering the soul of the man before me. Anger and distress build. I don't know why. John has been patient.

This is his first question. *It's the man's job to ask questions.*

"Jacoby, I can't help you if you don't talk to me."

My anger dissipates, replaced with exhaustion. There isn't hope for me. Not from my family, my friends, or even John. What can I do when speaking the truth is to provide the shovel for my own grave?

"Why don't you tell me, John," I say, defeated. "I'm sure you've already come to a conclusion."

The world sways as my head falls into open, sweaty palms. A sob halts at the back of my throat, and I release it through a pained breath. *I'm so tired.*

"I've interviewed those familiar with your case and looked over what documents have been submitted to my office, but I want you to know that you have a clean slate."

A pause. The room is silent once more.

"Look at me, Jacoby," he says with warmth. It's the first

time I've felt compassion from anyone since this nightmare began. "I'm not biased," he says as I look up, "as my only concern is for you. I'm open minded, so please, be open with me."

I laugh in silence as tears fall from the corners of swollen eyes. John watches without reaction, but I feel his concern. It isn't pity but an innate desire to help. I dare to allow a small light of hope to return.

I lock eyes with John, venturing toward the sharp, double-edge sword of trust. A most dangerous place. The weight of my burden ebbing in and out like a struggling tide, at war with hope and the prospect of peace.

I take my time, wrestling down another sob. "Even my family thinks I'm crazy." I recall their reactions, their faces, as I explained what was happening. One of those negative experiences. "That's why I'm here. If I tell you the truth, then you'll see why. You'll agree with everyone else."

"Crazy people don't know they're crazy…and you seem to be aware of your situation. I'm not saying we will agree as to what is exactly happening to you, but I don't believe you're *crazy*."

I run sweaty hands through oily hair and wipe the remnants of salty tears from my face. Funny thing about running into someone who genuinely cares, after so much judgment and callousness, it's hard to process. I want to scream, to sob uncontrollably into a pillow, but I don't have the energy. I feel dramatic, overreacting to the hand I've been dealt. Maybe I am. I deserve to be, but I hate it. No one can understand what I've been through. I lost my mother, then that demon of a beast decided to haunt me.

I imagine anyone would break under such torments.

Instead of exploding into an outburst, I take a deep breath and consider my life. It's not like things can get worse. Perhaps the psychiatrist can help.

"So, what do you think?" I finally ask.

John's head tilts to the right, perhaps surprised by the question. "You want an honest answer?"

I nod. *Everyone else has been eager to explain what's happening to me.*

"I believe your past has caught up to you."

You're not wrong. "How?" I ask after mulling over the statement. *John doesn't know the whole truth, at least not yet.*

John removes his glasses with practiced hands and sets them gently atop the table to the right, simultaneously dropping a large pen into a stylish, black notebook spread across thin legs. It seems dramatic, an attempt to show concern. My faith in John's purity wavers.

John closes the notebook after a deep breath and uncrosses his legs, closing the gap between us by settling at the end of his chair. "Past events, if not dealt with properly, will eventually work their way to the surface."

I scoff. *What a crock of shit.* "So, you think I'm lashing out or conjuring something to express compressed memories? That what's happening to me is triggered by something in my past? Typical. I've seen enough movies to know this is the go-to diagnosis for all things mental."

The man across from me simply stares, unblinking and unflinching at what was meant to be an insult, unwavering in the confidence of his response to my question.

"It's possible," John responds in an even tone, leaning back into the chair, "believe it or not, but I won't be able to decide until we talk more. Most movie writers spend a great deal of time with psychiatrists to accurately portray the profession." A surprising chuckle escapes through a small mouth. "But they do muck up a lot. Triggers are a real thing, however, and I assure you, they can be overcome."

"What's happening to me is crazy. This whole damn thing is insane," I say, waving my arms about. "I'm going to an institution, or something worse. You'd be crazy not to send me away...

if I tell you everything." I pause to catch my breath. "Sorry for swearing."

"No need to apologize. For the swearing. It seems an appropriate use for what's happening to you," he says with a wink. "As for the other thing. I'm not going to send you away. I have more than enough means, plenty of resources, to help you here and now." When I don't respond, John provides a reassuring smile and says, "How about you tell me what you're comfortable with? After time, when trust between us grows, then you can tell me more."

There's nothing comfortable about any of this. "Fine. Where'd you like me to start?"

"There's no better place than the beginning."

The beginning. "That would be a long time ago."

2
THE HUNT

Susan

The hard, wooden chair is unstable, wobbling at the slightest shift in weight. It smells of stale beer and despair. The building housing the chair is of similar condition, as well as its drunken patrons who slur their way through a fantastical story of their youth while attempting to forget their loneliness by persuading a fellow alcoholic to share in their misery. Even if it's just for the night.

None of it bothers me. Not the rotten smell seeping from damaged wood, not the damp feel of heavy air, or even the occasional ruckus of distraught men whose advances and underwhelming pickup lines are dismissed repeatedly and without mercy.

I have the corner of the bar to myself, and a mildly attractive bartender dedicated to keeping my glass full, who, so far, has intelligently opted to acknowledge my *fuck off* look and focus on pouring instead of conversing.

It's the perfect watering-hole.

I know nothing of the bar itself, failing to recall something as simple as its name. *The Drunken Parrot,* I think after downing my third glass of cheap whiskey. *That would explain all the weird bird pictures.*

I return to darker thoughts, throwing a hand in the air when in need of a refill.

"Well, aren't you just the prettiest thing I've seen this side of New York."

Damn. I noticed the man's zig-zag approach from the billiard bay, hoping his destination lay anywhere but with me. I should have known better.

"I just want to drink in peace," I say, eyes glued to my replenished glass.

"Come on, darling," he slurs out. "No one as pretty as you should drink alone."

"Thank you for the offer, but not tonight. Go back to your friends," I reply, refusing to look up.

The intruder stumbles forward, kicking the chair beside me. He laughs. I smell alcohol and cigarettes as he says, "We can be very good friends."

Fine. I tried. Lord knows I always try. I turn slightly and place an elbow against the sticky bar-top, resting my head against an open palm. My mind works quickly, analyzing the man's face, body, and posture. Something within works to support, filling in gaps, giving knowledge to things impossible to see. I grin when everything falls into place. The intruder misinterprets the grin. A mistake I'll correct shortly.

He wears a smirk of his own. One of false and drunken confidence that nearly elicits an audible laugh. "Still not interested," I respond with a bored and absent-minded tone.

"Oh, darling, you will be. I've got everything you need right here," he says, attempting to grab at his crotch but missing.

I give him the satisfaction of looking towards his groin. "I assure you, you don't."

He steps closer, leaning toward me, inches away now, too drunk to register my response. "What's your name, darling?"

I really hate being called darling. "Susan."

"Susan," he repeats, turning back toward the billiard bay. "Susan," he says louder. A few men chuckle and point.

I force down a laugh. "Not tonight. Don't be an asshole. I said no. Move on."

He manages to sway without toppling.

"I said get lost." Anyone within ten feet hears the command. I don't want there to be any surprises with what happens next.

He straightens, as straight as he can manage. *That one registered.* A confused look spreads across his less than memorable face like a slow tidal wave. Thick and wild eyebrows join as they furrow. "What did you say—"

"Judging by the size of your gut," I interrupt, "I'd say you're here drinking alone, what, four nights a week?" I smile as confusion surrenders to anger. "Bumming cigarettes and drinks when you can because you're a worthless shithead with nothing to your name."

I'm proud of myself for having given the man a chance to move on unscathed. Not everyone receives that mercy. There's something unnatural in my ability to read people. It comes on like a feeling, a distant memory of my own life. Combined with my temper, and the drinking, some would say I'm unpleasant at times. Most people, most times, actually.

With arms crossed, his throat burgeons as if about to say something but can't get the words quite right. I'm going to push him beyond what's necessary, but it'll satisfy my mood, so I don't care when both ears darken, and his small, dirty mouth tightens in anger.

"You also shave once a month, give yourself an uneven haircut every three months and have never had a serious relationship other than with an ancient blowup doll you tuck away in a dark corner." I look quickly at his teeth through a gaping mouth and notice discoloration on several fingers. "And you smoke two packs a day. All very charming characteristics to most women, I'm sure, but you'd best move along before I grow too bored of this riveting conversation."

I survey the bar, knowing where this ends. Two or three won't be a problem, but it will get interesting if this guy has a lot of friends.

No one seems to be coming to his aid anytime soon. In fact, those he ventured from are enjoying their game of pool in his absence, ignoring his latest voyage.

He stumbles forward, filthy hands clenched into white-knuckled fists. I cluck my tongue, wave a stern finger and slowly shake my head side-to-side. A confident and relaxed hand nonchalantly pats the side of my leather jacket. "Another step and I'll introduce you to Matilda."

Amused, he lets out an awful cackle. "Missy is packing some pepper spray, is she? Someone needs to teach you how to show some respect...and how to talk to a man. You prissy little bitch."

Slurring dumb ass. The bartender shuffles towards us. Not fast enough. For my suitor's sake.

Obviously drunk, it's several seconds before he manages a lunge, revealing the sluggish attack well in advance. The corner of my mouth twitches as adrenaline releases and courses through enlarged veins. Before he closes the distance, I pull back my jacket, remove the holstered gun at my hip, and use the butt of my pistol to smack the overzealous patron across the face. He goes stumbling, spewing saliva and blood as he collides with the bar and falls to the ground in the most ungraceful manner possible.

I look down at the ruined man, saying, "I warned you."

Alive but unconscious. *Thank God.* A murder charge would dampen my mood, and mission. Something tells me simple assault in self-defense will go unreported in an establishment like this.

I secure the weapon and quickly drop two, hundred-dollar bills on the counter. "Sorry," I call out to the bartender, who stands stunned at the violent outburst. A common reaction due to my outward appearance and reserved personality.

I turn and calmly exit out through the bar's western door, smiling to myself as I hear several patrons applauding the event's outcome. *Unreported it is.*

I'm a few steps into the small parking lot when I decide to turn and look at the half-worn and storm-battered neon sign sprawled grotesquely across a plethora of damaged shingles. Only a few bulbs are intact, but it's enough to convey the bar's name.

Covey's Hideout. Not even close to *The Drunken Parrot.* I fail to connect the reason for all the bird pictures.

I find my car and smile as the door opens. I bought the vehicle from a junkyard during high school and spent the better part of three years, and every dime I could earn—legally and illegally—piecing her back together. There aren't many of its kind on the road. Most were salvaged during the electric era push.

The '67 Mustang roars to life at the turn of the key, and I burn a good deal of rubber taking off towards a motel room that's eerily akin to the bar's innards.

I awake to an irritating and persistent buzzing.

I locate the source through blurry eyes. Damn thing has been going for nearly fifteen minutes. My head is pounding, and frustrations mount as I fail to reach the alarm clock. Finally, I find the cord and yank it from the socket, silencing the fuel for what's burning behind my eyes, the product of a half empty bottle of bourbon on the opposite nightstand.

After several moans and comforting stretches, I rise from bed in pursuit of a shower, first finding a bottle of aspirin. I plop the pills into a dry mouth and use the steaming shower water to wash them down. My body soaks in the heat as the water falls delightfully against raised skin, throwing off a shadowy haze as persistent and annoying as gum stuck to one's shoe.

"Coffee," I mumble, stumbling toward a small table along the far wall. The ancient coffee pot, and the less than gourmet liquid spilling forth, is the room's only amenity.

Nearly half the pot, even though scalding hot, is devoured within minutes. I dress into a comfortable suit and pull my midnight black hair into a tight ponytail. A quick attempt to make myself as presentable as possible. It's all I can manage until the aspirin kicks in.

I step toward the door before returning to the mirror for another look.

I inhale sharply, pondering the day's task while appraising my appearance. *They could be the ones to connect the dots.* A final nod, which is more acceptance than praise, another deep breath, then I'm out the door and moving south towards Canaseraga—a small town on the western side of New York.

It's a pleasant drive. My headache subsides as the sun rises and the coffee recedes. The landscape is one of rolling hills and winding roads. I avoid music so my mind can wander. I work through the pieces of this infuriating puzzle. Moving, prioritizing, reprioritizing, and reliving clues and information. The overall picture remains incomplete, but the instinct that lives within hums, encouraging, reassuring my path is true.

Several hours later, I pull up to an older ranch home in the middle of a quiet suburb. It's a small grouping of homes nestled within a span of green, rolling hills lush with never-ending forests. Trees line the paved road to either side, and the orange hue of the sun's rays paint a setting suited for magazines. There is beauty, but also an odd sense of claustrophobia as I peer down the road seemingly encircled by nature.

I remove a black, leather-bound notebook from the glove compartment and flip through several pages, each of which is full of ink but neatly organized. I find the desired page and steal a second glance toward the address on a dirty and slanted mailbox. It would appear a snowplow had its way at some point. I quickly compare the numbers against the notes, verifying I've arrived at the right house.

I can't help but detach the photos clipped to the page. I've seen them a hundred times, poured through each in detail, lost several meals when I grasped the evil within. I lift them toward the light and observe the pile of bones. The coroner's notes are found on the back. Notes I disagree with.

The agency's consensus is the flesh was consumed by animals, leaving very little but nails, tendons, and bone. Understandable since the body was discovered deep within an uninhabitable wood. However, the more I looked, the more I allowed the foreign voice to analyze, the more I disagreed.

The girl had been missing for only a few days. Not enough time for decomposition. Not enough time for the girl's body to be torn to the bone by scavengers. The voice within pushed without respite until the only plausible conclusion was settled upon.

The murderer is a cannibal. A practiced, highly intelligent cannibal. Pieces of flesh and shredded clothing were found scattered around the body, and analysis concluded puncture marks matched that of a wolf's bite. The only set of footprints found were the victim's own, and those of different types of animals. No signs of struggle or additional DNA were found. The coroner had no reason to declare the official cause of death as anything other than an accident.

The more I reflect, the more I see an art, a reverence to the act. A minor abrasion upon the femur and a chip in the mandible are all that indicate a tool was utilized to remove flesh from bone. That, and the fact I identified dozens of similar deaths over the past fifty years, across dozens of states, have set me down this isolated path.

Satisfied, I hop out of the car and quickly approach the front door, turning my collar to the chilly autumn air. I pass through a worn, decaying, white fence and unkempt flower garden. The house itself is in worse shape. Splintered wood hangs like icicles from the porch. Leaves engulf both yard and roof, dirt and grime coat what siding remains, and the windows reveal nothing but darkness.

I second guess the accuracy of my information. No one should be living here. Not in these conditions. I'm surprised the city hasn't taken possession. It's as if death passed over the home and a spirit of despair has taken up residence, which isn't too far from the truth as I think about it.

These poor parents. I can't imagine.

After shrugging off the dread and misery, suppressing an urge to flee this darkness, I ring the doorbell and wait.

There's a creak as the door opens slightly. A tousled woman peers through, revealing a small, withered face. "Yes?" she asks with a mix of anger and worry.

Here we go. Don't screw this up. "Hi. My name is Susan, and I'm an investigative journalist. I'd like to ask you a few questions about your daught—"

The door slams without warning. I hear the chain lock engage, then the deadbolt. *Shit.* I draw closer to the door and think for a moment. *Come on. Give me the words.* "Mrs. Baker, please, I believe I can help your family. I only need a few moments of your time."

"Get off our property now, or I'll call the cops, and have you forcefully removed," a gruff voice threatens from the other side of the door. *The husband. A father once.*

Dammit. "Mr. Baker, please, just a few minutes. I believe I can help get you answers about your daughter."

"Why do you people keep showing up here? She's gone. For three years. Leave us in peace," says the wife. The mother.

"I think I've found a clue. If I could only have a few minutes."

"Get the hell off our property," demands the husband. "I'm calling the cops now."

The threat of cops showing up is enough to push me from the home and into the Mustang. Being hauled into custody would end this little sabbatical of mine. The risk is too great. Too much depends upon connecting the dots. No one else is trying to.

I once again pull out the black book and find the page dedicated to Mr. and Mrs. Baker. I close my eyes, then punch the steering wheel, repeatedly. *This is too much. Why? Why is it this hard?* "Why is this so hard?" I ask whatever this thing inside me is—the thing that drove me here. "If this is my path, then could you make it a little easier? Please?"

A sense of calm washes over me. Not enough to take away the pain, but enough to regain my composure. I fight back tears and swallow my anger, opening the book. I pass several pages with line strikes, others with notes. I line strike Mr. and Mrs. Baker's page and place it back into the glove compartment. I already know where I'm headed next.

Sadly, there's always more.

3
FESTERING WOUNDS

JACOBY

I grab a beer from the fridge and head back out into the brisk night. I exit through the back of the house and land upon an oversized porch, which hosts a hot tub, multiple grills encased in stone, a massive brick fireplace, a sea of patio furniture, and a pool just beyond.

I pause and marvel, with a sliver of envy, at a space built to entertain. *Nice to have money.*

There's laughter off to the left. A girl's. I glance toward a rustling of leaves, but the darkness is thick, hiding the actions of my acquaintances within. That side of the house is for lovers. I shake my head and keep a straight line, heading for a beacon of light near the back of the property.

"Jacoby!" Mark hollers.

Jeff whistles, dramatically peering through the darkness. "Do I see a beer? You're finally manning up?" Jeff surveys those enjoying the warmth, anticipating a ruckus of laughter.

No one is laughing. It's not my first alcoholic drink, but I've strayed from drinking in large groups. You never know who will say what.

Prick. I salute the beer. "Refreshment...after time with your mom."

Snickers cut through the air like a knife as Jeff scoffs and leans back into his chair, short of a witty reply.

"Seriously," pries Mark, "why don't you drink?"

"I'd be suspended from the team if caught, and my chance at a baseball scholarship would disappear. It isn't worth it." *We don't have the money for me to mess up.* I'm hoping the beer will numb the dark thoughts. Today is a day of ghosts.

"Pussy," chides Jeff.

"Hey!" yells Alexis from his side, slapping his arm. "You know I hate that word."

I eye the two of them, clueless at their young union. *Jeff Slater of all people.* I've always liked Alexis. We were closer as kids, but high school can be rough on childhood friendships, especially when someone is carrying their weight in baggage.

Jeff shrugs and returns to his beer. Alexis stares daggers before giving up, crossing her arms and setting her gaze stubbornly toward the dancing flames.

"Anyway," interjects Mark, "Erika here gave us her scary story while you were in the house, so that means you're up."

"Still sharing ghost stories?" I ask.

There's a pull at the corner of my mouth. I've always been the tag-along friend, tolerated, but never the most popular—the landscape in a portrait painting. It doesn't bother me. I enjoy the position as it fits nicely within my introverted personality. I do welcome, on rare occasions, an opportunity to own the spotlight. Probably why I love baseball so much. A team effort won through periodic individual performances.

"It's Halloween. Show some spirit," encourages Erika.

"Yours any good?" My tight smirk slowly morphs into a wide smile as I gaze across the fire. *Stop smiling like an idiot.*

She laughs, a beautiful laugh, and shakes her head side-to-side. "It really wasn't. Won't take much to top it." She leans over long, crossed legs and returns the smile.

"Alright," I concede. *Can't say no now.*

Settled, I draw on the beer, a little too much, and struggle through a rough cough. *Smooth.* Thankfully the others, especially Jeff, don't notice.

My insides churn in turmoil as I search for a story. There isn't much to choose from. My life is normal, for the most part. Then, it hits me like a ton of bricks. It's an old story, one from childhood, but it's the only weird, scary experience in my life.

"I used to mow for my grandma and great grandma," I begin, "who both lived down the street from my parents. Every Saturday morning I'd hop on the mower and drive it a half mile down the road to where they lived."

"Already bored."

"Don't be an ass, Jeff. Let him speak," chastises Erika.

Allowing Erika to fight my battles, I return to the story. "So, one day, when I was about twelve years old, as I was riding down to grandma's house, I see a black dog sitting in the middle of the road. It was maybe fifty yards away, looking at me like I was its only concern in the world."

My eyes roam upward as I recall something about that day. A small detail I've never shared. "I remember it had white fur running from stomach to chin." I say, running a hand along the path of the fur.

I'm distracted by someone whispering and find Jeff leaning toward Alexis, who keeps waving him off in annoyance. A minor justice.

Prick. "I looked down at something," I continue, "and when I looked up, the dog was gone. I didn't think anything of it, but as the day went on, the dog kept appearing in the middle of the road and then disappearing. Always in the same spot. The only change was that it looked at me, no matter where I was.

"Now, before you laugh, I'm not crazy. The corn stalks were high, and I told myself that I simply kept missing when it ran off. What was odd, however, is that the appearing and disappearing act continued for hours."

I take a deep breath and another sip of beer, which is starting to warm, so I down what's left and flip the bottle aside. Several around the fire lean into the story, curious of its trajectory.

This is my scary and bizarre story, so bizarre I've often wondered if it even happened, or if I had manipulated the details to make it scarier than what truly transpired.

"I told my parents and sister about what happened because it weirded me out, but a few days later I forgot all about it. A few months passed and one Saturday morning, as I was cleaning out my parents' van with my sister, something odd happened. I remember that day like it was yesterday," I say.

I find each set of eyes, satisfied I hold everyone's attention, even Jeff's. I continue to withhold the rest of the story, inwardly smiling at the power I momentarily possess.

"Jacoby?" asks Alexis.

Now. "I stepped out of the van and went rigid. My blood turned to ice. My mind raced as I stood like a statue in the driveway. I wanted nothing more than to run, to hide, but I couldn't move. I couldn't even breathe. It was a paralyzing fear.

"There, standing in front of me, was the same black dog. It looked harmless and innocent enough, but something was off. It felt like I was somewhere I wasn't meant to be. That I had somehow landed in an alternate universe. I managed to gather my senses and yelled at my sister to get inside the house."

I pause to catch my breath. A coyote howls in the distance. *Good timing.*

"And then what?" asks Erika, eager for more.

The howl puts everyone on edge. A perfect backdrop to the upcoming climax.

"I ran into the house with my sister, but the weirdest part was yet to come. My mom was home," I feel a twinge at my side as I see her face, "and she looked through the front door with us. She wanted to say this was nonsense, but she felt it too.

"After a few minutes of silence, a van turned into our driveway and a man in a brown uniform stepped out of the vehicle. He motioned for me to come out of the house, neglecting the dog in our driveway, who hadn't moved. I remember wondering if he could even see it."

The air stills, silent, aside from crackling of wood as the fire burns, its light casting odd and animated shadows against wet grass. I relive the rest of the story with eyes shut, playing them out in my mind before putting words to the memories.

"I have no idea why I went outside, or why it wasn't my mom who left the house, but I did. It was me that went. The dog took a few steps forward as I left the house, but it quickly settled, stoically following my path toward the man in uniform."

An odd feeling washes over me as the story deepens. I feel encased, and even though it's an eerie feeling, there is something *right* with the timing of this tale. This event wasn't life-altering, so I've given it little thought throughout the years, but there is a strange sensation whenever I do recall the story.

"Is this your dog?', the man in brown asked. I told him no. He never gave a name, but eventually said he was with animal control and was responding to a report of a dog being hit and injured...like the one in our driveway.

"The man in uniform pointed towards the dog, but his eyes stayed on me. It was the first time he acknowledged the animal. I followed the man's outstretched hand to the dog, but I saw nothing wrong with the beast. It hadn't moved much, but there was no limp, no visual sign of injury.

"The man beckoned me closer, and I obliged. I still don't know why. He handed me a leather chain and told me to put it on the dog's collar. He said nothing else as I stared at him. He somehow knew I couldn't refuse, that I couldn't argue. I have no explanation for why I didn't...I just did as he said, and neither my mom nor sister opposed. They were still in the house.

"I went to put the chain on this mysterious dog with shaky hands, but when I was within inches of its neck...the dog pounced!" I yell, jumping from my chair in exaggeration.

Everyone around the fire startles. Some bring hands to their chests while others spill beer and other fruity, alcoholic drinks on colorful sweatshirts and coats. There's a lot of swearing.

I return to my seat, attempting to hide my amusement as the others moan and curse, most of whom smack pooling liquid from expensive clothing. I give everyone a moment to fall back into silence as I listen to the crackling of the fire. That isn't the end. Not yet.

"I fell back onto my ass," I continue, "hitting my head hard. Feeling the weight of two paws upon my chest, I found two pitch-black eyes staring back at me. There were no snarls, just that same emotionless face. It looked like a wax figure, but I could hear the breathing. No, I could feel it. It wasn't labored, but they were deep breaths, almost hypnotic in a treacherous way. I can't remember how long we stayed like that, but it was more than what should have been allowed.

"The man from the van never moved, and the dog's eyes never roamed from mine. It was as if the dog was waiting for something, contemplating an important decision. After what seemed an eternity, it simply turned and darted off into the corn field across the road."

"What the hell?" Mark says in a hushed voice.

I shake my head then continue. "Then, the man in uniform shrugged and got back into his van without a word. I looked it up later, Brighton didn't even have animal control at the time. Something about a lack of city funds due to a corrupt treasurer."

When I don't continue, Erika moves toward the edge of her seat. "You never saw the man or dog again?"

"Not since that day, no."

"What a crock of shit," Jeff blurts out. "There's no way that's a true story."

"Do you ever shut up?" snaps Erika.

"It was a lot better than your story about that half-naked clown with bagpipes you hallucinated," teases Mark. "Don't do drugs, man."

"I told you my dealer messed up. I don't usually do the hard stuff," replies Jeff, as if that's an acceptable answer.

"My mom and sister were there," I respond defensively, but quietly. I've only told that story a few times, but each time is met with the same skepticism. *I'm sure that's how it happened*, I tell myself with decaying confidence.

"I guess I'll just have to ask her when I come over..." Jeff trails off as everyone goes quiet. "I'm sorry," he says quickly. "I wasn't thinking."

I don't know how to respond, so I look at my feet. "It's okay."

"Shit, man. Sorry," Jeff reiterates.

"Seriously. It's okay. Umm," I'm stuttering, eyes downcast. "I'm going to take off. If you see Justin, tell him I said thanks for having me over."

No one protests my departure. Likely thankful to avoid a prolonged state of awkwardness.

My so-called friends say goodnight as I head toward the front of the house in search of my car. Once inside, I take a deep breath before turning the key, bringing the ancient mode of transportation to life. A few memories of my mother cascade through my mind before I back out of the driveway and head home.

The neighborhood is quiet and formless as I pull into the driveway, the antique and bruised engine of my car cutting through the silence. The car slowly rolls to a stall, the worn brakes screeching in protest, my face a mixture of concern and embarrassment.

Through the darkness, I envision enraged neighbors storming down the street with torches and pitchforks, hell-bent on riding the world of the creature responsible for their restlessness.

The living room light is on, a lone beacon in a house otherwise shrouded in darkness. Dad is most likely waiting up for me.

I linger within the car, battling the relentless knot gnawing at my stomach, product of Jeff's remark. Thoughts, memories of my mother pass quickly in a fractured timeline. After two more songs, I take a deep breath. I turn the key and head for the door.

I'm careful entering the house, moving slowly, quiet as a mouse. Slim chance the light is on by accident, but I don't risk the chance that everyone is asleep. Rest isn't something in abundant supply for my family.

I round a corner after locking the front door and see my father sprawled across the sofa. A couple of empty beer bottles congregate atop the worn and scratched coffee table, a few more on the rug below.

The knot returns when I see the scrapbook.

"Hey, Dad," I say after a moment, a heavy shoulder leaning against the door frame.

James Talavan is a good man, considering everything he's been through. He was a good husband, is a dedicated father, and works hard; an honest man with an honest living, having been employed as a production operator at a local manufacturing plant for nearly twenty years, as most people in Brighton seem to do.

There's little fault to be found with his character, except the drinking, which has exponentially increased this past year. Despite the increase in quantity, James isn't violent, just sad. He hides it well and is still a good father to my sister, Jocelyn, and myself.

James looks up from the rugged and worn scrapbook with a sad smile. "Hey, kiddo. How was the party?"

"Not much of a party, but it was alright." My eyes wander over the sleeved paper resting against my father's lap, and my heart aches. Inside that book are memories, once happy memories now sad as the result of horrible but uncontrollable events. "How are you?"

"Tumbling down the rabbit hole," James admits, eyes returning to the book. There's a shiver, a small one, but enough I notice. "I couldn't help myself," he mouths absently, his mind somewhere in the past. "Today is our anniversary, and I couldn't help myself."

"It's okay, Dad. I thought about her a lot tonight."

A tear forms in the corner of my father's eye, glistening in the low light, never breaching the bottom eyelid. The man cried often, initially, after the cancer took his wife, but such shows of sorrow have become rare over time. It seems only a certain amount of alcohol can elicit such emotions these days. It's a blessing. I don't do well with emotional displays.

I also cried a lot, after my parents told me what was happening, when our lives began to change. She was in so much pain then, struggling through chemotherapy treatments, surgeries, and more pills than I could count. I watched, helplessly, angrily, as she slowly transformed into a shadow of herself. It wasn't her fault, of course, but it ate at me. Not because I was angry with the person she became, but because it wasn't fair. Not for her. Not for our family.

I knew no one better. She was happy, always happy, until the cancer required regular trips to the hospital. More than half her energy drained from treatment while the other half fought to retain a sliver of the happiness that once defined her. I remember my parents talking one night when they thought we were asleep. Her voice was tired, ragged, worried. She felt guilt for becoming someone else, for the financial impact her sickness was causing, burdened that her struggles would become our own.

When she became worse, I cried secretly. There was an unsaid urge to be strong for my mother, for our family, so I waited for the cover of darkness and silently cried into my pillow. I put that weight on myself. Those were dark times, and the darkness grew until the day she didn't wake. I cried for hours that day, openly and into the shoulder of my father who didn't hide his own emotions.

Looking back, something within me broke that day. I can still feel, but what I feel, especially moments of sadness, no longer transfers to outward displays of emotion. I suppose I'm grateful. Being a rock, in control of myself, at least in appearance, was what my family needed. It's what I needed to survive that era of my life.

Jocelyn was there through it all, and more emotional than either of us, in a different way, a more dangerous way. She was reserved and confused through the treatments, but grew angry, at first, when our mother passed away. Usually full of life, she became short-tempered, prone to violent outbursts at seemingly random moments. In time, the anger dissipated until the void morphed into nothing but a cold sadness.

I battled myself to stay strong, somewhat for my father but mostly for Jocelyn. I spent countless nights in her room—talking, listening, and providing a shoulder to cry on. There was a circulating fear she would turn to unhealthy habits, so I gave her as much attention as I could. She turned out alright, as well as could be expected, and I'm eternally grateful for the outcome; that she's alive and healing.

"I miss her. Every day I miss her," my father continues, pushing off my comment.

"I know, Dad. I know. I miss her too." It's true. I may not cry anymore, but I loved my mother. I love her still. She was beautiful in every way.

Our family was happy, once. We weren't wealthy, but we wanted for nothing that mattered. Our house was full of love. A rare kind of love I took for granted. One I didn't realize or truly understand until the day it vanished. Warmth replaced by a numbing, dark cloud.

The book closes softly, with a distant love, as my father sits up. "Alright. Enough of that. You okay?" he asks sincerely.

It's amazing how, in the blink of an eye, the man can go from self-loathing to legitimate concern for another. A selfless nature tainted by shadows of a great loss.

"I am," is all I offer, looking absently toward my feet.

I am fine, at least that's what I tell myself. My response to that question varies, depending upon my mood. Lately, I find it awkward. It's a thing people ask, but they don't want the truth. The question is for them, so they feel good about themselves.

"Are you sure?" my father pries.

Not tonight. He wants to talk, hoping I break years of persistence and confer suppressed feelings about the absence of my mother, but I don't feel like discussing such a deep issue at such a late hour. If I'm honest, I never feel like talking about it, with anyone.

"Yeah. I think I'm going to head to bed," I answer quickly, pointing toward the direction of my room. "Adam and I are going to the field after school tomorrow to hit for a bit. I'll be home after."

"Jocelyn will take the bus?"

"Yeah."

My father sighs but nods. "Sounds good. I'll have dinner ready when you get home."

"Thanks," I reply over my shoulder, already running from the unwanted conversation.

The door before mine is ajar, a dim light breaches the small void. *No rest for any Talavan.* I knock gently.

"Yeah?"

"It's me. Can I come in?"

"Sure."

I push open the door and make my way to the center of the room, where I collapse at the foot of my sister's bed. Jocelyn has a tablet in hand but looks distraught. I give her a warm smile. We've always been close, but our mother's death eventually deepened our bond, even though we've kept the rest of the world at arm's length.

She's a freshman at Brighton while I'm a junior. I'm thankful for the overlap. Jocelyn is likely to disagree. I've been on the receiving end of several lectures for being overprotective, usually after scaring away a boy who summoned enough courage to ask Jocelyn on a date. I can take my sister's wrath with a smile because it's better than seeing her hurt by a high school teenager with only one thing on his mind.

I would know.

"Reading anything good?"

"*1984*. Mr. Potter's English class."

I grin like Christmas morning. "What a great book. It's what got me into reading. One of the only books I've read twice."

"You *would* like it," she says with disgust.

I laugh a little. "I gather you don't?"

"Not at all. It's boring and unrealistic. And…it's so old."

My grin sours, a tirade at the tip of my tongue, but I manage to calm myself before correcting her misguided opinion.

"It's a dramatization of what Orwell saw for our future. You have to understand the time at which he wrote that book, then you'll understand the genius of the potential future he saw.

Especially when you compare it with our society today. Sure, a lot that didn't happen, but there are similarities."

Jocelyn looks bored with the conversation. I've often wondered how she manages to be in the top five of her class. She's a tremendously bright student, but she complains over every subject, book, and assignment. On the surface, you'd guess she's lazy and possesses little interest in school. Reality is quite the opposite, and a surprise to those who somehow manage to get to know her.

"Just...do me a favor. Read the whole book with an open mind and we'll talk about it afterwards. I'll even help you with whatever paper is assigned to the book. Deal?"

She may not like, or appreciate, Orwell's writing, but the offer of help spawns a smile. "Deal."

Not that she needs my help, and she'll likely re-write whatever suggestions I make, but she's also street smart. She knows literature is my strongest subject, so she'll shave a few hours off the project by allowing me to produce the meat while she works toward a conclusive argument.

"Good. Now get some sleep. I'll see you in the morning."

The door to my bedroom opens with a creak and the faint light of a half-moon casts vague silhouettes of what lies within. I flip on the light and head for the dresser across the room. Eclectic walls flaunt varying interests: Star Wars posters, fatheads of idolized baseball players, framed pictures of old rock singers, signed copies of favorite books, and a vinyl record player atop a large shelf mounted to the far wall.

I'm abnormal, more an old soul than a contemporary one. My room is spotless, organized, and neat. It's a clean room, which brings me peace, and nothing like the common perception associated with teenage boys. It's a pride thing, not in the general sense of the term, but more a feeling of accomplishment in caring for what's mine.

I fall violently upon the bed after changing into a pair of

athletic shorts. My mind races, pulling on thoughts of both the past and present. Memories of my mother wash over me, but only the dark and painful ones linger. With eyes wide shut, I follow the dreadful timeline, building towards the moment she left, and then to the months of turmoil that followed. Thoughts of my mother segue to those of my father, then to my sister, and I feel helpless in making our family whole again, powerless to recall our happiness.

I shiver with pain. Pain from a deep hole with twisted, thorn-laced roots where my heart once beat, and I continue to sulk until my body's need for sleep overcomes my restless mind.

4
A SHADOW

JACOBY

I wake in a sour mood, taking my breakfast in silence. Dad is at work and Jocelyn senses my distraction. She knows me well enough to leave it alone until I'm ready to talk.

With less than a handful of words said between us, Jocelyn and I finish readying ourselves for school and hop into the car. We usually sing along to whatever we're in the mood for, but today we drive in silence. Jocelyn says nothing and spends most of the time looking out her window.

"Sorry," I finally say.

"For what?" she asks, peering into the darkness.

"Had a rough night. Something Jeff said made me think about mom."

She snorts. "Jeff's an ass."

"Mouth," I chide with a sideways glance. "But, yes."

We laugh a little.

"Want to talk about it?" she asks evenly.

Part of me wants to. Another, more adamant part wants to move on. "I don't think so. But thanks. I'll be okay."

Jocelyn returns to the window. "Okay."

The short response isn't a slight. We've shared enough moments since Mom died to respect each other's process. We've done this song and dance before. Many times. We know when to pry and when to wait.

We travel the last handful of minutes in silence, arriving at school with plenty of time to spare. I hate being late. Even the potential of being late stresses me out. Jocelyn couldn't care less but arriving a few minutes earlier than desired beats the hell out of riding the bus, so she doesn't complain.

We enter the building together and bump knuckles before heading down separate hallways.

"Later, princess," I say.

"Later, nerd," she quips.

I'm the first to arrive for class, and I take advantage of the silence by allowing my mind to wander. I permit a few moments of self-pity before moving on and accepting life for what it has become.

The first period bell rings, and I pull forth my tablet as the other students settle into their uncomfortable wooden restraints. I despise chemistry. Equal parts teacher and material. I'd rather start my day taking a throat punch from Edward Scissorhands.

Mrs. Rolland stands at the front of the class, swaying side-to-side, wearing a fool's smile. She irks my disposition, but I've never been able to put a finger on why. Perhaps it's her overzealous nature and go-happy attitude. The woman is an unstoppable force determined to not only improve our grades, but our lives as well. Other students appreciate the attention, but I find her intrusive and overbearing. I don't need such help or attention, and I've adamantly shrugged off her attempts to alter my stance on the matter.

It's an odd class. Time passes quickly, but intermittent moments come and go where the world stops on a dime.

Thoughts of my family—what's left of it—distract me from Mrs. Rolland's ramblings, but they're unpleasant distractions. I think of the man in the brown uniform. The memory has blurred over time. I can no longer conjure details of his face, the van, or much of the scene. The same can't be said of the dog. I see him clearly. A shiver down the spine electrifies my skin.

Male? Female? I ponder. I assumed it was a boy. The moment was a little too chaotic to conduct a formal check. I decide it's unimportant.

The scene playing out in my mind isn't as I remember it. Here, the beast is moving, circling. His eyes on mine, searching, hungry. Everything else fades away. We are alone.

It's disconcerting when the bell rings, announcing an end to the period. The unpleasant daydream dissolves. I have no idea what Mrs. Rolland covered the last half of the class. I send up a silent thank you, grateful I wasn't called upon to answer a question. I recall thumbing my tablet and nodding my head now and then, but I retained nothing.

I place the tablet into my bag. *I'll have to re-read that chapter tonight.* Mrs. Rolland is notorious for dropping a pop quiz, and something tells me there will be one first thing tomorrow morning.

I exit the classroom and step into the bland, white-washed hallways of Brighton Community High School. The structure of the institution is a cage, devoted to nurturing gossip, cliques, and overall discomfort, which makes sense as it was designed by an architect known for his skill in constructing prisons.

Not a natural comparison I would have made. No wonder so many kids despise high school. Not like we have enough problems to worry about, but those problems and feelings fester for eight hours a day in an environment better suited to restrain than motivate.

I was a few weeks into my freshman year when I stumbled

upon that bit of information about the architect. I find it more annoying now than I did then.

The building itself has several interlinking square sections with no entrances, or exits, except through carefully placed doors locked from the inside during school hours. Again, not an enriching environment for what is supposedly our most important and formative years.

"You alright?" someone asks from behind me.

I turn after making it to the far wall. "Yeah. Why?" I ask.

Mitch cocks his head, considering the answer but apparently taking my word for it. "You seemed off in class is all. You were somewhere else."

"Mrs. Rolland," I say with a forced laugh. "Hard to pay attention."

"No kidding. Still on for after school?"

I nearly forgot, and my mood brightens. "Absolutely. Meet at the field?"

"That'll work," he replies, throwing two hands in the air as he turns and yells, "Go Sparrows!"

Fucking sparrows. My head drops and shoulders slump. We had a better mascot, once, but it was deemed insensitive. Fine. But whomever decided upon a sparrow as a replacement deserves a prolonged bout of medieval torture.

I watch my best friend—the closest thing I have to a best friend—trot off before turning to make my way to calculus with Ms. Jamison, who is significantly more pleasant to look at than Mrs. Rolland. It doesn't hurt that Erika will be there.

I take a right at the end of the hall and descend a flight of worn but illuminated stairs. I take a left once my feet find the main level and travel another hundred feet before venturing into what is known as *Math-Alley*. Every math class a student can take, from freshman to senior year, is nestled within this section of the school.

Here, along what I personally describe as death row, the

teachers stand erect outside their respective classroom walls like the Swiss Guard. Fluttering eyes are all that move, and they roam the mass of passing students; monitoring, ready to pounce at the slightest injustice and reprimand those who would dare act out against the established rule of law. Math-Alley is an island, a government of its own, operating upon its own set of norms and expectations.

I walk cautiously with my head downcast, attempting to navigate incognito past gargoyle-looking statues. Ms. Jamison may be pleasant on the eyes, but she scares the crap out of me, especially when joined by her coworkers between periods.

She's a serious woman, disciplined in all facets of life. Anyone with eyes can observe a toned physique, the product of countless hours spent mastering grueling training regimens. She is often found, both before and after school, at the school's gym. Rumor has it she once asked the school's quarterback for a spot while squatting, who immediately ran to the locker room to change shorts. I never believed the story. Doesn't seem like something Ms. Jamison would do, and discipline would have followed such an inappropriate request. Such is high school, where rumor and gossip are currency for inclusion and fame.

As if imposing looks aren't enough, Ms. Jamison possesses a sharp mind and is often matter of fact in her communication. I've never seen her make a mistake, and I've certainly never seen someone attempt to correct her. She is desirable and horrifying at the same time, and for all the same characteristics.

I enter the classroom with a sigh of relief, taking note of Erika's empty chair. I find my own and attempt to stare at something other than the door.

There's a rush of excitement as she crosses into the small classroom, and another when she graces me with a smile before taking the anterior seat. Tablet in hand, she quickly turns in her chair.

"I had fun last night. How about you?" a warmth immediately swallowed by horror. "Sorry. I forgot about Jeff. I don't think he meant it."

I glance toward Jeff's seat, which is still empty. *I don't think he meant it either. Still an asshole though.*

Erika has long, brunette hair and dark but soft eyes. She is of average height and in amazing shape, having ran varsity track for two years and started as the school's shooting guard for three. The attraction is more than looks and athletic talents: it's the way she cares for people, her innocent but fun laugh, her openness and desire to see the best in people, and moral stance. She never judges, but she has her beliefs and doesn't waver.

"It's okay. It was fun, other than that. Sorry I missed your story."

"It really wasn't that good," she says softly. "You didn't miss much."

"Still wish I would've heard it."

The bell rings.

"Perhaps later," she says, twisting toward the front of the class.

"I would like that," I respond, more to myself than Erika's back.

"Still don't think it's true," says Jeff, who dramatically plops into the adjacent chair after whispering in my ear.

"Whatever," I squeak out the side of my mouth, turning toward the front of the class. That's all Jeff is going to get from me.

Ms. Jamison enters the classroom, and everyone involuntarily straightens. "Let's begin," she says.

I force myself to focus on the day's lesson, but I quickly lose the necessary stamina. My mind wanders to Jeff's comment. *Asshole.* Didn't take him long to get over bringing up my dead mother. I rub my eyes, shooing off negative thoughts. I replace them with Erika.

I know our conversations are harmless. She's nice to everyone, except maybe Jeff. But a guy can dream. A small part of me hopes there's a sliver of interest there. Either way, replaying our earlier discussion is enough to brighten my mood.

I'm daydreaming of Erika and I's first date when the scene darkens. Erika disappears first, then the restaurant, followed quickly by everything else. The world blurs. I see a dark shape, a shadow on the move. It begins in the corner, then flows up the far wall until it hangs from the ceiling. I stare into the black cloud. Something within stirs. The world I know returns after a violent bout of battling eyelids. Nothing. I close my eyes with a deep breath and find the face of the beast.

I'm still shaky as school ends. Real or not, seeing the dog so clearly scared the shit out of me. Luckily, I played my physical response off as a much-needed stretch.

Mitch makes his way to the field well after the last bell. I've already stretched and ran a few poles by the time he comes running up to the cages, flaunting a mischievous grin.

"You're late," I chastise.

Mitch shrugs. "Megan really wanted to say goodbye."

"Goodbye, eh. That was a long goodbye."

"Indeed," he answers with a sideways smile.

I shake my head but laugh. Mitch begins to elaborate when I wave him off. "I don't want to hear the details."

"You sure? They're good details."

"I'm sure. Let's just hit."

I roll up the sleeves of my sweatshirt and fasten a batting glove across each wrist. It's the first day of November, but the weather is beautiful. A cloudless sky, and the sun's harvest-flavored light paints a beautiful canvas atop the baseball diamond to the right. A tickling wind fills the air with the warm scent of freshly cut grass. I can't help but smile.

Although metal bats are permitted for high school, we use wooden bats for practice to preserve the lifespan of our aluminum barrels. Connecting down the handle hurts a hell of a lot more with a wooden bat, but I don't mind. It doesn't happen often, and there are very few things in life more pleasing than the smell of fresh pine-tar atop a wooden handle. A sensation impossible to describe to someone who doesn't play baseball.

There is a beauty in baseball no other sport can match. From the look of a diamond to the unwritten traditions. In no other sport is an athlete considered essential when they've failed seventy percent of the time. A team sport where each player stands at the center of attention three to four times per game. It's an infuriating game, filled more often with heartbreak than elation. Alike golf: a single victory, a ground ball with eyes, a home run, an outfield assist, is enough to propel a ball player through errors and slumps.

Neither of us feel like chasing balls around the field, so we duck into one of two netted cages. Mitch is thirty feet away, tucked safely behind a web of metal bars and green ropes, throwing short toss as I selectively choose pitches to hit.

Taking balls, and even well-placed strikes, has always been my fault. I'm a power hitter, despite my average build, with an undisciplined strike zone. A shortcoming I've internally vowed to correct before next season.

We switch after I've taken a couple-dozen swings, and we continue to alternate until we've each hit well over a hundred balls. A small speaker sits outside the cage, blaring a hip-hop song I haven't heard. I bite my tongue. I prefer rock music when practicing or working out, but picking the afternoon's playlist isn't worth a fight. Mitch is overly defensive in his taste of music.

We exchange a few coarse jokes, but other than that we've said little to one another, except when there's a request for pitch location or general swing advice. I'm adjusting one of my batting gloves when Mitch stands.

He says something.

I find the speaker and turn down the volume. "What?"

"I heard about the party. What Jeff said."

"Of course you did. Everyone hears about everything here."

"Sorry I wasn't there. I've always wanted to hit the guy," Mitch says, and I believe him.

"He isn't worth losing our second-best player," I say with raised eyebrows.

He lobs a ball at me. "Twenty bucks says I end up with a higher batting average."

"You were almost thirty points behind me last year. Deal," I say, throwing a ball back at him. It hits the net, but Mitch flinches anyway.

"Speaking of balls," he says, "you ever going to find your own and ask Erika out?"

"Not this again," I reply, annoyed. *Yes. No. Maybe.*

"Yes. This again. The whole school knows you have a thing for her, which means she does too."

I hate high school. "The whole school?"

Mitch nods with exaggeration.

I don't want to talk about this, but I can't help but wonder if he knows something. "So?"

He sighs like an instructive father. "So. If she knows and isn't into it, do you think she would still talk to you as much as she does?"

"She's nice. She talks to everyone."

"You're an idiot," he says, exhausted. "She talks to you more than any other guy in school."

I take a couple of practice swings in silence.

"Want me to talk to her?" Mitch asks.

"What? No. Hell no," I blurt out, equal parts demand and plea. Mitch has no shame, and he would absolutely lay bare my heart's desire. I'm horrified.

"Just a little talk. See what she thinks about you."

"Mitch. Don't."

"Jacoby," he responds flatly. "I'll give you a few weeks to ask her out, or I'm going to do it for you."

My cheeks redden at the brisk air, but I'm also blushing, and this conversation is starting to annoy me. "We will talk about this later."

"A few weeks," he reiterates.

"Just throw."

Mitch lobs a ball, and I take an uncontrolled swing. He drops the issue, and we return to our routine.

The sun sets and the temperature is dropping fast when we finally leave the park and part ways. He doesn't bring up Erika, neither pushing nor apologizing for the earlier conversation. I know he's serious on the timeline.

Tomorrow's problem.

5
GOING HOME

SUSAN

A bored knock raps against the room's moldy, slim door. Slowly, quietly, I place a half-empty beer can on a table next to the bed and stand. Joint and bone crack as my ear and shoulder touch. The knock is earlier than expected.

My now free right hand goes to the small of my back. Confidence conquers concern as I find the cold metal nestled between shirt and jeans. Matilda. A loyal girl. Always there when I need her. The instrument an extremity, an extension of myself, with its own personality.

I swiftly approach the far wall and settle between the door and a slanted set of windows, analyzing dozens of variables along the way. The action instinct through training and real-world experience. Most of that experience being recent.

Standing in front of the window will give away my position, and if the door were forced open while I'm standing behind it, I'd be struck and rendered defenseless. That sense within is quiet, dormant, but a girl can't be too careful these days.

With a finger over the trigger and the safety off, I lean and peer through the peephole.

"Who is it?" I ask quickly.

"Loui Yammer's Pizza. I have your delivery." The voice mirrors the knock, a teenager forced into a job he hates by parents he largely ignores.

I know little of my prey, but that thing within, even though silent now, has warned of an evil I can't explain. A feeling responsible for many restless nights. I've been known to point Matilda toward harmless shadows, cursing my paranoia as I down shots of something that warms my insides. I have no idea what I'm dealing with, or what the murderous cannibal is capable of.

"What kind of pizza?"

"What?"

Strike one. The gun rises as I say more slowly, "What...kind...of...pizza...did I order?"

A moment of silence magnifies the tension. *Strike two.* My finger itches at the metal guarding the trigger, my nail tracing its arc. It's been a long time since I've taken a life. *You can do it again.* I hope for my sake, when the time comes, that I do. Damn whatever feelings follow. They can't be worse than the nightmares plaguing me day and night.

"Uh....," the boy finally responds. "I have a medium pepperoni and sausage."

Probably not a cannibal at my door, at least not the one I'm looking for. They do say every serial killer lives next to someone. "What style of crust?" I'm only slightly serious at this point, capitalizing on an opportunity to have a little fun.

"Hand-tossed," he answers more quickly.

I unhook the chain and release the deadbolt, then slowly open the door, Matilda hidden but close. I give the boy a once-over, step back into the room to holster the weapon, then reopen the door and step into the night. He back-steps quickly as I look left and right. Satisfied we're alone, my eyes return to the teenager, who looks slightly bemused but mostly annoyed.

"How much?" I ask in a let's-hurry-this-along way.

He shakes his head, the motel light catching patches of peach-fuzz over an otherwise smooth face. This is probably the most interesting and confusing delivery of his short career.

I only take slight pleasure in baffling the young man, but the precautions are necessary, and good laughs are hard to come by.

He clumsily fumbles over the receipt and eventually mumbles, "Thirty-two dollars and thirty-eight cents."

"Steep."

He shrugs. "They say we are world-famous."

"What do you say?"

"I'm lactose intolerant."

I can't help but audibly laugh. I hand over forty dollars and take the pizza. Before he can say anything in return, I slam the door and return to bed, and more importantly, my beer.

I casually flip through the limited number of channels offered by the dinky motel as I pull a slice from the box. *Not worth forty bucks,* I think after a bite. *World-famous my ass.* A news report catches my eye, and I quickly elevate the volume. It's a local channel. However, the case of a missing South Carolina girl, for whatever reason, has the entire nation's attention.

I've yet to discern the criteria for a missing persons case to garner widespread media coverage, while so many others are forgotten within days. *Likely money.*

I forget about both pizza and beer as I listen intently to a skinny blonde anchor, who probably can't spell the word *anchor*, give an update on a story I've been following with great interest.

"We have now received word that Juliana Marrow, the

young girl who has been missing for over a month, has been located and is in good health," says the blonde.

I inch forward in bed, anxiously waiting for the details. *How did she escape? Did they catch who took her?* My heart races, palms slick with sweat.

"There are confirmed reports," the anchor continues, "that Ms. Marrow, a senior at Pearl Glenn high school in South Carolina, ran away to California with her college boyfriend, Michael Kraff. Their relationship was kept secret out of fear that Ms. Marrow's parents wouldn't approve, due to the age difference.

"Ms. Morrow," continues the anchor, "is reportedly returning home. There are no planned press releases from either Ms. Morrow or her family at this time. A lawyer representing the family has asked for privacy as the family reconnects."

"Damnit," I grind out. I crack the other side of my neck, then slam my head against the headboard.

Damnit.

I continue to listen as the anchor gives an updated report on the situation. There are interviews of people with no stake in the matter, followed by statements of neighbors and supposed lifelong friends. When nothing more is to be said about a girl who simply ran away from home, the blonde woman transitions to a story about a pregnant monkey at a nearby zoo.

Dumb girl. I'm happy, of course, that Juliana is safe and unharmed, but the circumstances surrounding the girl's disappearance were perfect. Similar to all the others. Her discovery upended my assumptions. I pull out the black, leather-bound book from a backpack beside the bed and flip to one of the last marked-up pages. I find the page dedicated to the Marrows and make a note toward the bottom of the page, indicating the daughter has been found and isn't connected.

My confidence wanes. I eye the book sprawled before me.

What if they're all the same? I have no hard evidence that supports my theory. Most of these cases are either unsolved or ruled as accidental. Every victim could be independent of one another. I am the only person in the world who thinks differently.

Guilt sprouts as my concern deepens. The thing within awakening, imploring my determination to win out. More will die if I fail, if I quit. I will not stand by and do nothing. The parade of death must stop. I carefully scroll through previous pages, scouring for another family close to Westchester, Pennsylvania—now that I won't be visiting the Marrows.

Somewhere near the middle of the book, I stumble upon an entry for a small town in eastern Ohio. The Turners. I read through the details quickly, then open a military-grade laptop.

After a little research, and rediscovering my beer, I make up my mind. *The Turners it is.* I look back toward the television, thinking of Juliana. "Looks like we're both heading home."

I arrive at an old, dilapidated ranch two days later.

The Mustang roars beneath a rusted, arched gateway made of worn iron as the early morning sun dulls against the earthy mineral. It's a surreal moment, and a beautiful setting. The sun hides behind the gate, a flicker of light cresting the top arch, a brilliant star upon a miniature horizon.

The antique mailbox beside the gateway reveals no name, but a barn inside the property displays *Turner Horse Training* in faded and chipped white paint along its side. I sigh in relief. The residence's location was somewhat of an educated guess, derived through hours of research.

The house itself is out in the middle of nowhere, hidden from any form of GPS. My efforts were further hindered by the family's decision to become hermits. From what I could find online, the family begged for privacy after the discovery of their daughter's missing body, which the city honored by doing their best to conceal the Turner's whereabouts. The family retreated from their suburban home to an uninhabited family estate after the city buried any record of it.

Small towns.

I can't help but scale back the maps application and stare at the surrounding area. This is the closest to home I've been in nearly ten years. Southwest lies New Philadelphia. A home that once held everything dear to me. Now, a name associated with memories I drink into oblivion.

The car bounces its way up a long gravel road lined with a diverse setting of shrubs and trees, all of which have grown wild. A cloud of dust rises like a storm in the rear-view mirror as rocks and dirt bounce off the car's undercarriage. I cringe, hoping there are no chips on one of my own—the Mustang is Matilda's older sister.

At the top of a small hill, I exit the car with no intention of approaching in silence. I know enough about the countryside to understand that stealthily walking about someone's personal property warrants the handling of a shotgun by said property's owner.

This adventure of mine is risky enough. I don't need to compound the threat by acting carelessly and inciting a gun battle with someone I want to help.

Do I really want to help the families of the slain girls? Would killing the cannibal really bring them peace? Walking toward the house, I try to put myself in their place, and I doubt anything in this world would bring me peace. I have searched tirelessly within for what drives me to solve this case. What I settle upon depends on the day. All I know is that I can't stop. The pursuit a function of survival as critical as the need to breathe. If I were to stop, I would pass out, wake up, and resume.

After a few steps toward the front door, a middle-aged

man exits the house. "Can I help you?" he asks. There's a pain embedded in every word. His voice is soft but weathered.

A gust of wind catches the end of my scarf. I stop and tackle it into submission.

"My name is Susan McGraff."

"Good for you."

I sigh. Not a good start. "I'm an investigative journalist." When the man says nothing in reply, I decide to continue. "I'd like to ask you a few questions about your daughter," I say carefully.

"Fuck you." His voice slices through the wind. Calm but threatening. The anger that seeps from each word is a jarring contrast to an otherwise relaxed form. "How'd you find me?"

"I'm good at..."

He waves a hand at me. "Doesn't matter. Get the hell off my land," he says, turning his back to me. Dismissed like a wild, harmless animal.

No. No, no. "Mr. Turner, please," I say, braving a step toward the retreating father.

There is a slow in his step, a heavy sigh that ripples around us. "I'm going to get my gun now. You had better be gone when I return." His voice level, a hint of sadness.

Push. Gently. "I want to find the man who murdered your daughter. I am not looking for a story. I'm looking to stop a murderer, and I think you can help me."

He turns and we stare at one another, waiting for the town clock to strike noon. He rubs rough hands against a wrinkled forehead. "Why? How? What can an investigative journalist offer that the police couldn't?"

"The police have stopped looking for the person responsible. They say the case is still open, but you and I both know they're no longer devoting any resources toward catching the killer. I've come across some evidence the police don't have,

49

that they won't consider, and it could help me track down your daughter's killer. But I need your help."

A flock of geese cackle above. Mr. Turner follows their path then stares into the rising sun.

I send up a silent prayer. I'm tired of hunting down the victims' families. I'm tired of dead ends. I'm tired of uncovering disappearance after disappearance. *Please. Please help me, so I can help others.*

Mr. Turner turns back toward the door. *No!* I can't be dismissed again. "Want some coffee?" he asks over his shoulder, never breaking stride.

I inwardly smile. *Finally.* "I would love some," I reply, taking off after him. "Thank you."

The wooden floor moans as I cross through the door and close it behind me. The inside of the house is a catastrophe. I'm caught looking at piles of discarded items.

"Sorry for the mess. Rachel left about six months ago, and it's been hard…on the upkeep," he says with a sweeping gesture.

The wife. "I didn't know. I'm sorry." I instantly feel for the man. A daughter murdered eighteen months ago, and then his wife left. Life has dealt him a shitty hand. Most couples don't survive the loss of a child, especially an only child.

"Not many do, and thank you, but don't be sorry. It wasn't your fault. It was no one's fault…except the son-of-a-bitch who took our daughter from us. Rachel couldn't cope with the loss, and everything here reminded her of Nancy. Even me."

"Mr. Turner—"

"Call me Tom. Have a seat on the couch and I'll bring out some coffee."

I pull out a notebook as I hear, "Cream or sugar?"

"Splash of cream, please."

He returns from the kitchen a few minutes later with two white cups, heat rising in waves over the brim and into the dusty air like smoke from an idle but lit cigar.

I can't help but take stock of the room. *I thought my life was a mess.*

He hands one of the cups over with shaky hands, and a forced smile.

"Thank you," I say sympathetically, wrapping cold fingers around the cup's warmth, savoring the sensation it brings. The coffee, surprisingly, is good. "What is this?"

"Good or bad?" he asks.

"Very good."

"Good. I used to be in the coffee business. It's from a nonprofit headquartered a couple of towns over. I cut most of the world out, but I couldn't cut out this coffee."

"Understandable." I mean it. I eye the many framed pictures nestled atop discolored banisters, then the ones that hang from dirty walls, most of which show a happy and whole family. I feel Tom's eyes on me, and I dare to look in his direction. I find the defeated face of a father with no power, no way of changing past events. No matter how much he tries.

"I hired personal investigators, when I started to get the feeling the police were giving up."

A piece of information I didn't know. "Did they find anything?"

He sips from his own cup. "Not a damn thing. I spent most of our money on those thieves. Rachel wanted to focus on grieving. I wanted revenge, so I plunged my time and money into finding whoever did this to our baby girl. I think it was too much for Rachel. Instead of being there for her, I was consumed with finding the killer. I was the final nail in the coffin."

"Do you think you can get her back? Seems like you moved on from revenge."

"The desire for revenge is still there. I only moved on from the investigators because the money ran out." He thinks for a moment. "But I think I'm different now. Even if I had the money, I wouldn't spend it the way I did before."

"Sounds like hope to me," I encourage.

"Maybe. But that's not why you're here. As for Rachel, I think that's over. Too much pain here. This place and me. I can't leave. I've tried. Lord knows I've tried. I still feel close to her here, and I won't give that up."

"You moved here after?"

"We did. Rachel and I, but we spent time here as a family when Nancy was younger. A lot of fond memories. I can still hear the laughs."

I feel his gaze as I find a picture of the three of them.

"We were a happy family, but it seems like a lifetime ago now. I don't get many visitors, so please forgive my manners and the state of our...my home," he corrects. "Believe it or not, most people honored our request to be left alone. It wasn't something we expected. The quiet allowed me time to think, for the desire of vengeance to grow."

There is a low laugh, more of a huff, which I take as a replacement for a sob. "You never know how to respond," he continues, "or what your next action should be...in a situation like ours. There is no playbook. So, I leaned into my anger and desires."

A clock somewhere in the distance barks out a cadence of some sort, indicating a new hour.

"I can't begin to imagine what it has been like for you. I'm sure you have reservations about me, and my motives. But I assure you, I'm here to help."

"Why haven't you taken what you've found to the police?" he asks.

"To be honest, I don't think they would believe me."

Tom waits patiently before realizing I don't intend to elaborate. "Huh," he huffs out. "Vague."

"Sorry," I say. "Habit. My theories are...unpopular."

"I see." He's beginning to doubt my usefulness.

"If it were easy, or a popular motive, then your daughter's murderer would have been found by now."

Tom considers my position on the matter, likely reliving his own failures. "Fair enough."

"I know I'm onto something. I know which doors are locked; I just need the key, and my only motive is to stop this monster before another girl is taken."

"I don't care what your motives are. If you're really trying to catch the bastard, we don't have a problem. So, tell me, how do you think you can help? What key do I unknowingly possess?"

I place the coffee cup on a table, locking eyes with Tom. "Here's what I've found."

6
MANIFESTATION

JACOBY

I'm standing barefoot at the back door, peering into a dimly lit night for no reason. I'm unsure of the time. It's dark, so maybe the middle of the night? There's a fog in the distance, thickest atop a far hill, which sways and moves with a menacing purpose. It consumes everything in its path. A feeling of unease ripples violently throughout my stiff body.

I'm aware of my trance but unable to influence it in any way. Eyes numbly stare into the night, waiting for this story to unfold. Then, just as boredom settles in, movement. A dark figure emerges from the hill. The fog reveals nothing except a monstrous shadow—a night shadow cast against the low clouds from a hidden moon.

The unsettling feeling grows, deepens, spreading like wicked vines. The shadow form is familiar. I'm speechless, my feet in mutiny, anchored to the cold ground below.

I want to scream. I want to run, to lock every door and window in the house, but I fail to speak, to move.

The eyes are first to appear. Yellow and emotionless. The

fog parts, bending to the will of the beast as it creeps forward in slow confidence, cresting the hill and working its way across the declivity.

The beast slithers forward. An unnatural site in an already unnatural setting. A stewing sense of dread spreads like wildfire, the vines fuel for an inferno that engulfs every bodily function.

It's the dog of my past. My scary story has come again.

I awake drenched in sweat and with strained, heavy breathing. I'm frantic as my mind transitions from dream to reality. A muddled and confusing convergence, but the fast-paced beating of my heart slows as I register the familiarity of my bedroom.

An antique clock atop a nightstand to the right glows with red, block numbers in an otherwise dark room. Two hours until the alarm is set to go off.

A small sigh escapes through grinding teeth after twenty minutes of tossing and turning. I relive the dream every time I close my eyes, making sleep impossible. I decide to do something useful and go to work on an assignment due later in the week.

Each page I write is a grueling task.

I fail to understand why the dog has returned. It was a long time ago, and many years have passed since it affected me in any way. In the end, I chalk it up to sharing the recollection at the Halloween party, and I inwardly vow to never speak of it again.

I arrive at school energized, which is unexpected after losing a couple of hours of sleep. A sense of angst and discomfort are in tow, so much so the hairs on my neck randomly rise at the slightest chill. I see yellow eyes every time I blink.

Later in the day, a hand grabs at my shoulder as I'm making my way down the school's main hallway. The touch of another startles me. I lurch forward with an embarrassing gasp. Taking a moment to recover, I turn to find an amused face.

Mark Miller laughs.

I exhale. "You scared the shit out of me."

We're getting sideways glances from passing students as Mark continues to laugh, louder with each passing second, snowballing until he can't speak.

I shake my head back and forth, blood boiling. It isn't a day to be laughed at.

"I'm glad you find it so funny."

"Sorry, man. I didn't mean it. I yelled your name a handful of times. I thought you were ignoring me."

"I wasn't. Just a lot on my mind."

"Fair enough." Mark manages to reel himself in. "Listen, about the other night, I'm sorry for yelling your name and giving Jeff something to be a dick about."

I snort. "If it wasn't you then it would have been something else. All good."

"Hey guys," Melissa interrupts. Jenny falls in beside Melissa with a sideways smile, a pink encased tablet clenched against her chest.

"Well, hello," replies Mark. His attempt at smooth embarrassing for everyone. Of the two girls, Mark notices only one.

Jennifer Albert is likely our class's salutatorian, with enough time left to perhaps overtake the current valedictorian, who is a rather unpleasant human. I'm not Jenny's biggest fan, but I'm rooting for her in this matchup. She'll have her pick of university. Although highly intelligent, she's mostly known for her wild side. A combination that's had Mark head-over-heels for the better part of two years.

I jump in after an awkward silence. "You two were missed at Justin's."

"I was behind on Mr. Bueller's physics project. I bribed Jenny into coming over to help me get caught up."

Mark, fixated on Jenny, says, "That was nice of you."

I hear the sadness. Mark had hoped to woo Jenny out into the woods that night - the area reserved for couples who do couple things.

"What's going on, guys...and ladies?" asks Jeff. He throws arms over both Melissa and Mark.

Mark flashes a look of disgust, then attempts to nonchalantly maneuver out from under Jeff's hold. I smile. *At least I'm not the only one.*

"Not a lot, Jeff," I say with contempt. My slight goes unnoticed as Jeff head-nods my direction before returning to the group.

Ignorant ass. What a waste of a cliche.

There's a twinkle, a desire, in Jenny's eye, and I want to puke.

Jeff meets her gaze. "Hey, Jenny," he says.

"Hey," she responds shyly. An abnormal trait that doesn't suit her. "Where's Alexis? I haven't seen her today."

He shrugs. "She felt ill or something. Didn't come to school."

Jeff and Jenny exchange sly smiles before Melissa steps into the center of our little circle. "Anyone want to go to *HeBrews* after school? I could get some more studying done, and a yummy coffee sounds good."

Those who think it's a good idea voice their approval as the three-minute warning bell rings throughout the school. The crowd disperses, each heading toward their next class. Melissa and I fall in beside one another as we move in the direction of Mr. Farrow's tirade on ancient civilizations.

"How's the team look this year?" she asks when we're alone.

Melissa is a cheerleader—a member of Brighton's varsity team. Her decision to join the high school squad was more for the social aspect than anything else. Her talents far exceed that of the average cheerleader, proven by a plethora of trophies from time spent on a highly competitive travel cheer squad. She is also a gymnastics phenom, and rumors held that she would have her pick of no less than a dozen Division 1 colleges.

She knows sports, probably a wider understanding than anyone else at the school.

"We look good. Losing regionals last year was tough, but I think we have a chance this year."

"You're returning six starters, right?"

I smile. *Girl loves baseball.* I considered asking Melissa out a couple of years ago. We share a lot of the same passions, same worldviews. The more we talked the more we realized it wouldn't work. I can't explain why, but we found ourselves satisfied with the friendship we've developed.

"We are. Not too deep at pitching, but we will figure it out."

"Good," she says. "I'm sorry we don't cheer at baseball, but I'll definitely be in the stands."

I can't help but laugh.

"What?" she responds quizzically.

"No offense, but I'm glad we don't have cheerleaders."

I think I'm in for a rebuke, but she eventually returns the laugh. "Yeah. I guess baseball is a lot like soccer. Action takes too long to develop for us." There's a slight tilt in her stance. "Although...I'm sure you wouldn't mind seeing Erika in a short skirt, cheering you on."

My cheeks immediately flush. I guess Mitch isn't wrong. Everyone knows. "Well...I...I don't—"

"You should ask her out." Melissa runs straight for her seat at the back of the classroom, leaving me open-mouthed with nothing to say. My mind runs wild. Part of me hopes she knows something, that Erika has said something to her.

I somehow stumble into my chair, which sits beside a set of high windows that look out into the parking lot. Mr. Farrow begins with his usual, overly animated lecture and rambles on for a while before taking a break to wipe sweat from his brow.

The man is a machine, rambling on for extensive amounts of time without so much as a water break. I'm wide awake, although distracted. My mind flutters between the dream and Melissa's comment about asking Erika out.

Someone to the left drops their tablet. The sudden and unexpected noise shakes loose both thoughts. There is a distant roar of thunder, drawing my attention to the window. The sky has darkened and a light, slanted rain falls against the gray, cracked asphalt.

Indiana. Never know if it's going to rain or snow. Thunder in November is different.

I find a small, grassy hill toward the back of the parking lot, just beyond the last row of student vehicles. Something tugs at my insides, and I watch the hill for a moment, heart quickening.

My vision tunnels, and a familiar trance takes hold. Everything but the hill falls away. Mr. Farrow, my classmates, the rain, and even the cars cease to exist, insignificant against what looms in the distance. I inch forward as breathing comes faster and heavier. I blink, for the first time in what feels like hours, and there it is. I shake in fear and confusion.

Atop the hill, perched like a predator, is the black dog.

The world blackens, shattered by a stroke of lightning as my jaw clenches. *This isn't real. It can't be.* "It's a different dog," I hear myself mumble. Cautiously, I dare a closer look at the beast in the distance. Despite being so far way, I see the beast clearly. It's there. "No." The white fur rises from stomach to chin. It's the same dog.

I jump from my chair. "What the..." I yell out, interrupting whatever Mr. Farrow is covering.

Creased eyebrows and dazzled looks meet my gaze as I look around the room, quickly realizing I'm now the center of attention.

"Is everything alright, Mr. Talavan?" There is a mixture of concern and annoyance in Mr. Farrow's voice.

I look to my right. "Jon, do you see that dog?" I point out the window.

The dog hasn't moved.

Jon, an introverted soul with similar friends, is horrified at being called out with so much attention. After a glance out the window, he quickly shakes his head and returns to the tablet atop his desk. He visibly attempts to shrink into his chair.

"You don't see anything?" I ask, voice laced with desperation. Reality crumbles, withering away as the question goes unanswered.

"What's going on, Mr. Talavan?"

My hands are shaking. "Yeah...umm...I need to..." I mumble as snickers and hushed voices fill the silence.

A drip of sweat pools somewhere on my forehead. I scratch at the liquid when its weight succumbs to gravity. I turn to the window and find the beast on the move. I stumble backward as it somehow closes the distance in mere seconds, impossibly floating just outside the window. I twirl in silence, my stomach in shambles, and watch in horror as no one reacts.

Mr. Farrow stands with hands on wide hips, wearing an annoyed and expecting face.

I cough. "I need to see the nurse...or use the restroom."

"Which is it, Mr. Talavan? The restroom, or the nurse?"

I chance a sideways look to the window. Inwardly, I beg for this to be a dream. I blink repetitively until I realize I've done it enough to raise additional questions. The dog is no longer floating halfway up the glass, having returned to earth at some point. The beast is calm, relaxed even. It's eyes on me. I lean left then right and watch as my torment mirrors the movements.

There is a growl inside my head. *Your fear is misplaced.* The voice isn't my own.

"Whichever will get me out of here," I say too harshly, but it works.

"Very well." Mr. Farrow scribbles away on his tablet, signing for a hall pass.

I act quickly when my tablet pings, notifying me of the approved hallway pass. Tablet back in hand, I'm out the door before anyone can formulate a full sentence, but not soon enough to hear the start of rumblings by classmates in amusement of my peculiar behavior.

"Where were we?" Mr. Farrow asks as I step out of the class.

After clearing the classroom door, I take a right and crash against a wall of blue lockers. I painfully slide to the floor and attempt to catch my breath, which comes in short and hurried gasps.

"What was that?" I whisper through gasps. The fear is overwhelming. I want to cry, scream, but nothing comes out. Seeing something unexplainable is one thing, no one else able to see it is another. I panic at the thought of being alone, of what others will say about me.

"Jacoby?"

The voice startles me. I take a deep breath and count to four, rising upon wobbly knees. I nearly collapse, but I steady myself by throwing a hand against a locker.

"Hey, Mr. Andrews," I reply with a wheeze.

A comforting hand falls upon my shoulder. The touch is unexpectedly calming. "You okay, son?"

"I think so." *I'm definitely not.* "I'm not feeling the best." *Damn understatement.* "I have a medical pass—"

"I don't care about the pass. You're obviously hurting. Do you need help getting to the nurse's office?"

"I think I can make it," I answer, embarrassed that someone has stumbled into my meltdown.

Calm, I tell myself. *It wasn't real.*

"How about I walk with you. Would that be okay? I get

bored from time-to-time and roam the halls like a ghost. Don't tell anyone," he says with a smirk, "or they'll make me do actual work."

I force a laugh. "What is a vice principal doing roaming the halls? I heard you have a pool table stashed away somewhere for those bored moments."

This time, Mr. Andrews is the one to laugh. He leans toward me after a few steps and says, "None of the teachers here can play to save their lives. Winning all the time gets boring."

"Are you sure they aren't letting you win? You're the boss."

"How dare you accuse the teachers here of going soft on me," he says with a smile.

We talk about school, sports, and prospective colleges until we arrive at a tan colored door at the end of an endless hallway. A gold and black nameplate across the top announces we've arrived at the nurse's office. I'm thankful for Mr. Andrew's distraction.

We shake hands and part with a joke I find inappropriate for a vice principal to share with a student, but it makes me laugh, nonetheless.

In the span of nearly twenty-four hours, rumor and dramatization have passed through the entire school. Mercifully, I was absent for the game of telephone. After groveling for what seemed hours, the nurse permitted an early exit to recover from whatever illness had befallen me. I ready myself for a bombardment of concern and gossip, formulating a series of reasonable explanations.

I find Mitch waiting at the main entrance. "Hey man, you alright?"

We bump fists. "Talking about yesterday?"

Mitch nods silently.

"Yeah, I'm good. Just got sick all of the sudden and started seeing things."

"Like...hallucinations?"

I open my locker and remove a few books, enough to get through a couple of periods. "Yeah, something like that," I answer absently, playing it off as nothing serious.

"I heard it was crazy. Something about a dog, and you asking Jon if he could see it, but he couldn't. Poor Jon, probably the most he's said all year."

I slam the locker, already tired of this conversation and growing distraught at the likelihood of similar ones to come. "I'm not crazy," I say through clenched teeth. "The nurse gave me some meds and sent me home."

"Alright, man. Sorry. I didn't mean anything by it. Just looking out for you is all." Mitch allows me a minute to cool off. "You feel better now?" he asks carefully.

I relax a little. "All better, Mom."

We both laugh.

"Hear about the new kid?" he asks.

"What kid?"

"Some senior named Brian, I think. Alexis pointed him out yesterday."

"What," I ask, seeing his eyes roll.

"She thought he was hot."

I can't help but roll my own eyes.

"I hear he plays baseball too, but I haven't talked to him yet to find out for sure. Coach is the one who told me about baseball."

"Did you think he was hot?"

Mitch pushes me but laughs off the comment. "Shut up."

"Hopefully he can play. I can think of one or two he could replace," I say without regret.

Mitch snorts. "No shit. Let's see if the rumors are true, then we can see if he's any good. Another arm would be helpful."

"That'll work. Point him out some time, so I know who he is."

We enter chemistry class in unison and take up our assigned seats. Yesterday is thrown in my face as I'm welcomed with whispers and curious eyes. Those judgmental eyes quickly divert to something else when I take notice.

I squirm as the whispers continue and classmates discretely nod my direction. I feel broken, that something, deep below the surface, has always been off, and now everyone else knows it. I'm embarrassed, frustrated, and angry—all at the same time.

By the time the day is over, I've given the same speech to Melissa, Jeff, Alexis, Mark, and Erika as I had to Mitch. I stuttered a few times when explaining the situation to Erika, who seemed genuinely concerned. There was an innate desire to come up with something heroic or brave, but I decided to stick with the original story to avoid discrepancies when everyone eventually talked behind my back.

No one else asks me about yesterday. I'm thankful for keeping a small group of friends.

Mitch heads to Megan's after school to do who knows what, so I decide to take a day off from baseball. An easy decision because I'm to spend time with Erika—not in the way I'd prefer, but it's something.

I joined Yearbook Club a year ago, after winning two Indiana statewide awards for some artwork I submitted through one of Brighton's advanced art classes. The awards caught the attention of Mrs. Edwards, who was the yearbook supervising teacher at the time. When she discovered my talents towards graphic design, she somehow convinced me to give the club a try.

I decided to stay after discovering Erika was the club's president.

A half-hour after school ends, I climb to the second floor and enter a small lab off a forgotten hallway. There are several waist-high tables at the center of the room, each sporting a row of high-powered computers. No matter how advanced tablets and phones become, nothing beats the power of a stack of chips, wire, and metal.

The room itself is always locked and keys are given to a select few deemed as authorized, Erika being one of the select students. It's a multi-purpose room for various clubs and projects, not just for yearbook. Tonight, however, we have the entire room to ourselves.

"Hey," comes a soft voice from somewhere behind the bank of computers.

I round the middle desk and there she is. Muscles tense, and my entire body freezes at the sight of her. My brain and mouth battle, no longer working together, as I relive the conversation with Melissa.

Part of me wants to ask her out, but the remaining, larger part is craven in a way I've never known.

After several seconds of silence, she turns from whatever she is doing on the computer. "You okay?" she asks curiously.

"Yeah, sorry. I'm good. Uh, how are you?" I bumble out.

The awkwardness, and my bodily struggles, continue as I fail to decide whether to sit or remain standing. The anxiety melts away when I convince himself it isn't the right time to broach the subject of dating. Relieved, like a boulder is lifted from my struggling back, I take the seat next to her.

She smells of cinnamon. I want to move closer, to touch, but I do what I always do: nothing.

"I'm doing well. Excited to finally start making progress on the yearbook," she says.

Erika is wearing large but oddly attractive glasses that disappear somewhere beyond thick, brunette hair.

"Me too," I say. "I didn't know you wore glasses?"

There is a subtle change in her demeanor, and her head turns in what seems like embarrassment. "I don't wear them often. Lost a contact last period. They're hideous, aren't they?"

"No. No, not at all. They look great. In a sophisticated librarian way." *In a hot librarian way.*

"A librarian, huh?"

"Well...I just meant..."

She laughs. "Don't worry. I know what you meant." She turns toward the computer, then briefly looks at me sideways as she asks, "You're into librarians?"

"Sophisticated ones." I surprise myself with the bold statement. Pride quickly turns into terror as I decide it was way too forward.

It could be wishful thinking, but I think she blushes, which gives me hope I haven't crossed a line and ruined our friendship.

"Well then," she coughs out, "I'll take it as a compliment." It's a shy response, and I wonder what's going through that head of hers. "You have the cover?" she asks when I say nothing.

The moment is gone. The chance to escalate the flirt into an ask disappears before my eyes. I nod, going to my bag to retrieve a small flash drive. "I do."

"Well, let's have a look."

I thumb a button on the side of the monitor, bringing the machine to life. I then plug the memory device in at the back, and the computer quickly reads its contents. I try not to fidget or look Erika in the eye. That was the moment. I'm embarrassed by failure to seize the moment. She probably would have said no, but that was as good a time as any to make the ask.

"Did you hear about Jeff and Alexis?" she asks while I eye the screen.

"No."

"Well...I got a text before you made it up here. Heather heard that Alexis found Jeff making out with Jenny. Something about Jeff saying he had to stay late for school, and Alexis, who is apparently feeling better, wanted to surprise him. She was going to wait by his car after school, but he was already in the car, with Jenny."

A mix of emotions roll through me like a tsunami, which convolute my feelings on the matter. What Jeff did makes me sick. I also feel sorry for Alexis and can't imagine what she's feeling. However, there's a small part of me that's pleased. Jeff's sins are exposed, and now others truly saw him as I did—as a complete asshole.

"Doesn't surprise me," I finally say.

"Why?"

I open the cover art and expand the screen. "Aside from him being an asshole?"

Erika squints at my question.

I exhale a deep breath and decide upon a more tactful answer. "It was the both of them. Jeff was too flirty, and she couldn't keep her eyes off him. It doesn't surprise me with him, but I can't believe Jenny would do something like that, knowing he was with Alexis. It'll devastate her."

"Not me," she says.

"What do you mean?"

"Being surprised. I know Jenny has a party-girl reputation, but she also enjoys catching boys who are trouble. I think this is just the first time she has been caught."

"Nice guys finish last," I say under my breath.

Erika's expression turns serious. "Most of the guys who say that aren't nice. For the ones who are, they wouldn't finish last if they weren't so shy."

I can't help but think she's talking about me. I live in my head for too long, to the point I forget to say anything.

"Don't get me wrong," she continues, "I'm mad as hell at both Jeff and Jenny for what they've done to Alexis, but maybe those two deserve one another. Alexis is flighty, but she is a great girl and deserves better than Jeff."

"She does. So, ready to go over the yearbook?" I desperately want to move on to a less complicated topic.

"Sure."

We work together for a couple of hours and only discuss issues relevant to the project, then we depart with an awkward goodbye that culminates in something that was a part hug and part handshake. It was awful. I run to my locker to unburden my backpack with items I no longer need. Feeling twenty pounds lighter, I stroll out of the school and run into a setting sun and an evening air that bites sharply at my skin.

The lot is empty except for a group of basketball players huddled together fifty feet away.

Nathan Greenwald, the school's center, gives a cat-call whistle. "Hey, J.J. You're here late. Baseball?" He's an odd kid, but just odd enough. We usually hang out a couple times a year, which we both find to be an efficient number.

"Nah, just working on a project."

"Alright, man. Have a good night," he yells.

I wave. "Thanks. You too. See you, guys," I say to the other players.

I fumble the keys and eventually drop them, cursing my coordination until the keys are back in hand.

A slight gust of wind brings about a rash of goosebumps, but there is more to the reaction than the unpleasant air. I am cold to the core, and my heart races, faster and faster as I stand frozen in place.

Your fear is misplaced, a deep voice sounds in my head. It's distant, traveling over water from a great distance. Something moves in the reflection of the backseat window. After what seems like an hour, I rotate my head enough to get a better look at the reflection, finding a blurry figure some distance away. My bladder begs for release as my stomach knots.

The last thing I want to do is turn and face the beast, but

that's what I do. It's a slow turn, body and mind at war with one another. I want to run, to get into my car and flee as fast as possible, but something forces me to stay. Something I can't explain. It's as if the beast holds control over my actions.

Face me. The voice calls to me, an anchor I cannot resist. It's in my head. It must be.

Midway through the turn, I squint as hard as possible, sealing my eyes. *If I don't see it, it isn't real.* After a few breaths, I dare a look. *It isn't real,* I tell myself repeatedly. Paralysis and fear overcome both mind and body, but I'm not surprised by what I see. Deep down, I knew what awaited.

About sixty feet away, in the opposite direction of the basketball players, is the black dog.

We stare at one another, neither blinking nor moving. I hear voices behind me, probably the basketball players, but I don't care. They don't exist in the moment. Somehow, without consciously being aware, I gain some composure and slowly unlock the car, never taking my eyes off the beast. At the click of the lock, the dog rises from its seated position and steps forward, silently baring its teeth.

Face me, the voice says again, distant and faint, somewhere in the back of my mind.

"Hell no," I respond out loud.

The menacing look is unsettling. To say the least.

I sidestep to allow enough clearance for the car door to swing open. But, before I can pull the handle, the dog takes off at a sprint. Its mouth widens, lips curl around barred teeth. It makes no sound as it sprints forward. A silent reaper driven to collect its soul. *Embrace me.* The voice louder than before, a weight to the words as they nearly drive me to the ground.

As the beast quickly closes the gap between us, I stand paralyzed, the car door shut. I can't explain my inability to disappear into the safety of hard metal. I can't move. The reason is beyond fear. Something within, deep and with conviction, roots me in place. My eyes fall shut when the beast is near, and I wait calmly for teeth to find flesh.

Something shakes me. I open my eyes and find Nathan, along with a few of his teammates. "Dude, what the hell?"

"Huh?" I ask, shaking uncontrollably.

Nathan is frantic, arms flailing like a stringed puppet. "You were screaming like a freaked-out little girl. You stared off into the distance for a few minutes and then, all of the sudden, you lost your damn mind."

I'm unaware of any screaming, but I take them at their word. They are as freaked out as I am. "It was the dog. Where did it go?" I look left then right, but see nothing, no animal of any kind.

"What dog?"

"The one that was coming at me," I say with a hint of panic. Partly for fear of another attack, but more so that the whole thing was a hallucination.

Two guys off to the right whisper to one another as Nathan looks confused, and worried. I quickly realize I'm the only one to have seen the beast.

"Never mind," I say, quickly turning to my car.

"Woah man, should you be driving? You seemed really messed up for a second. I heard this is what happened in class the other day."

"I said it was nothing," I yell, maybe even scream. The guys back off as I slam the car door. The basketball players jump out of the way as I punch the accelerator.

My breathing matches my speed as I roar onto the road. I make it halfway home before slowing down to avoid a speeding ticket, or death.

I punch the steering wheel with both fists, repeatedly, splitting flesh atop my knuckles. "What the hell is happening to me?" I yell into the windshield, begging my own mind to respond, to tell me that it will be okay.

7
THE COLOR OF EVIL

SUSAN

A simple, gray cell phone jumps quickly from one hand to another. The next course of action requires a difficult choice. I stare at the phone and contemplate the consequences of every possible decision.

What a shitty motel, I think, looking around the room. Having stayed in many questionable establishments, there is something to be said in calling this one exceptionally grotesque. The bed creaks like a collapsing home, the walls coated with who knows what, and the carpet is stained to the point that its natural color is unknown. Quality of living is just one of the many sacrifices I've made during this cross-country trip. I have very little in terms of money, which results in less than favorable living conditions, in all facets of life.

I did manage to keep enough aside to support my medicinal panel of several types of alcohol. I'm good at prioritizing needs.

Wallowing in the filth is a distraction, an attempt to stall the impending but required verdict on how to proceed. Who I call, or don't call, could determine the success of my mission.

Closing in on the target is exciting, but the increasing danger is nerve-wracking.

Once again, I'm at odds with myself.

I caught a break in the discussion with Mr. Turner. He recognized a name on the list. There wasn't conviction in the recognition, and he couldn't recall why it seemed familiar, but I believed him. I had to, and that thing burrowed deep within the recesses of my mind agreed.

The revelation, absent any hard evidence, puts me in an uncomfortable situation. I need help tying the pieces together, but I'm unsure who to trust. Even a sliver of trust will work. There is risk, no matter what I decide to do.

After an hour of merciless anxiety, I steel myself and dial the number.

It rings twice.

"Susan! Is everything okay?"

"Hey, Joyce. Yeah, everything is okay. How are you?"

"I'm good. We're good. About to sit down for some dinner." There is a pause. A deep breath. One that comes mid-thought. "We all miss you. Are you sure you're okay?"

"Yeah. I'm sorry for calling so late and interrupting dinner."

"It's alright. Don't worry about it. We haven't sat down yet."

Children in the background are yelling.

I need to get to the point before I lose my gall. "Good. Listen, I need your help." I cringe when she doesn't reply.

There is no going back now. "Joyce?"

"No," comes a cold, stern, matter-of-fact answer. "I don't want any part of what you are up to. There have been rumors, but I didn't want to believe them. I want plausible deniability. Please, don't put me in an awkward situation. Don't make me choose between you and my career."

"Joyce—"

"Susan, *you* listen to me. I wish I could tell you that I wanted to help, but I don't. I can't afford to be part of this, to end up like you. This is your demon to fight. Don't you pull me into it."

"I'm calling in my favor." It's a low blow, but I'm out of options. I feel sick at what I've done, that it must be this way between us. To force the hand of my only friend. To know that this would forever change our relationship. But the quarry is the most important thing in my life, and Joyce is the only person who can help without bringing law enforcement down on my head.

"How dare you call in that favor for this," she says in a strained whisper.

I feel my friend's seething but controlled anger through the phone, and I'm immediately thankful we aren't having this discussion in-person. It would take more strength than I possess to push, to ultimately force, Joyce into helping if she were sitting across from me.

"You don't even know what it's for."

"I'm sure I *do* know what it's for."

"Joyce, I need this, and you're the only one who can help. I'm using my favor, and you can't tell anyone what I've asked you to do."

There is a deep sigh. "Do you know what this will do to our friendship?"

"I do, but I hope you'll understand, one day…when this is all over."

"I doubt I will, but I owe you. What do you need?"

"I need you to set up an alert for a list of names. Contact me if any of them are used or flagged."

"Fine. Preexisting?"

"Only if they have hit once, no more, and in the last five years."

"Any particular state? City?"

I rattle off the names and states of interest.

"Anything else?" Joyce asks.

"That's it."

There's a click before I'm able to say anything more. The suddenness of the hang-up births a spout of self-doubt, which leads to a feeling of disgust. But the cards have been played, and I will have to live with the consequences.

It will be worth it, if I'm successful. The ends will justify the means, or at least that's what I tell myself.

Relief from my despair comes in the uncomfortable form of a stomach growl. I throw on a jacket and head for the door, grabbing keys and downing what's left of a cheap bottle of whiskey on my way out. There is a hole-in-the-wall Chinese restaurant, situated between a dry-cleaner and electronic repair store, within walking distance. They probably deliver, but I need some fresh air, so into the cold and dark night I venture.

The street is empty of both pedestrians and traffic. Newspapers and other paper products float like something out of a movie, directed by the will of the wind. The dim glow of sporadic streetlights—of which only a few are operational—paint an eerie picture of an apocalyptic ghost town.

I walk along exterior walls of worn-out and decaying businesses, most of which are adjoined. Experience pushes me as far away from the street as possible, hidden in shadow and darkness, fingers never more than a few inches from either knife or pistol.

On the far side, two men move in unison, heads downcast, talking to one another in incoherent ramblings. I dart into an ally and watch them with strained eyes. An aura of something mischievous surrounds them, an omen, revealing plans yet to take place. The aura impossible to describe, but it resembles a yellow mist, or steam, radiating off the two men.

The sight is nothing new, an extra sense, and I've learned to trust my instincts—they have saved my life several times.

There is something unnatural about those instincts. A personal belief I've never discussed with anyone, but they are impossible to hide. While others operate with facts, I tend to formulate theories based upon feeling, meaning I rarely possess tangible proof for my actions. My peers, and more importantly my superiors, often refer to me as a maverick, an unpredictable gunslinger, a loner who is careless and unobservant of best practices and procedures.

I'm not held in high regard, especially in recent years, which explains my current situation.

After stealthily sliding out of the ally, I cross to the other side of the street. A hundred or so feet separate me from the two men. They are close enough to see but far enough away to remain ignorant of my pursuit.

Fingers coil around the cold metal at my hip, but I think better of it and reach for the knife. Hard to trace a knife.

The two men abruptly stop and look right, peering down what appears to be a small service road. I press up against the wall of an out-of-service pawn shop and watch. Preemptively committing to a confrontation, no matter how much I trust my instincts, isn't a solid plan.

No, I will wait until they act.

As I wait, my mind tells me I don't have time for this shit. My instincts push back, arguing this is the right thing. A determination to intercede overshadows the doubt, as it always does. Something violent is about to transpire, and I can't ignore it, no matter how hard I try.

I tell myself it's the right thing to do. The thought wrapped in a thin blanket of disgust. Ironically, I've always felt my true personality is best described as a self-centered hermit, but that bitch of a thing that lives within me won't allow it. It's exhausting being at war with yourself.

It helped that I'm also an action-junkie, and whether by a curse, divine intervention, or lucky circumstance, this instinct overcame my natural born personality through an offering of violence. In a way, I can see things before they happen, and the feeling that comes along with the sight drives me to follow evil into the depths of hell.

The combating forces—flight or fight—have led to turmoil in both my personal and professional life. So, naturally, I drink, which often leads to self-destructive behavior. Helping people is nice, but those positive feelings are short-lived, and then the war within me resumes. Someone with severall advanced degrees would probably call that a vicious cycle, my life likely an avenue for fame if I were to become a willing subject.

One of the two men turns, and I fear discovery. Dark eyes roll over my position, but they don't linger, his attention returning to the road. I remain unseen, and a deep exhale escapes through pursed lips. The men talk in whispers. They take off at a sprint at the sound of metal colliding.

"Shit," I murmur, emerging from the darkness.

I run with all that I have, lungs straining against the cold, heavy night. Transparent clouds of quick breathing push out into the night, dissipating within seconds. I hear sounds of struggle before I round the corner. I yank the knife free and turn down the access road, never slowing.

The two men stand atop a bloody body, punching and kicking, hurling line after line of insults. The victim is an older, Asian man curled into the fetal position, moaning against each strike, crying out for mercy, begging for someone to save him.

They never see me coming.

I jump into the air and extend a knee, striking the back of the largest assailant as he goes for the man's wallet. The force of the impact sends the guy stumbling forward, tripping over his own feet before toppling, where he rolls several times.

After landing on the balls of my feet, I square my shoulders and find the second attacker. The smaller man is lanky but lean. He has taken a step back, obviously surprised by the interruption.

"Who the hell are you?" He looks to his partner in crime

when I don't respond. "You'll pay for that, bitch." He braves a few steps forward and throws a right hook.

With the knife in hand, I duck beneath the swing and complete a full circle, bringing the knife around and thrusting it into the man's thigh. I twist the handle slightly before removing the blade. *That won't heal for a while.*

A scream of agony shadows flailing hands. He quickly topples over. There is a string of curses intermixed with childish whimpers as he convulses along the far wall.

"I'll kill you," he keeps yelling.

"Sure you will," I mutter as I turn.

Somewhere to my right there is a shuffle of feet against pavement, so I complete my turn quickly and find the larger man working his way back to the fight, bearing a knife of his own. He is shaking, clumsy and uncomfortable. I surmise this is his first knife fight.

I don't mean to smile.

I nonchalantly relax both shoulders and let my own knife fall to the side. I lock eyes with the uninjured assailant as he continues his advance. I raise a hand, and he slows. Without breaking eye contact, I point to his counterpart, who has moved on from yelling in syllables to outright threats of what he is going to do to me. "You have one chance to leave. Take your crying friend and go."

Eyes flicker for a moment, considering the offer, then his hesitation gives way to determination. "I am going to cut you up," he says through labored breaths.

"Good luck."

He moves first, like some epileptic dance. I meet his flailing charge in one step and kick him in the chest before he's able to raise the knife. Stumbling backwards, he trips over uneven ground and falls, hitting his head against the pavement. He rolls onto his stomach, reaching slowly for his head. I kick him over onto his back and straddle his chest, pinning both arms with my knees.

"Who are you?" he asks with dazed eyes, nearly unconscious. No doubt he has a concussion.

I say nothing. I feel bone and flesh crack after the second punch. His body goes limp.

He won't wake for some time.

I turn. The man I stabbed is standing, sort of. He's leaning heavily upon the building's wall, both hands busy against the knife wound. "You want some more, bitch?" I ask with a smirk, knife raised.

He shakes his head and limps back out into the street, leaving his buddy behind. I turn toward their victim and find the older man on all fours, blood seeping from his mouth.

I kneel, level but still a few feet away. "Your car close?"

He nods, a hand going to his ribcage.

"Can you drive?"

"Yes," he manages through a cough.

"Good. I'll walk you to it, but then you will get in and forget my face. Deal?"

We lock eyes. He wants to protest, maybe ask a series of questions, but he nods. "Thank you," he says through gulps of pain as I help him stand.

8

THE NEW KID

JACOBY

"What the hell?" I ask on repeat, burning a path into my bedroom's carpet. What's happening to me makes no sense. I'm not sick. I haven't had any trauma to the head. I can't understand why I'm suddenly seeing a weird dog from a weird experience years ago, proven unreal since I'm the only one seeing it.

My brain aches. A different pain than a normal headache.

Since the parking lot, I've thought of nothing else but the dog, and how I'm the only one who can see it. No matter the explanation I've contrived, the root cause is always the same: I am going insane.

There is a soft knock at the bedroom door.

"Yeah?" I ask nervously.

"It's me, son," my father answers with a whisper. "Can I come in?"

There's a twinge somewhere deep within my stomach. I

need control. If not, I'll need to come clean about this madness. To my father. To others. My father will pry and push until the issue is brought up, but I'm not in the mood to talk. Not yet.

I plan to solve this madness on my own.

I rub my eyes against an audible sigh. My father's worries will deepen the more I shrug him off. I collapse on the bed. "Yeah. Sure."

Treading lightly, my father enters and grabs the desk chair. He settles beside the bed, where I lay outstretched like I've got the world by the horns.

"What's going on? I've called the school for two days now, like you begged me to do, and told them that you're sick and staying home. But you won't go to a doctor and you've been sulking up here in your room the entire time. You've barely said two words to your sister...and me."

"It's nothing. I just feel off. Like a cold or something."

Across from me, unconvinced eyes blink slowly. "It's more than nothing, isn't it?"

An urge to scream is muted by exhaustion. I struggle to decide whether to tell my father. The thought of unburdening myself, to pull someone in close, provides an unexplainable relief. My hands begin to fidget, and my father notices.

"Come on, kiddo. Talk to me."

Several deep breaths help. I settle upon disclosing enough information to unburden the both of us. "Do you remember that story about the dog that showed up years ago, and the man who claimed to be animal control?"

He's surprised. I suspect this wasn't the direction he anticipated. "I do," he answers curiously. "Kind of an odd day if I recall. What's that have to do with this?"

An unexpected breath escapes as I contemplate the most efficient way to summarize what has occurred. "Well, I dreamed about it the other night. The dog." I look nervously around the room, expecting to see the beast. I find nothing abnormal. "Then I saw the dog."

"You saw it in your dream?"

An involuntary, sarcastic laugh drips from chapped lips. "Yes. At first. But then I saw it in the parking lot. At school." He doesn't need to know I've seen it twice.

"You're sure it was the same dog?"

"Yes, I am. It matched exactly, but I don't think it was real."

Dad's curiosity turns to confusion and concern. "I don't understand."

"I think I hallucinated it. There were some basketball players in the parking lot. They didn't see it."

"I see," he responds carefully, somewhat judgmentally. Silence hangs in the air while my father considers the confession. Hard features soften, and I feel a hand upon my shin. "You've been out late a lot, kiddo. Whether with friends, practice, or clubs...and I think you probably just need some sleep."

"It isn't normal, and it scared the shit out of me. Dad, I don't know what's wrong with me." The walls are crumbling. I hate that the siege, the enemy, has won. I fear what I might say, and the consequences of those words. My mind digs up old wounds. I see my mother's face. All the walls I've built over the years are in scope at this moment. The dam is punctured, threatening to dissolve entirely.

I take a deep breath, driven to repair the ruptures. This is enough emotion for one night.

"It sounds scary. I'm sorry you're in pain. Try to sleep. I think you'll feel better. Alright?"

I fail to hide my frustration. The words are encouraging, but I feel dismissed. Like everything else in this family, everyone is too afraid to dig deep, too afraid of what we might discover. I'm left feeling small, that I'm overreacting because what's happening to me is as common as getting a cold, an ailment relieved by a good night's rest. Part of me hopes it's true, but another part, a very small part, wants it to be real—an unnatural event with some supernatural meaning. At the very least, I know what haunts me is uncommon, and I want to know why it's happening to me.

I tell myself to calm down. To move on from this moment unscathed. "Alright. Thanks, Dad."

"No problem. I'll see you in the morning."

As expected, word about my breakdown has circulated throughout the school in my absence, proven when I'm accosted by several friends, who each have a handful of questions, before I make it to my locker.

My issues are my own. They are private, mine to deal with, but I'm certain my episode has spread like wildfire via text message and social media. I've always possessed a subtle distaste for my own generation, which seems to have a need, a desire even, to share everything about their lives on social media—to friends, acquaintances, even strangers. Nothing is private anymore. No. That isn't correct. People attempt to hide their hideousness while outwardly portraying their best. The family that posts pictures of their smiling faces while traveling the world only to find out the dad is abusive, and the mom is a junkie. Or the most popular kid in high school with thousands of friends who commits suicide because something deep down is broken.

Many people share carefully selected, sometimes staged, blocks of their lives while others await, device ready, to share the more human, personal, and vulnerable parts—the parts we wish to keep private.

That's the worst part about social media—the ability of others to share the lives of others, against their will or even knowledge. It isn't right or fair, and we, as humans, have normalized, promoted even, hatred in return for likes, followers, and money. Life has become a judgment of others via algorithms catered to an individual's worldview. I fucking hate social media.

I do my best to shrug off the inquiries, once again referencing how the nurse sent me home to deal with an ailment. I assure all interested parties that I've taken the magical pills, gotten some sleep, and am feeling much better. That something as simple as a prescription and sleep worked miracles on an overworked mind and tired body.

Halfway through chemistry, an office runner knocks on the classroom's door. Most teachers would fume over the interruption, but Mrs. Rolland stands from the desk and happily retrieves a slip of paper from a nervous looking girl, who then darts back to whatever member of the office staff she slaves for.

Mrs. Rolland reads over the document and then places it upside down on the desk. "Now, where were we?" she asks with a smile, eyes glancing my way. It's a rhetorical question, and she continues with the lesson before anyone manages a blink.

Class is miserably slow. The urge to sprint out of the building and hide from the world is overwhelming. Hitting a couple dozen balls would help clear my head, but it's unbearably cold outside, so I fantasized about retreating into the warmth and safety of my bedroom.

In the end, I wrestle down the anxiety because there's no escaping this prison. A merciless prison where everyone knows everyone else's business.

I'm the last to rise and head for the door when class is dismissed, hoping the delay allows a solitary escape of my friends and their judgmental questions.

"Mr. Talavan," my teacher says softly.

Mrs. Roland's face is one of a concerned mother. "Yes?"

The document she acquired from the runner manifests.

"This is for you," she says shyly, as if handing back a failed assignment.

"Uh, thanks." Flipping the document over, I skim over numerous boxes until I find a section designated for comments. I'm to report to the school counselor's office. Must be bad. These types of requests are typically sent via tablet. "What's this for?" I ask while re-reading with more attention. The document is vague.

"I'm not sure. But it asked that I wait until class was over to give it to you."

How thoughtful not to call out my issues in front of the whole class. "Great," I mumble.

Mrs. Rolland provides a sympathetic smile. "Everything okay, dear?"

I sense additional questions on the tip of her tongue. Her resolve to better my life is commendable, but I have no desire to give her the opportunity. "Yeah. Thanks for asking," I say quickly, which comes out harsher than intended.

The document is folded and stuffed into a pant-leg pocket. A restroom is across the hall, and I dart into one of the stalls, opening a Texas Hold'em game on my phone to pass the time. The bell rings after a few rounds, signifying the hallways should be empty. I prefer no one see where I'm heading. I close the application and head toward the counselor's office.

I meander up to the office door and attempt to calm myself. *I hate this.* I hate this part of the school and the memories it elicits. I'm a nervous wreck, contemplating the reasons for my visit. I come up with nothing but my recent freak-outs. I pace for a good two minutes then double-check the note, hoping I misread the summons, which I haven't, then enter.

A receptionist sits behind a large desk at the center of the room, violently scribbling on a notepad. She is the gatekeeper for the *Lion's Den*, that's what most students call it—the office being home to the principal, vice-principal, athletic director, and counselor.

I've spelunked this cave before, barely ascending with life. I've interacted with each of those who call this office home, on numerous occasions, usually to receive some sort of athletic award. The counselor was a different type of encounter, our unpleasant conversations restricted within the walls of her office. Apparently, it's school policy to make the loss of a parent as discomforting as possible, requiring several sessions with the school's counselor to relive a horrific event, repeatedly, and to put words to the associated feelings.

I'd hoped to never return.

The dark-haired receptionist, different from the one a year ago, looks up as the door closes with a jingle. "Good morning. How can I help you?"

I'm given a quick once-over with a forced smile. My presence annoys her. I'm sure she's been told to smile, to be warm and welcoming, which she feigns while internally hating both herself and this job. Personally, I'm happy to spare the pen and paper a few moments of agony. It's like she was trying to start a fire.

"Talavan. Jacoby Talavan." *What the hell was that? You're not James Bond. You idiot.* This place has me all out of sorts. "I—"

"Ah, yes. Mr. Talavan. Mrs. Johnston is ready for you," she says without looking, having returned to her notepad.

"Okay," I manage through a quick back spasm and shaking hands. I realize, unable to take a step, that I'm more nervous than anticipated.

The receptionist notices my failure to move. "You can go on back. She's the last door on the left."

"I know the way. But thanks," I quip.

I'm rooted where I stand.

"Umm...," the receptionist mutters. "Do you need assistance?"

Shit. No. Maybe. I don't want to make another scene but my legs won't work. I rock my entire body like I'm doing the wave. I manage a step as my hands crash downward. I turn to the receptionist, who appears absolutely befuddled, "I'm good," I say, slightly embarrassed.

The office sits twenty or so feet behind the receptionist's table, and I knock after taking several long, deep breaths. The door opens and I'm met by a middle-aged Hispanic woman.

Mrs. Johnston. I've seen her around the school, following the sessions regarding my mother, but I've made it a priority to avoid coming close enough to talk. We haven't said anything to one another since our last meeting.

"Mr. Talavan. Please, come in." she says, extending a hand.

I awkwardly take the outstretched hand and notice a slight shake in my own. I follow her into the office without a reply and take the closest chair, which faces another, a nondescript desk separating the two.

"It has been a while. How have you been?" she asks quickly, as if we are old friends catching up. I find it hard not to throat punch her. She was responsible for so much turmoil in my life, the bane of my existence for weeks, endlessly torturing me through the reliving of a traumatic event. After all that, she asks how I've been? *You're a psychopath.*

I fail to respond. Her question is insincere, a practiced conversation starter. She has no real concern toward my answer. It's obvious she has decided upon my answer before I ever entered her office. So, I say nothing.

"Please, don't be nervous," she offers with a warm but distracted smile.

Great. Nervous is an admission of guilt. I'm screwed.

"Do you know why you are here?" she asks while typing something out on her laptop, ignoring the fact I never answered her first question.

Straight to business. I think a moment. "Does this have something to do with what happened in class the other day?" *Vague enough.*

"Where you suddenly stood and asked for either a medical or bathroom pass?"

I shake my head while playing with a fingernail. "Yeah."

"Yes. It does. In part."

In part? I need to get ahead of this conversation, to finish it before she has a chance to ask too many questions. "The nurse sent me home. I wasn't feeling well. But, I stayed home the past couple of days, and now I'm feeling much better."

"Uh-huh," she hums out, opening a manila folder after finishing with whatever she was doing on her computer. I'm both infuriated and relieved I haven't held her full attention. "Mind telling me what happened in the school parking lot?"

Damn basketball players. They can't keep their mouths shut.

She notices the flash of anger, quickly raising both hands defensively. "You're not required to tell me anything you're not comfortable with. Just as before. I'm here to make sure you're okay. I talked with the nurse and those who were witness to your...to both of your outbur—"

"Outbursts?" I ask angrily.

"I'm sorry, I didn't have a better term, but I'm not sure what they were. That's what I called you in here for. To discover what's going on with you. You're a good student, a smart kid, a good athlete, and haven't gotten into any trouble here at Brighton.

"We have talked very little, except for the few sessions after your mother passed. So, sadly, I admit that I don't know you very well. I'm hoping you can tell me what's going on, so I can provide whatever help you need, or are not getting."

"I'm fine. Really. I've already received all the help I need."

The politeness, either real or forced, in her voice falls away like a snake shedding its skin. Gone is concern and in comes something more parental, more administrative. "We can't have students interrupting class or going well over the speed limit in the parking lot!"

"That's what this is all about? Someone is upset that I interrupted class, and that I drove out of the parking lot faster than I should have?"

Mrs. Johnston's lip twitches and a long breath follows, but she collects herself. "Partially. We are an educational institution. Here, we provide students with the means to further their intelligence and prepare for life. They can't do that if faced with distractions during class. We also need to ensure the safety of our students, which is where you high tailing out the parking lot comes in.

"You're not in trouble, Mr. Talavan. I'm just trying to help in any way that I can, to ensure neither of those incidents happen again. That you and the other students here at Brighton have the chance to safely educate themselves."

"Everyone at this school is so helpful," I say sarcastically.

"That is an unfair and unwarranted comment," she responds sternly.

Just do what it takes to get out of here. "You're right, and I'm sorry. It has just been a rough couple of days. I didn't feel well, and I wasn't getting much sleep. I honestly believe that was my problem. I slept well last night, and I feel much better. I promise that those events are behind me, and I'll do better."

"High school is full of a lot of pressure, and I know life has been tough for you over the past couple of years."

"You mean my mother?"

She nods.

"That has nothing to do with this," I say defensively.

"I didn't say that it did."

My eyes narrow. "It felt like an accusation."

"Jacoby, it wasn't. You went through something terrible, and it's natural for the loss of a parent to affect us in ways we couldn't have even imagined. These events could have roots there."

"She has nothing to do with this."

"Perhaps we should have talked more after she passed," she says to herself.

"I said she has nothing to do with this." My tone turns sour, and I'm readying myself for a full knock-down-drag-out.

I cringe beneath her gaze. Rational thoughts return, and I realize this is getting out of hand. Nothing productive would come out of a screaming match with the school counselor. She is looking for any excuse to make my life miserable. *Don't give her a reason.* "You could be right. But I really believe that this was something else. Something different, not related to my mother's death. I also believe that I am much better, and my... outbursts will cease. I promise to come back if this ends up being more."

My answer softens her determination. "I just want you to know that you can come see me anytime, to talk about anything you want, or need. Everything discussed here is private, unless it involves a crime, or bringing injury to yourself or others. Sorry," she continues when my eyebrows furrow, "it's a disclaimer that we have to make now. I don't believe you fall into any of those categories, so you have nothing to fear."

"Thank you for the offer, and I'll be sure to keep it in mind. Can I go now?" I ask, probably too quickly.

"You may. It was nice to see you again, Mr. Talavan."

"And you, Mrs. Johnston."

I leave quickly, with a fervent desire to never return to that office, inwardly vowing to myself, right then and there, that if the dog were to show up again, I would simply ignore it. A few steps down the hall, contemplating how quickly my life seems to be spiraling out of control, I notice Mitch walking beside a kid I don't recognize.

"Hey, man. All good?" Mitch asks.

"Yeah," I answer tiredly. "Nothing like a good mind-fuck."

"Great." It takes a moment for Mitch to realize what I had said. "Wait. What?"

"Don't worry about it."

"Okay. Well...This is Michael, the new kid I was telling you about."

We shake hands. "Michael. Not Brian, huh?" I ask with a smirk.

"Yeah, yeah," says Mitch.

"I'm Jacoby. So, I hear you play baseball."

Michael retracts his hand with a smile. "I do. Love the game. Been playing since before I could walk."

Jacoby nods. "We're going to be good this year, but we're always excited to get better."

"I heard you guys had a tough loss last year, but most of your players are returning. I'm excited to be a part of it."

"What position do you play?" I ask.

Michael's smile turns into a smirk. "I pitch and play short. Better at short than pitching, but not by much," he adds with a shit-eating grin.

Instinctively, I feel myself turning defensive, but I'm cut off before I manage to say anything.

"Sorry to break it to you, bud, but J.J. here was All-State shortstop last year as a sophomore."

Michael gives a whistle. "Well, that sucks for me, but I've played the corner before as well."

"Third base?" Mitch asks hopefully.

Our third baseman was one of the few seniors last year, and the kid slated to fill the spot isn't very good. If Michael is as good as he claims, then we might have the talent to make a run at a state title.

"Yep."

"That's great news," I say. "The spot is pretty much open, and we could use someone worth a damn there."

"Hey, Michael, mind if I catch up with Jacoby for a minute?" Michael nods but doesn't move. "Alone," Mitch eventually adds.

"Sure. I'll see you around. Nice to meet you, Jacoby."

"You too."

With a nod, Michael wanders off and Mitch turns.

"What?" I ask.

"Dude, what the hell is going on? I heard you had another breakdown? You didn't answer any of our texts or calls. You worried the shit out of us, man. Mark was betting that you died."

"Well, Mark will be pissed."

I'm slapped with a disapproving look.

"It wasn't a breakdown. I just still wasn't feeling well. But I got some sleep these past couple of days and took an unhealthy number of meds, and now I feel a whole lot better," I say jubilantly, dramatically.

"You better be. Seriously, man, don't just fall off the grid like that, after something like...whatever that was."

I'd do anything to be able to fall off the grid. "I know, but all is good. I promise."

"Alright. But let me know if you need anything."

"I could use some practice time soon."

"Agreed. Weather is getting crappy, but we can always throw and take some ground balls in the gym."

"That'll work."

"Just shoot me a text when you want to set it up. I'll try to get some of the other guys in on it as well. It's never too early to start preparing for that state championship run."

"Absolutely."

"Alright, man. I need to go find Megan, but I'll catch you later."

"You're so whipped," I tease.

"You would be too if you asked Erika out."

"Yeah, yeah. Get out of here." I want more than anything, aside from an end to the hallucinations, to ask her out, but the time is never right.

"Talk to you later," says Mitch.

I watch Mitch head down the opposite hallway while I imagine a different life for myself. One where I brought Erika home to meet my mother.

9
AN ENDLESS ECHO

Susan

There are things to do, so I reluctantly turn the knob, desperate to savor every second. The hot water ceases its therapeutic cleanse as a small shiver releases at the sudden absence of warmth. A fog of steam engulfs everything while the bathroom falls silent, except for an infuriating drip from a worn and rusty fixture.

I reach for a towel hanging outside the shower and hear a soft but persistent *ping*. I dry quickly and wrap the towel around my form, moving swiftly into the motel's only other room. The potential of another breakthrough births excitement, which transitions into sadness, then anger, when I consider the implications of an alert.

The computer beeps until I dismiss the alert. A customized program built upon dozens of variables has flagged a recent news article. I read quickly. The bodies of two young females were discovered somewhere in southern Indiana.

I'm suddenly aware these murders are relevant. It washes over me in waves, each burst strengthening in intensity until it's abundantly clear these girls were murdered by the beast I'm hunting. My brain applauds in excitement as my stomach tightens with nausea. I've relentlessly prayed for a lead, but a heavy price has been paid.

"I'm going to find you. I'm going to kill you," I mutter to myself. A promise that became a mantra over time. I promised long ago there wouldn't be a trial. No prison. No interviews. No opportunity to defend so much death. No. My face would be the last this man ever sees.

Doubt seeps into my mind with long, dark vines. *It may not even be him. What if the killer isn't a male? Don't doubt yourself. The names are all male, and that's the profile.*

The article claims a man and his dog were hiking in a heavily wooded area outside of Terre Haute the day before, where, at some point during the hike, the dog had slipped his owner and found the remains by digging for several minutes. The discovery of the bodies happened sooner than the others, at least those that have been found. Likely pure coincidence the girls were found so deep within a rather remote forest. Not necessarily a mistake by the killer, but it's a turn of events I plan to capitalize upon.

Both girls were missing for nearly three months, sickening to consider, but I can't deny the importance of the story. Guilt accompanies a sliver of hope. If truly relevant, these murders are the most recent case in my theory, by a long shot.

Since this crusade began, I've been nothing more than an observer, as both years and states have separated me from my prey. Like turning on a murder movie and watching the story unfold without any ability to alter the course of events. I've been a groupie several shows behind.

The search has been both frustrating and disheartening more times than not. There is no distinguishing pattern, regarding the path of the murders, other than they trail west. Sometimes it's clear the victims were murdered, other times they appear to be accidents. But, either way, chunks of flesh were always missing.

I began this hunt too late, too far removed to catch up with the killer, let alone head him off. These girls, God rest their souls, could be the break I need because it puts me mere months behind the killer. Taking into account the timelines I've put together, he's searching for his next victim.

Trust but verify. I trust my instinct with my life, but it doesn't mean I forgo all evidence. I've found the more I help myself the more the instinct kicks in to fill the gaps. The instinct rarely raises its head from nothing. So, I search for information, dig, until the instinct comes alive to help set the path.

I scroll over the highlighted words, seeking to understand the relevant variables. You can't imagine how many murders take place daily in the United States, let alone the world. I read somewhere, long ago, that the human brain is incapable of comprehending the sheer horror.

I read through the highlights: the girls disappeared at night, both were brunettes, the bodies were hard to find, and their cell phones were missing—all of which match every other case in my theory and fall within the parameters of the program.

I read on. The girls occasionally hiked the area together, the journalist states, but never that deep into the forest. The bodies, once unearthed, were unrecognizable, resulting in a need to verify the remains through dental records.

Despite the system's notification, the instinct, and eerily similar circumstances, I'm admittedly skeptical. Murders like this aren't necessarily uncommon. It's the more nuanced details that matter; a subtle calling-card important only to the killer, or a specific style that goes unnoticed by most investigators. I need to see those details to believe it's *my* killer, and to justify the time and money it will take to investigate this case. One wrong move could set me back months.

I have acted on less in the past, but money is waning, which means I need to make intelligent decisions about which cases to pursue. A time is coming when I'll need to stretch the evidence and pray for some luck, but not yet. There is still time, and a few unexplored options. I stare at the picture of the crime scene, picturing the two girls lying naked, lifeless upon the cold earth. Maybe less time and less options than I want to admit.

The noticeable difference between this case and the others, and the reason for skepticism, is the presence of two bodies. All other cases involved one missing, or murdered, female with brunette hair. Committing two murders in the same town, let alone at the same time, is a drastic deviation from the killer's profile.

Is he growing bored? Was it by accident? Did he mess up? No. He's too smart to mess up. If it's him, then this was on purpose.

The questions flow until, in a rare turn of events, I decide against my instinct. The presence of two bodies is too much of deviation. This isn't the man I'm hunting.

Biting my lip, I decide to take a risk before putting this story out of mind.

I open a link and insert the requested credentials to gain access to a secure database. The case remains local, so logging in to poke around shouldn't garner too much attention. *I'll be quick*, I tell myself. It takes some time, more time than I anticipated, but I eventually find the desired folder and double-click, opening a mirage of crime scene photos. I quickly scan through the first few images. The search takes too long, and I'm willing myself not to look at the phone—anticipating a rather unpleasant call—so I'm distractedly, fervently, flipping through the pictures when I suddenly stop.

I jump from the chair. "Holy shit," I yell aloud. I pace the room, water from still wet hair thrown about the room as I jump and twirl.

Once calm, I return to the chair. "How about that," I mumble, staring more closely at the screen. The initial shock, and the rush of excitement that followed, melts away. I feel small, uneasy, as if I'm looking the devil straight in the face.

The pictures are horrific, especially the one on-screen, but I've seen worse. Both bodies are covered in blood—their own—the result of an indiscernible amount of knife wounds. Chunks of flesh are missing in various places, likely to be attributed to wild animals. I can't help but picture the killer consuming their flesh. I nearly puke, but I steel myself and press forward.

Always a knife, I think, eyes glued to the screen. The number of wounds differed from victim to victim. Every case I've run down possessed similar circumstances and three items: each victim had a knife wound somewhere along the throat, and the body, or bodies, were dumped where wild animals had access, likely a strategy to hide the killer's cannibalistic tendencies. The third similarity is what I've labeled as the killer's calling card.

Under all the blood, I find a smear pattern most would dismiss, that everyone has dismissed, at least in connecting the murders to a single killer, which I see due to countless hours spent looking through similar photos. The hidden pattern is foundational to my theory—the one my superiors found lacking in evidence—and the primary detail used in filtering cases.

With enough patience and focus, one can see a skewed handprint on both girls' necks. If tested, the mark would prove to be the hand of the victim, most likely believed to be the reaction to a wound somewhere in the area. My superiors argued anybody would throw a hand to their throat if it was spitting blood. Their point is impossible to argue with, obviously, but the marks are too similar. I visualize the killer pressing the victim's hand to a pool of blood then carefully wrapping the hand around their own throat while he did unimaginable horrors.

I zoom in and out of the girls' throats. It's always the victim's left hand that wraps around the throat, which eventually falls or is placed off to their left side.

At first, before heading west, I believed the discovery was an end to the case, that the handprint belonged to the man responsible for all this death. Now, I know better. Tests will prove otherwise, as they all have, and I've come to realize I'm hunting a highly intelligent serial killer who wouldn't risk exposure by placing his own, naked hand on the victim. The killer will have guided the victims' own hands as he carried out unimaginable, horrific acts of violence.

The importance of the gesture, the calling-card, remains unknown, but it's common across every case I've investigated. At least the cases where the body, or bodies in this case, were discovered. The missing person cases are obviously different and require a degree of guesswork. Absent a body, and the handprint as a result, these cases are difficult to confidently declare relevant to my theory. But, like the murders, there are details that set them apart.

Staring at the photo, I mull over my options. *I need to be there. Maybe there's a trail.*

Recently found bodies produce a circus of cops, journalists, and other forms of media attention. All of which make it difficult, and risky, to conduct an independent investigation. Especially for me, when I'm supposed to steer clear of all cases.

Biting at my lip, I measure risk versus reward.

I quickly pack my things and check out of the motel. The Mustang roars to life soon after as I take off for southern Indiana.

The blue and white classic car roars into the small town of Cedar Groove five hours later. A worn and dirty sign marks the city's territory, welcoming visitors to the small town known for producing a *Ms. Basketball* I've never heard of. A population tracker at the bottom of the sign appears neglected and likely inaccurate.

A few hours of daylight remain, so I decide to make a run past the crime scene. I send up a silent and rare thank you to the media for noting the location the victims were found.

The dark and barren woods playing home to the murders is remote and hard to find. The perimeter flaunts rusty gates, collapsed fences, and a string of *Private Property* signs that look several decades old.

Considering the setting, the killer likely thought the bodies would remain hidden for years, which is consistent with the other cases I've deemed pertinent.

Cops, tape, and orange cones block off the only road that runs along the woods; all of which serve to divert traffic and to ensure no one stumbles upon the crime scene, either accidentally or on purpose.

I drive past the access point and complete a U-turn about half a mile down the road. On the next pass I notice I've garnered the attention of a certain cop. Midway through the stare-down, the woman steps out into the road and throws a hand in the air.

"Shit." I slow the car and put it into park, using a crank to lower my window as the officer approaches.

"Good afternoon," she says, leaning an elbow against the Mustang.

Get off my car, you smug, small-town wannabe cop. "What can I do for you, officer?" I ask, dramatically naive.

The cop isn't thrown. "It's sheriff, actually. Sheriff Gosnel."

"Alright, Sheriff Gosnel, to what do I owe the pleasure?"

"Well, you see, this is a crime scene, and I noticed you drive down the road this way," she points west, "then back this way," then east. "I just want to make sure you're aware that you should stay clear of this area."

I've dealt with several small-town police personnel in my short career. Enough to harbor a certain expectation, or lack of expectation. I immediately note Sheriff Gosnel as different. I decide to tread carefully. "I admit, I was curious about what's going on. I heard it on the news. Such a tragedy. I won't let my curiosity get the better of me again. I'll make sure to keep my distance."

"That's all I ask. Have yourself a good day, now." I cringe as she taps the hood of the Mustang.

I consider making an issue with the sheriff but ultimately decide there are more important items to tend to, so I avert my eyes and drive on. The crime scene likely has little to offer at this point. I have what I need from the photos to pick up the trail, if there is one to be found.

There is a cheap and dilapidated looking motel about ten miles south. I coast onto cracked pavement and kill the engine. I grab my bag from the trunk and head toward a faltering light. A bell rings as I pass into a small room. The air is thick with exhaled smoke and my nostrils flare at something pungent.

A rather thin man with greasy hair sits behind a desk to my right. I approach and shrug off a head-to-toe analysis from appraising eyes. "Well..." he says, clearing his throat. "How might I be of service?"

Eyes up, asshole.

"I'd like a room."

"Full night?" he asks. A pause. He wants to ask something else. "By hour?" he finally manages to spit out with raised eyebrows, hopeful.

My right-hand clenches into a fist. Fingernails bite into flesh. I imagine shattering the man's nose, straddling him to deliver punch after punch until he goes limp. *I'm supposed to be avoiding attention.* A deep breath loosens coiled muscles. "Full night."

We stare at one another for an uncomfortable stretch.

"Full night," I reiterate, voice stern.

His demeanor shifts. He sees something in me. Something beneath the surface. "Right. Cash or card?"

"Cash." I hand over the required amount, grab the key in haste, and go in search of room 7.

The door opens with a low, horrible groan at every inch given. I sigh, expecting an uninhabitable environment. I flip the switch and, to my surprise, discover a room far improved from the motel's exterior. The bed is tidy and appears clean. A modern TV is mounted along the far wall. A simple but new coffee pot sits atop a strong end table. The place smells clean. *Not bad for a cheap motel in a shit-hole town.* It isn't paradise, but it will do.

I unpack my bag and find the shower. The water is hard but warm. Traveling carries a haze, a stench I've always removed as soon as possible. I dry and dress, contemplating my next move. The sheriff knows my face, so I decide to lay low for a couple of days. There is plenty of research I can garner from the safety of a motel room.

No time like the present. After typing in the victim's names—Shelby Herring and Natasha Daniels—I hit enter and read quickly. Interviewing the parents with widespread attention on the case is impossible, so I look for affiliations the police might miss or will have already considered.

Pulling out the black book, I write down whatever information might be useful, and after several pages of notes, along with a few beers, I close the book and go in search of sleep.

It's a restless night, a familiar dream returns. In it, I'm in a crowded place, walking, invisible to everyone around me. I gaze upon contorted faces, a jigsaw puzzle yet to come together. I feel their pain as they meander. Gunshots echo throughout the building. The crowd panics. They run for exits, screaming. More gunshots. I wade into the current of the crowd. I'm pushed, and I push back. I make it maybe twenty feet when I suddenly stop. I raise my weapon and fire.

The scene changes. A new dream. I'm hunting a demon with no face; more shadow than human. The landscape is dark.

I see only what is immediately in front of me. Even then, something is wrong with the air, a slithering fog works itself in and out of my vision. An echo of a voice ripples across a vast ocean, mounted atop ominous waves. It sounds like a medieval chant in an alien language. There are drums, a slow beat that escalates with each step I muster. A hand rests upon my shoulder. I'm turned with force. The demon revealing he was the hunter all along.

10
IF DREAMS COULD TALK

JACOBY

I'm within sight of my destination. The engine is running, but I miserably fail to find the courage to pull into the driveway. *Her* driveway. I'm as nervous as a middle school boy at his first dance, and it's aggravating.

Just get on with it, I tell myself, but I go nowhere. "Where you going?" I ask, quoting a movie. "Fucking nowhere," I answer in defeat. My reaction is childish. I think I've forgotten to breathe several times.

This is ridiculous. You're going to be late.

With a few swipes of the thumb, I find a familiar playlist. A song contrived of blues, rock, and hip-hop plays through unreliable and old speakers. The crackle reminds me of vinyl, so what others find as a lack of clarity brings me joy. Looking around the vehicle, I frown. *I should have cleaned more. What a piece of shit.*

My head rests against the torn mesh of the seat's headrest, confidence rallying as I listen to the quickening beat. After a few songs, and no shortage of inspirational speeches to myself,

I find the courage to shift the car out of park and slowly pull into the driveway.

Get out. Don't sit here like a weirdo.

I begrudgingly step out of the car and take stock of the elegant property. The house wears white, vinyl siding with stressed brick layered throughout. A four-car garage sits to the left, while a magnificent porch wraps around the right side of the home. Large windows rise two floors, and the massive structure sits atop a small hill, with a walkout basement most likely visible from the back.

The parents are obviously loaded, which somehow makes this situation even more disconcerting. The buildup of confidence from my playlist diminishes, self-doubt and anxiety returns like a raging flood.

Although I've desired to step foot inside this house for years, today is my first time even seeing it. This visit, although somewhat fulfilling, isn't for the reason I've always imagined.

With hands tucked into pockets and head downcast, I sulk up to the front door like a whipped puppy. Mercifully, the door opens before I have a chance to knock or ring the doorbell.

"Hey!" Erika says, glowing.

Her brunette hair is pulled back into a ponytail and a stressed sweatshirt with a wide collar hangs loosely over both shoulders. She's in light blue jeans that sport several holes along both thigh and knee, the fabric tight around toned legs. A vibrant face full of life. In a world of glamour, photoshop, and cosmetics, Erika stands apart through simplicity and natural beauty. In terms of makeup, she wears only a light eyeshadow, which is enough.

I try like hell to return the smile, but it feels out of place. "Hey...umm, ready to go?"

"Sure! Let me grab a coat." She retreats into the house and emerges a few seconds later with a stylish gray peacoat that falls below her knees. "Be back later," she yells into the house. The door closes before I hear a response.

I make it back to the car without tripping or stumbling. A win in my mind. Without thinking much of it, I open the passenger side door. Certain manners, a sense of propriety, were instilled in me at a very early age.

"Wow. Thank you, sir," she says, bowing her head.

"You're welcome," I reply shyly, positive I'm blushing. *Act confident you moron.*

"Chivalry. The lost art no longer," she says playfully, falling into the heap of metal that I call a car.

I allow myself a quick smile as I walk along the lopsided and scuffed grill. "So, where are we heading?" I ask, settling in behind the wheel.

"You know Market Street?"

"In Crater Lake? We're going out of town?"

"That's the one. Don't be so dramatic. It's only fifteen minutes away."

"I know the street."

"Good. Head down Market until you get to Darren's Repair Shop. Take the next right and his house is about a mile down the road. It will be on the left."

"Easy enough."

The drive begins quiet and awkward, but we quickly find our step. The transition from awkward to comfortable a natural development. I can't speak for Erika, but it seems similar for her. It's been this way for years. I lose my mind at the sight of her, she overcomes my shambles with kindness and patience, and I eventually return to a normal, functioning human again.

We continue to laugh and talk about anything and everything, except the two occurrences at school, which I'm thankful she doesn't bring up.

We eventually pull into the driveway of a simple, single-story home on what must be a couple of acres of open land.

"So, tell me again. How can this guy help? And why are we at his house?" I ask.

"He's apparently a web genius, but he operates out of his home."

"How did you hear about him?"

"Found him by accident. Saw a sign in the yard and thought he did electronic repair. My personal tablet was acting up," she offers with a shrug.

"And we're sure we want to do an online yearbook in conjunction with a hard-copy version?" I exit the car and head for her door, which she opens before I can reach for the handle.

Erika steps out and closes the door. "What?" She follows my eyes to the door. "Oh!" she laughs out. "Sorry about that. Next time, sir." She sighs slightly as we ascend the porch. "We already talked about the online yearbook. We can start small this year and see where it goes. Wouldn't it be cool?"

"Sorry. I just want to be sure this is something you wanted. It will be a lot of extra work. I do think it could be cool though."

"I want to give it a shot. I'm glad you're on board."

"Always," I mumble as Erika knocks a few times. We both take a step away from the door when we hear movement somewhere within.

A few seconds pass in silence before the door swings open. The man on the other side stands a little over six feet with a short, groomed beard and long, wavy black hair. Fitted slacks fall over black, polished shoes while a button-down shirt goes untucked. He doesn't look much older than a college student, and even I can't discredit his looks.

"Good morning," he says, voice deep and full. There is a slight accent that I fail to place.

Erika shudders with a wide smile that instantly sours my mood. "Good morning, Chris."

Everyone looks at one another for a moment. "So, this is?" Chris asks with a smirk.

Erika shakes her head and rotates with an outstretched arm. "Sorry, this is my friend, Jacoby. The one I told you about."

Chris extends his own hand, retaining the same smile, flaunting pearly-white teeth. "Distinguished from the Jacobys you haven't told me about," he manages the joke tastefully. "Nice to meet you."

I desperately want to dislike the guy, but I fail to find an immediate flaw. It eats at my core, my insides churning in anger and envy at Chris' ability to influence Erika. It's pure jealousy, I know that, but I don't care. Infuriatingly, and without noticing, Chris has somehow managed to disarm my initial feelings with a few words. He is charming and genuine, someone who truly cares about anyone and everyone he crosses paths with.

"Nice to meet you too," I say. I sound more like an avid fan than a jealous want-to-be-boyfriend.

"Please," Chris says, retreating into the house and turning sideways, a warm and welcoming gesture, "come in."

We pass through the doorway and into a small foyer. Dark wood runs between most walls, providing a comforting environment. Natural light floods each room, revealing a mixture of colors that speak of sophistication and autumn.

Chris closes the outer glass door but leaves the inner open. "Living room is just that way. Would either of you like something to drink? Coffee? Water?"

"Water for me," says Erika.

I'm unaccustomed to waking this early on a Saturday, so some caffeine, and warmth, sounds like a treat. "Coffee, please."

"Cream? Sugar?"

"Black."

"Good man. A proper coffee."

"Umm...thank you." I find myself outwardly polite and internally at war. I want to hate the man out of envy, but I can't.

"You're welcome. Take a seat and make yourself at home. I'll grab the drinks."

We both give another round of thanks and sit on a leather sofa at the far end of the living room. I sit first. Erika next. She leaves the middle seat open. I'm once again agitated. *Get out of your head. It doesn't mean anything.*

The house isn't much to look at on the outside, but the inside is a different story. Simple but elegant is a proper description. A sophistication suited for a home and garden magazine.

Chris returns a few minutes later and disperses the drinks, taking both a coffee and water for himself as he sits across from us in a high-back leather chair a shade darker than the couch. "So, what can I do for you two?"

Erika leans forward and clears her throat. "Well...as we spoke the other day, we're looking to develop a web page for our school's yearbook."

"Interesting idea. Still going to do the traditional hard-copy yearbook?" Chris has no issue making firm eye contact, with either of us, but Erika frequently diverts her own. Her cheeks redden, and I tell myself it's all in my head.

"That's the plan," she answers, glancing my way. "We were thinking something small and simple for the first year. Maybe just a drop point for some additional pictures and a few articles. We're also thinking the two should work in conjunction with one another. Meaning students can only access the website if they purchased the hard copy, which is where we really need some help."

"That's easy enough. I can build a simple site that will give you some freedom. That way, you can easily upload pictures and format the site to your specific needs. I can also set it up to require an activation code that you can place inside each hard copy."

"Can you set it up so that the code can only be used once?" she asks.

Chris' fingers interlock as his left eyebrow rises slightly.

"That way someone doesn't pass around the code and give everyone access?"

I'm impressed she thought of the possibility so quickly.

"Exactly," she affirms.

"I can program 500 different codes, or however many you need, and only allow each to be used once."

"That sounds amazing," I interject, wanting to be part of the conversation. "How much for all of this?" I look nervously to Erika. "Yearbook doesn't have the largest of budgets."

Chris casually leans back into the chair, dramatically contemplating the value of his time and work. "Nothing," he finally says, another smirk somewhere just beyond the corner of his mouth.

"Nothing?" we ask in unison.

This is a lot of work to be offered up freely. I find it too good to be true.

"Consider it my donation to the school for the year."

Erika looks thankful and impressed and infatuated. "You donate often?" she asks.

Chris slips a slight chuckle. "No, to be honest. I haven't lived here long to make much of an impact on the community." He raises his coffee in the air and says, "But here is to new traditions."

I really despise how much I like the guy. Chris is the guy you want to sit around a fire with, shooting the shit and drinking beer. "That is very generous. Are you sure?"

After a slap on the knees, Chris locks eyes with my own. "I am. I think you two have come up with an awesome idea, and I'd love to play a small role in it."

"Well, we can have your name put somewhere on the website, so that it can be a marketing tool for you," offers Erika.

"That won't be necessary," he says quickly with a raised arm, waving it about. "I have made, and continuously update, websites for a lot of major companies throughout the U.S. I honestly have no desire, or time, to take on more work. I would like this to be an anonymous donation. If that's okay with you two?"

"We can do that," I answer quickly, feeling a need to agree before Chris changed his mind about giving away time and effort. "Sounds like you do a lot of work. What brought you to Indiana?"

"I've moved around quite a bit since college. I tried the big city. Too loud. Too crowded, and I hated the traffic. The air here smells like it should, and I like the openness."

"And we're very thankful you're here," adds Erika.

"It'll be my pleasure. I'll mock something up within the next couple of weeks and send it to both of you for consideration. Don't be afraid to ask for changes or additions. It won't take me long once the framework is built."

We talk over some details while everyone finishes their drinks. When everything seems settled, we thank Chris for his help and head for the door.

Chris gives yet another wide smile as we leave. "Erika, it was nice seeing you again. And Jacoby, it was a pleasure to meet you. I look forward to our little project."

"Likewise," I say, once again shaking Chris' hand. I'm the first out the door with Erika following close behind.

"We do too. Thanks again, Chris," I hear her say.

"Be safe."

The door closes behind us and we head back to the car, where I'm damn sure to open Erika's door.

She put a hand on my arm before getting into the vehicle. "Consistency is nice. Thanks."

"Not a problem." *Not a problem. What kind of response is that?* I think while metal groans in protest.

Erika attempts small talk between bouts of silence. I'm considering what I might have done wrong, or if her thoughts are consumed with Chris, when she says, "I'm kind of hungry," sounding like herself once more. "Want to stop and get something to eat?"

I find my watch. "I would love to but...I'm supposed to meet up with Mitch in thirty minutes." *Mitch or Erika? Come on man. Just tell Mitch this came up. He would be happy for me.*

"Oh. That's okay. Maybe another time." She fidgets a moment before turning to add, "I mean to go over yearbook stuff."

"You sure? We don't have anything special or important planned. I can cancel with Mitch."

"Don't cancel your plans for me. We can do lunch later, after Chris sends us what he comes up with."

See. She just wanted to go over yearbook stuff. Not like I had a chance. "That'll work. I'm excited to see what he comes up with," I say with as much enthusiasm as possible, hoping to veer from the topic of lunch.

"Yeah. Me too."

There isn't much talking after that, and thankfully, we arrive back at Erika's house a few minutes later.

"Thanks for the ride," she says, quickly jumping from the car. I don't have enough time to muster a response.

Well, that went well.

I'm happy to be home. The day was long and I'm exhausted. My time with Erika replays over and over again against tired eyes and a stressed mind. Even my time with Mitch offered little distraction.

"Hey, kiddo. Dinner is the fridge," my father says as I shake off my coat.

"Thanks."

Dad strolls into the kitchen, taking a seat at the table.

Looking over the top of a magazine, he asks, "You doing alright?"

"Yeah. I'm good." It isn't a lie. Life has returned to a form of normality. Well, as normal as could be expected. I'm dealing with issues every teenager encounters, but I can handle those. The optimistic tone possible due to the fact I haven't seen the dog in over a week. I cringe just thinking about dark fur and yellow eyes, but I'm thankful the nightmare has passed. A lack of rest was apparently the culprit.

I find the fridge and remove a bowl of pasta.

"Have a good day?" my father asks.

I set the microwave timer and turn. "I did. Yearbook stuff went well and hanging out with Mitch was nice." That part isn't necessarily true.

"Good," he murmurs, returning to the magazine. "You went with that Erika girl, right?"

I'm leaning against the kitchen counter with pasta in hand. "Yes," I respond in more of a question than answer. *Where are you going with this, Dad?*

I feel my father's sly smirk through the magazine. "I've only met her once, but she seems nice."

I cough. "She is."

Dad recognizes my discomfort and mercifully rises from the table to grab a beer from the fridge, seemingly dismissing the topic. "Alright, kiddo. I'm off to bed."

I breathe a sigh of relief. I would have bet my life he was going to push the issue just to mess with me, to see his son blush and squirm. Despite my newfound optimism, I'm not in the mood to talk about girls, or to be given a hard time about girls.

"Jocelyn upstairs?" I ask.

"Nope. Staying the night with Candice."

"Harrington?"

"That's the one," he says through hefty gulps. "I think. I'm sure she's fine."

Dad disappears around the corner as I wolf down what pasta remains. I place the container in the sink and head upstairs. Sliding into bed, I grab a baseball from the nightstand and begin throwing it into the air, struggling to keep it straight as my mind is elsewhere. I alternate pitches, fingers finding the relevant seams, and I become lost in watching the rotation of the ball as it heads to the ceiling and back again. The ebb and flow of gravity synchronizes muscle and mind, throwing and catching becomes an afterthought.

The events of the day dance repeatedly across my mind, mostly my time with Erika. I begin to spiral and decide enough is enough. I place the baseball on the nightstand and roll over onto my side.

Sleep comes quickly.

The darkness remains, but a slight shimmer of light slowly develops. There is no source, just a slow recession of black all around me. I'm inside. Somewhere warm. My surroundings reveal themselves, and I recognize my home. I look outside, somehow aware I'd freeze to death the moment I stepped outside. It's either late at night or very early in the morning. I can't say for sure. I have no memory of traversing to this place, no explanation as to why I'm here, staring blankly through a muddled glass window.

A few moments pass. The cold lays siege to my home, seeping through old wounds. I see my own breath. A familiar hill looms treacherously in the distance, revealed by the echoing light.

The moon comes next, and its pale glow casts an eerie aura through a dense fog. Everything is familiar, but I can't place how or why. What comes next at the tip of my tongue. Staring into the night, a shadow within the fog emerges, then it comes to me. I know the shadow and what form it will take. The beast rises from the hill's peak and walks toward the house, the fog parting before each step.

Your fear is misplaced, a growl says at the back of my mind. *Let me in.*

"No," I yell in response.

I tremble in fear and my heart races. Paralysis holds firm, despite my desire to run and hide. I'm trapped. The beast continues its menacing progress, head downcast with every confident step. Halfway between the house and hill, the dog's eyes rise to meet my own. Beams of yellow cut through the night like a flashlight, and I know those eyes are for me alone.

I swear the beast smiles. My bladder nearly releases at the horrifying and unnatural look.

Soon now.

I awake drenched in sweat, breathing heavy, just as before. It takes a moment, but I slowly transition from the dream to reality.

It's getting closer, I think, still trembling.

❧ 11 ☙
A FACELESS NAME

SUSAN

The laptop screen brightly displays a dormant search engine. The only movement in the last hour being a swipe every so often to keep the computer from going to sleep. Staring absent-mindedly, I zoned out some time ago, feeling lost.

I've been in Cedar Grove for a week, most of that time spent cooped up in this motel room. But the police remain heavily involved with the two murders, and I can't risk another encounter. I fear, feel, the trail turning into ice. Anger turned into desperation, which has recently turned into something I despise: defeat.

Screw this, I think, fed up with doing nothing except drinking myself to sleep. Drinking when emotional results in an even shorter temper, which isn't good for anyone. It's a character flaw I have no intention of confronting or correcting.

I pull up a saved document and scroll through the list of names and connections. Settling on a friend of the victim, I close the laptop and throw on some warm clothes.

The Mustang roars into the Cedar Grove high school parking lot about twenty minutes later. I work my way around to the eastern side of the small campus, to where the school gymnasium is located. The glove compartment snaps open, and I pass over the black, leather-bound book to grab a half-empty bottle of bourbon. After a few pulls on the bottle, the chair falls back as I prop my left foot atop the dash, taking another healthy shot of the warm, amber liquid.

Here we go, I tell myself thirty minutes later. I push open the driver side door and quickly emerge from the vehicle. My head swirls, the world spins. I might have fallen if not for the hood of my car. *I didn't drink that much.* I manage a focused thought, seeing the empty bottle atop the passenger seat. *Maybe I did.*

I return to the car in search of food and find a half-eaten candy bar in the backseat. I can't remember when I ate the first half, but it doesn't matter. Nearly a full bottle of water washes it down.

Feeling grounded, and only slightly tipsy, I move to intercept a group of girls exiting the gym. All of whom flaunt rather risqué cheerleading outfits.

"Tracy Hernandez?" I direct toward the girl in the middle.

The entire group halts. "Yes," a tall, dark-haired girl answers, more question than answer. "And you are?"

"Susan McGraff. I'm an investigative journalist. I was hoping we could talk alone," I say, eying the others.

Tracy looks nervously to her friends. "About what?"

"Shelby and Natasha."

Half the posse disperses while the other half rallies around their friend. "No way," she answers quickly. "I've already talked to the cops, and my parents said not to talk with anyone unless they were present."

Smart girl. Smart parents. "I'm aware you've talked with the cops. I work with them, and I'm usually brought on to ensure they didn't miss anything." *I will need to move quickly when this is done.*

"I see." Walls begin to crumble. "I still think we should do this in front of my parents."

I eye the girls that remain. "Would everyone mind giving me a moment with Ms. Hernandez? You can all stay within sight if you wish."

I'm met with several quizzical looks. A girl to my right finally looks at Tracy when it's apparent I'm not leaving. "Will you be okay?"

Tracy nods. "Yeah. I'll catch up with you later."

When we're alone, I guide Tracy towards a bench across the parking lot. It's cold but there is nowhere else to go. Being alone with a student inside a car, with so many eyes on us, would not bode well once questions about my identity were raised.

"Listen," I say warmly. "I understand your reservations, but I'm here to help. I have another lead that I need to get to, so time isn't on my side. I just have a few questions. If you don't want to answer, or feel uncomfortable at any time, you can scream and go running. Sound like a deal?"

Tracy gives a half-hearted smile but nods. We both take a seat on a wobbly, wooden bench that overlooks a rough-looking, unkempt, baseball field.

"Okay. Ask away." There's a hint of regret in Tracy's voice. She crosses arms and legs defensively, but she will answer my questions.

"You were close with them?"

"More so with Shelby. We cheered together. Natasha was more Shelby's friend than mine, but we would all hang out sometimes."

"I'm sorry for your loss."

Tracy looks to the sky, and I grant her a moment of grief.

"This may seem odd," I continue, "but I have a list of names that I'd like you to look at. Now, you probably haven't met any of these people on the list. The name would have been mentioned more in passing from either Shelby or Natasha. So, don't worry about mentioning any classmates, unless they have moved recently." I hand Tracy a printed copy of the names, first names only, and wait as she fingers each line.

Tracy makes it to the bottom of the list and my heart sinks, until the finger ascends a few spaces. "Max."

"Max was mentioned?"

Tracy nods, eyes still on the list.

"By who? Do you know the last name?"

Tracy is startled by my sudden excitement. "Umm...Shelby mentioned a Max. No last name. She said they met at a writing thing and that he was cute. Something about he was attending college for creative writing and offered her some pointers, but I never heard anything more about him after that."

"Do you remember when this writing thing was? Do you have an idea of how old he was?"

"I do remember, but I can't say for sure his age. Shelby wasn't that detailed."

I raise an eyebrow. The anticipation is unbearable. *Keep it together. Don't scare her off.* "So, when was this writing thing?" I urge.

"It was in May. Right here at the school. I remember because Shelby came out to the game and told me about Max right away." Tracy looks out over the field. "My boyfriend plays baseball. It was one of the last games of the season, when he tore his ACL. That's why I remember."

I gently retake the paper from Tracy's hands. "Thank you so much for your time, Tracy." The teenager looks surprised the conversation is over.

Max Reynolds, my mind repeats. There is no need to read from the paper because I know Max's last name by heart—like all the others on that list.

"Also," I say while rising from the bench, "this will be tough, but I need you to keep this conversation between us. That includes friends, parents, and teachers. You can tell them I asked all the same questions the cops did, but don't mention anything about the list of names. Can you do that?"

"Why?"

"To be honest, I work in the gray. There is no real evidence to support that list of names I gave you. I need to follow up on the name you gave me before we do anything else. If you go running around, telling everyone about what we discussed, it could send the cops on a wild goose chase and the real killer could disappear. It wouldn't be good for anyone involved. Do you understand?"

Tracy nods her head and stands. "I hope you find the guy. I can't imagine who would do something like this to Shelby. To either of them."

"I'll find the guy. As long as you say nothing. I won't stop until I find the guy. That much I can promise you."

We part ways in the parking lot, returning to my car while Tracy rejoins her friends and leaves school grounds. I look at the list of names for twenty minutes before deciding what to do next.

It's a risk, but I have to.

I leave the Mustang in the parking lot and find the school's main entrance, which is on the other side of the building. An older lady with a bored face sits behind a large desk just a few feet beyond a set of double doors.

The receptionist gives a slight smile. "Good afternoon. How can I help you?"

I flash an ID; one I've hoped not to use during this investigation. But desperate times called for desperate measures. No matter how much trouble it will cause down the road.

The receptionist, wearing a Velma nametag, looks at the ID with disdain, or sadness. I can't say for sure. "You're here about Shelby and Natasha?"

"Sadly, I am. May I speak to an administrator?"

"Hold for one moment," Velma says, picking up a phone. After a quick discussion, she stands from the desk. "Principal Grines had to leave earlier today, but Vice Principal Weinstein will see you."

"Thank you."

"Of course. I'll show you the way."

We pass through another set of double doors and turn left. After a hundred feet, we turn right and stop at an office with many windows. Lockers line the back wall while more offices occupy the space ahead. We enter without hesitation and are met by another receptionist who, after seeing the two of us, says, "You can go in. He's waiting for you."

Velma nods and continues toward the back of the room, where open doors reveal the further back one ventures the larger the offices become.

I stand at Velma's back as she knocks once. The nameplate fastened to the door reveals we've arrived at the vice principal's office. Velma doesn't wait for an answer and opens the door, sliding off to the side to grant enough room for my entry.

"Thanks."

Velma nods and closes the door behind me.

A well-dressed, middle-aged woman remains seated behind a desk anterior to several windows that look out into a wild and untamed field. "Please, take a seat," she says with an outstretched arm pointing toward a chair across from her own.

"Thank you," I say, taking the offered seat. I blink several times, adjusting the chair to avoid rays from a setting sun.

The vice principal watches my discomfort with little interest.

"What can I do for you?" she asks.

"I know you've had discussion with several cops about Shelby and Natasha—"

"Yes, I have. Although, you are the first federal investigator we have seen. Why are you here? There is no cause, and we don't need, or want, this type of exposure in our community, or school."

Be careful. This one isn't a pushover. "We like to follow up. And because the person responsible hasn't been found yet. We want to have as much information as possible in case they strike again, which is highly unlikely, but we like to be prepared."

"So, we must grind through all the same grueling questions, like the dozen times before you? To relive our failures in protecting two girls that were adored and loved here? All for the sake of something that will most likely not happen again?"

You have no idea, and your smug ignorance is going to piss me off. I shake my head. *She doesn't know. It's not her fault.* "I only have a few questions. They will seem odd, and I promise no one else has asked them, but I won't ask you to relive your pains. Please stay with me even though you will doubt the importance of the questions."

Mrs. Weinstein looks across the table curiously. A three-diamond ring on her left-hand sparkles against the setting sun as her hands interlock, blinding me once again as it catches the light.

A few seconds pass, and I take the silence as permission to ask. "Did you have a writing conference, or something of the sort, here at the school last May?"

"I'd have to look at the records, but I'll say that sounds about right. It was for the county. An annual competition for various literature genres open to any student in the area."

I do my best to hide a smile, struggling to remain realistic. The probability is small that I'll find Max's name on a conference sign-up sheet that took place months ago.

What if there wasn't a sign-up sheet? "Did you have a sign-in sheet or was it open to all?"

"It was open to all but there were some requirements. We

required students to have a completed project and register online to be granted entry."

"Can you access the registration list?"

"We should. I'll be back in one moment." The vice principal returns ten minutes later with a stapled packet and hands it over without hesitation.

I thumb through the pages while periodically eyeing the vice principal, who opts not to return to her own chair and, instead, has chosen to remain standing uncomfortably close.

I want nothing more than to find Max's name on the registration, but I can't focus with the vice principal rubbernecking over my shoulder.

Finally, Mrs. Weinstein says, "I don't know why you want this, but I hope it's everything you need."

I stand. "It is. Thank you." *Just leave. There's nothing else but trouble you will get from her.* If the name isn't on the list then there's nothing else to be gained from the Vice Principal, or the school.

"Have a good day," Mrs. Weinstein says, deciding the conversation is over. She returns to her seat of power without so much as looking at me again.

I have no qualm with Weinstein's behavior and happily accept the silent dismissal. It's only a matter of time before someone starts questioning, or attempts to verify, my identity and purpose for running around a school, asking odd questions about the murder of two girls the police are still investigating.

Back at the motel, I'm finally able to look through the registration list, which has well over three-hundred names attached to it. Apparently, this is quite the competition, and numerous scholarships are awarded at the end of the day. On the second-to-last page, I find it; not only the first name, Max, but also the last name Reynolds. It's him.

"Yes!" I stand a clap several times. *I've got you, you son of a bitch.*

It's unlikely anyone can put a face to a name. This Max Reynolds would have blended with the crowd and had likely changed his appearance before and after the murders. Shelby, and maybe Natasha, were probably the only ones who could have provided a description.

I pound the desk with both fists and quickly stand, pacing from wall to wall while taking deep breaths. Excitement and anger and a whole host of other emotions rapidly wash through me. I'm on a roller coaster ride. I'm not sure how I feel, except a burning desire to end this hunt before another murder occurs.

I'm getting close.

Evening is settling in when a knock comes at the door. I eye the door in my periphery and grab *Matilda* from the nightstand, sliding the safety off. Each revelation, every clue, brings me closer to the killer. The proximity flows both ways. Just like my dream, the prey could become the hunter at a moment's notice.

I slide toward the door, once again placing myself between the door and windows, then stretch to peer through the door's peephole.

Oh, shit.

Securing the pistol at my back, hidden beneath both shirt and jeans, I open the door. "Sheriff," I say nonchalantly, arm leaning against the frame.

"Ms. McGraff," she replies firmly. A hand rests over her own weapon, which hangs off the right hip.

How did you come across my name, I wonder? We stare at one another for a time before I break the silence. "How can I help you?"

"You've been busy since we met. Yes, I remember you. And something tells me you failed to mention some important details about who you actually are."

"Want a drink?" I offer, turning sideways in the doorway.

"Why not. Technically been off shift for a few hours, and

tomorrow is Thanksgiving. I don't have anywhere to be." She comfortably and confidently enters the room. I notice her hand never strays from her hip.

"Me either. Whiskey or beer?"

The sheriff smirks. "Beer. You're not really my type."

"Fair enough," I huff out, handing the sheriff a beer from the fridge. I can't explain why, but I already like her. "So, why are you here?"

"I want to know why a federal investigator is poking around my town...without telling me."

We both sit at a small table along the far wall. I slowly sip at a beer of my own. The cold metal at my back instills confidence, not that I have any intention of using it against a law enforcement officer, but it's comforting anyway.

I sight dramatically. *Play it up. Win her over.* "My visit to the school gave me away?"

"It did. We are too close of a community for someone not to tell me about your visit, and conversations."

"It was a calculated risk. To be honest, I'm not on official business. As a matter of fact, my actions, if discovered, would be frowned upon. To say the least," I admit with a shrug.

"That was very trusting and overly honest. I could end your little crusade with one phone call."

"You could," I say, without so much as a flinch in response to the threat, "but I'm hoping my honesty will grant me a little leeway."

The sheriff leans back, and I can see the wheels in her mind spinning. "Why should it? This is my jurisdiction. My case. You are interfering with this investigation, upsetting this town's residents. Why shouldn't I call your superiors, and have you reprimanded."

"I don't respond well to threats," I say, taking another swig.

"You're going to have to respond to this one, or I'll make your life miserable."

I smile again. "We can be friends...and I'll stay out of your way. I won't interfere, and I'll also inform you before I talk to anyone in this town. Good?"

"Good," she responds, looking somewhat surprised by my willingness to cooperate. "Now, tell me why you're here for a local murder."

Tell her just enough to get her off my ass. "Murders," I correct. "I don't think they're just local murders." The sheriff frowns in disbelief. "I believe they are two in well over a dozen murders carried out by a single killer." I intentionally downsize the number of deaths to keep the conversation alive.

"And you have evidence of this?" she asks skeptically.

"Sort of. I'll tell you, and I'll honestly stay out of your way if you agree to keep this conversation between us. Deal?"

Eyebrows furrow, but she eventually nods. "I can do that."

"I noticed some similarities in various cases spread out over several states. It's a long story, but I eventually came across a man known for creating fake identities. After some...aggressive negotiation, I was given a list of names he created for a man he'd never met."

"So, you know what the guy looks like. The one you're looking for? The one you believe responsible for all these murders?"

"No. This guy is smart. He only ordered the names from the man I found. He must have had someone else assemble the identification documents with pictures and those names. Someone I haven't been able to find."

"You believe it's a man? And how did you know this identity forger was linked to your killer? How do you know the names weren't for someone else?"

A hell of a tale for another time. "It would take too long to explain, but everything just clicked into place. Yes, I believe it's a man. The profile matches that of a male, between 17 to 30

127

years of age, but I wasn't sure about the list of names. It was more of a gut feeling, until today."

The age profile is bothersome, but I've kept those worries to myself since this whole thing started. The murders span decades. The killer would have to be 70 years old by now, at least. Something doesn't fit, and the profile discrepancy is one of the initial reasons I fought an urge to pursue this case. Eventually, the assurances outweighed what I'm unable to currently explain.

"What happened today?"

"I found one of the names on the list was used here in town."

"How?"

So, the vice principal called you, not Tracy. "One of the victim's friends told me that a Max was mentioned after a writing conference at the high school. I cross-referenced the name with the registration list and found it. It could be a coincidence. It's not an uncommon name, so I have some more work to do."

"What's your next move?"

"It's a stretch, but I need to make sure that name has moved on. I will be pursuing a thread of evidence separate from your investigation."

"Which means you'll stay out of my way," she says in warning. "This is a wonderful theory, but it sounds like nothing more than a theory at this point. I'll let you pursue it, but I'll be tracking down actual evidence and not looking for some mythical serial killer."

Ignorant, just like everyone else. "Yes. I promise not to interfere. If something comes up, I'll be sure to give you a call."

"Best of luck, then."

12
THE HOOK

JACOBY

I've been sitting in bed with the light on for at least an hour, most of that time spent staring at the far wall. Once again, sleep is a distant reality. The dream has become relentless, repeating itself throughout the night, every night. The mere thought of sleep elicits physical discomfort— knowing I'll find yellow eyes closer than the dream before.

The beast is close now, just a few feet short of the home's property. The recollection draws chills, and I shake off an icy and lifeless wind.

I work my way to the kitchen after the alarm goes off, yanking my mind from dazed wonderings, in search of cereal. I'm surprised at the flavor, having absentmindedly filled the bowl.

Jocelyn strolls into the kitchen a few minutes later with a smile and purposeful bounce in her step. "Good morning," she blurts out.

I mumble a response; more grunt than words.

"What's with you?" she asks. She looks me up and down. "You look terrible. And you're losing weight."

Angry fingers squeeze against the spoon, coiled like an anaconda about to feast, as my jaw clenches. "Not much sleep," is all I offer, returning to my cereal, focusing on the crunch it makes as I chew.

"Again?" she asks, carefully.

"Yes. Again," I answer in frustration. Jocelyn turns and focuses on her own breakfast, a couple of pastries.

We stand and eat in silence, until our father comes stumbling in. "Good morning," he says, almost as chirpy as Jocelyn.

I take two steps toward the sink and throw my bowl, still half-full of milk and cereal, into one of the basins.

My father stops mid-stride and looks nervously around the room. "Woah. What was that?"

"Yeah. Great freaking morning. I'm glad everyone is doing so good."

"Sit down," my father states, a sternness to his voice I'm unaccustomed to handling. I move to leave. "Jacoby, I said sit your ass down."

I dramatically, and violently, pull back a chair and take a seat at the table, crossing my arms and looking anywhere but at my father.

"Jocelyn, please excuse us," my father says in an eerily calm voice, but stern enough to ensure he hears no argument.

She takes her plate of frost-covered fake bread and leaves. She's probably standing outside the kitchen door, eager to eavesdrop on the upcoming conversation. Yelling at her to move further away isn't worth the energy.

My father and I sit across from one another, and when neither of us speaks, I dare to look him in the eye. "What?" I ask sarcastically, defiantly.

"Don't you *what* me. What the hell is going on with you?

This past week you've been irritable, stewing mess. You haven't been yourself."

Just this past week? Much longer than that, Dad. "It's nothing. I'm fine."

"No! No, you're not. Is it something at school? Baseball? Friends? Please, let me in. Tell me what's going on"

I sigh and clench both fists. The urge to cry is equal to the rage. I find it confusing. The torrid mix of emotions is new, foreign, and I can't process them fast enough. However, no matter how much I want to lash out, there is no point in arguing, especially with my father. It isn't his fault.

"I'm still not sleeping," I say after a time.

"Because of that dream? The one about the dog?"

I shrug. I don't want to say it aloud. To talk about it means trusting others not to judge. What can anyone do for me? Can they dive into my mind and remove the dream? Can they somehow ensure I won't ever hallucinate the dog again? No one can promise any of that, so it's better to keep it all inside. I may self-implode, but at least it will be without the aid of others.

"Have you tried taking something to knock you out at night?"

That piques my interest. "Like what?"

"Anything for the nighttime. I don't usually dream, or I can't remember dreaming, when I take something for allergies, or a cold. A shot of something warm mixed in with the medicine usually helps," he says with a sad smile.

"You want me to take nighttime medicine with liquor?"

We've never talked about anything of major life importance, whether it's alcohol or sex. Intimate conversations are not our family's thing, although they were more common when Mom was alive. Everyone has been reluctant to bring up such conversations since she passed. It feels better, more comfortable, to act as if certain aspects of life don't exist.

Even though James Talavan has become borderline alcoholic, I'm surprised he's offering alcohol as a solution.

"Worth a shot," he says, laughing at an unintended pun. "Just don't overdo it. That could be dangerous. Okay?"

"Okay." I look to the far wall. "Jocelyn," I holler. When no answer comes, I yell a little louder, "Jocelyn, I know you're there. You can come back in."

She trots back into the kitchen. Not a shred of embarrassment to be found. I don't call her out for snooping as she finds the sink and disposes of her plate. No one says anything more until I rise from the table to grab my backpack.

"Try to have a good day," my father says with concern.

"Yeah," I reply over my shoulder. Jocelyn is in tow as we head out the front door.

The drive to school is quiet. A practice becoming more common. I say nothing to Jocelyn and she says nothing in return. Guilt mixes with anger. I hate pushing my family away but there is nothing to say. What can I say? I'm lost and angry and scared. No one can understand. How can they? I don't even understand. The insanity is mine alone to bear, and I would find my own way back to normality.

The school day is a haze of walking and sitting and unremembered motions. There's an echo of rage flying around my mind, transparent and impossible to grasp. I recall a desire to lash out against a handful of people at different points in the day. I can't recall what they did to elicit such a desire. Probably nothing.

The only saving grace is a modified practice after school. Mitch has managed to persuade nearly half the varsity team to meet in the gymnasium after last period to go through some drills and hit. It won't be a long practice, just enough to get the guys back into the swing of things.

Several years ago, a former student gifted the school with enough money to purchase two indoor batting cages. The cages were mounted to the ceiling of the gym's upper deck and descend per a mess of pulleys and motors. It was a significant purchase, not only in terms of money but also the effect they had on the team's performance. The cages granted opportunity for baseball players to take batting practice year-round. The results were improved batting and more wins.

A few guys are stretching when I walk into the gym. I enter slowly, head downcast, but my spirit lifts at the prospect of hitting and throwing.

Mitch comes running up with a smile on his face. "What's up, man?"

"Just glad to be here," I answer tiredly.

Mitch's neck tilts to the left. "You good? You look like shit."

"Thanks. And you're still a prick."

There is a quiet laugh. "Just looking out for you, man."

"You need to stop doing that. It's just pissing me off." I can't help but smile a little. It feels good to be doing something normal, even if it's only teasing with a friend. It helps to forget what haunts me.

I run a few laps and stretch as more teammates roll into the gym.

"Hey," Mitch says from my side.

"Yeah?"

Mitch nods toward the gym's entrance. The new kid, Michael, is heading toward a group of sophomores off to the left. He's noticeably tall. Solid build. Looks more suited for college than high school.

Mitch clears his throat before continuing. "Umm...well..."

"What? Out with it."

"I heard he talked with coach."

"Okay?"

"Rumor is that he told coach he wanted a shot at shortstop. It was just a day after the three of us talked in the hallway."

I scoff out a half-laugh, not because I find the information funny. I'm surprised and angry. *Who the hell did this kid think he is?* Mitch and I had stood there, listening to Michael surrender his desire for shortstop, then express happiness at having a shot at third base. Instead, he is coming after my job.

Going to the coach about taking my job would have pissed me off regardless, but I'm already in turmoil. Everything is piling up, and I'm spiraling, stuck in a never-ending horizon of quicksand—the harder I fight the more I sink.

"You had better not be messing with me."

Mitch shakes his head but says nothing.

"After telling us both he was happy with third."

"Yep," Mitch says quickly.

"I'll enjoy putting him in his place."

After a solid warmup, I quickly break those in attendance into two groups. I run the group that remains on the gym floor while I put Mitch in charge of those heading to the upper deck for batting practice.

Encircled by my group, I say, "Outfielders with John and infielders with me."

John claps violently, startling those around him, and takes off around the circle, smacking the outfielders' asses as he passes. John's group heads toward the back of the gym to work on footwork and fly-balls.

I measure out the bases and create an ad-hoc infield. I tell Julio, a senior with a net for a glove, to head over to first while everyone else lines up at short. The rotation is easy: I hit a ground ball, the first in line at short will field the ball then throw over to Julio, who will then one-hop the ball back into myself.

I start simple, a decently struck ball hit right at the infielder; however, after three repetitions, Michael steps up and I can't hide a smile. *Let's see what you got.* I, not wanting everyone to recognize my grand plan, act like I miss-hit the ball and send a dribbler toward Michael.

Michael charges with unnatural speed and fields the ball cleanly off to his left while continuing full speed ahead. He's low to the ground when his glove strikes against the floor, sending the ball skyward, where he plucks it from the air and makes a near-perfect, off-balanced throw across the infield to an awaiting Julio.

It all happens so quickly.

I can do all of that, but I've never considered bouncing my glove off the floor. It's amazing and infuriating to watch.

There are whistles and murmurs as Michael trots past the plastic mound and veers toward the back of the line. Fearing what else Michael is capable of, I decide to treat him like the rest of the group going forward.

The two groups exchange locations after thirty minutes.

The cages are fifty feet long, so all indoor batting practices is short-toss—meaning the distance between the batter and pitcher is much shorter than in a game, but it's better than not hitting at all.

I'm on the floor stretching when I notice Michael approaching. I have no desire to talk to the guy, so I stand and turn toward one of the cages, where Julio is at work from the left side of the plate.

Keep on walking, buddy. Just keep on walking. Despite my hopes, Michael quietly comes up beside me.

I frown, still angry but wanting to be the bigger man. "What's going on?" I ask.

Michael turns with an arrogant smirk. "Just having a good time. You don't have too bad of a team here."

"Thanks. Glad you're a part of it." *Maybe I'll have one of the pitchers throw at your head.*

"Oh, me too. Say, I was wondering..."

"Yeah?"

"Well...the girls here, they aren't too bad either."

My mind immediately finds Erika. "No. No they're not." I'm

smiling despite being in the presence of a guy I'd rather beat to death than talk girls with.

"I actually have a date coming up. Which is something because I rarely date. I'm more of the meet up when convenient type. For fun."

Just what we need, another Jeff. "Good for you," I mouth out.

"I agree. She's a brunette. I have a thing for brunettes. And she's an athlete. Smoking hot."

Wait. What? No. "What's her name?" I ask frantically.

Michael turns toward the cages, but my heart skips a beat as I watch that arrogant smirk turn into a devilish smile. "Erika," he finally answers.

You bastard. My grip on the baseball bat tightens as I seriously consider taking a swing and sending that shit-eating grin into another zip code.

Does he know? Is he doing this to mess with me? Does he really have a date with her? I managed to avoid taking the hardest swing of my life and say nothing. Something happens with my vision. Everything goes out of focus, the cage a convoluted mess of rope.

"You know her, right?" he asks when I say nothing.

He knows.

"Well," he continues, as if we're having a casual conversation, "I've got some plans for her. I'm thinking a few drinks out in the middle of nowhere, then she'll be eager enough to try everything I've thought about since—"

The bat falls in what should have sounded like a solid strike against an oversized church bell, but I hear nothing. My fist tightens as I subconsciously realize I'm no longer in control of my own body. My arm lags but whips around with rapid speed, striking Michael's face.

To me, landing the punch seems an eternity, the violence playing out in slow motion. In reality, it's over within the blink of an eye, and I don't realize what's happening until it's too late.

Michael crashes against the floor and rolls a few feet, frantic hands grabbing at the left side of his face, moaning and swearing. I straddle him with still clenched fists, muscles tight and shoulder locked, ready to strike again.

Arms wrap around my own chest before I'm able to deliver a second punch, and I'm pulled away from Michael's squirming body.

People are yelling at me, but their voices are echoes over a vast ocean. Even Michael fades into nothing.

I'm shaking uncontrollably. There is so much movement, but everything is out of focus. When I realize I'm no longer being held back, I turn and head for the gym's exit.

My teammates, friends, continue to call my name, but I don't look back.

The group downstairs is still practicing, unaware of what's happened above them. I manage to slip out the back exit unnoticed.

Once inside my car, I scream, louder than I've ever before. I punch the steering wheel repeatedly until knuckles bleed and my adrenaline is exhausted.

Tears come next, then an awareness of aching bones and angry muscles, especially in my hand. I snapped, I knew that much, but I can't piece together everything that just transpired. Someone else took control of both my mind and body, then blurred the events to protect my mind.

The weight of my actions slowly creeps into understanding, and it scares me.

Practice is ending soon, and I have no desire to face any of my teammates, so I fire up the car and head home.

Thankfully, my dad is pulling a double shift at the factory and a disheveled napkin with faded ink marks atop the kitchen table says Jocelyn is staying with a friend. I wet a towel and wrap up a few murky ice cubes, placing it over my hand as I pull a beer from the fridge and collapse on the living room couch.

I'll need more than one to sleep tonight, Dad.

A dim hallway light is the only thing staving off complete darkness.

I cry some more, continuing to do so until I'm too tired to go on. I eventually make my way to the bedroom and slowly work myself under the cool sheets without changing or showering.

I go to place my phone on the nightstand and notice fifteen unread text messages and eight missed calls—all from various people. I roll over without responding to any of them.

Word about what happened will spread like man's discovery of an alien species, which makes even the thought of going to school seem like medieval torture. Confronting anyone who knows about my violent delight will be awkward, let alone Michael. But not going to school tomorrow will be worse. People already question my sanity, and not showing up will raise additional questions. I would rather face it head on than have people come for me armed with inaccurate assumptions.

No. I won't cower from my actions. I shake at the thought of being suspended. The thought of watching my college career disappear behind a jail cell.

All I can hope for is that Michael, and everyone else who was present, agrees not to file any complaints. I could be expelled, suspended, kicked-off the baseball team, or even worse, be sent to jail for assault.

Michael wants my job. He turns me in and I'll be suspended. Shortstop will be his, I think in contempt, and worry, as I roll again, restless. *Erika.* Despite the events of the day, and the growing number of concerns swirling around inside my head, sleep eventually comes for me.

I awake to a beeping alarm, which warns I've overslept by a few minutes. I'm both thankful and sad I'll make it to school before the first bell. I push off the bed with a grunt. My right hand is black and blue, with a dusting of dried blood atop swollen knuckles. After cleaning myself up, I dress and head to the kitchen.

The door to my father's room is shut, but he will wake shortly for work. I decide I want to be long gone before that happens, so I eat quickly and head for school, determined to face, and overcome, whatever is waiting for me.

I pull into the school's parking lot and flip the hood of my sweatshirt up and over my head. It's an ill-attempt to conceal my identity, but it's better than nothing. I consider running the opposite direction when I see Mitch waiting at the entrance, who, not fooled by the hood, barrels his way through the mass of students.

"What the hell, man?"

I say nothing, head downcast.

"You okay?" my friend asks with more concern. "I tried calling you, like a thousand times last night. You didn't answer. You had us all worried. Again."

"Didn't feel like talking," I say quietly without making eye contact. I wanted to hit Michael, to cause him physical pain. I thought I'd feel different in the aftermath, but my emotions are mixed on the fight.

"What did he do?"

That garners my attention. "Michael?"

"Yeah. He didn't really say anything after you left. We just kept practicing. It was kind of weird."

I want to ignore Mitch, to act as if he didn't exist, that he isn't walking beside me stride for stride. But I feel Mitch's piercing gaze and know my friend won't let up until he has answers.

After a sigh, I finally turn and say, "He talked about Erika. I don't know. Everything just came together. Him vying for my job, then that. It was too much."

"Shit. Sorry, man. I had no idea. He's shaping up to be a real asshole."

I unintentionally let loose a snort. "No kidding." I'm optimistic about avoiding jail as Michael didn't immediately call the police after my violent outburst.

"Don't worry. I got everyone together and no one has any intention of reporting it to anyone. Even Michael agreed to keep his mouth shut."

"How? Why?"

"Don't worry about that. Just know we got your back."

A sense of relief triggers a high. The unknown was slowly eating away at my soul. I had hoped for the best but played out every scenario, most of which led to a ruined life.

We'll see, I think skeptically. "Thank you," I manage as we enter the school. "This means a lot."

Mitch answers with an awkward arm pat. "Not a problem. You would've done the same for me."

I nod because it's true.

After a quick trip to my locker, I make my way to chemistry. Luckily, I don't have any classes with Michael, although we're bound to run into each other at some point in the day. I have no idea how I'm going to respond when that encounter unfolds.

Mrs. Rolland is on the phone when I fall into my small seat. Only one other student is in the classroom, who is either sleeping or in need of immediate medical attention. It's hard to tell.

I'm not down for a minute when Mrs. Rolland rises from behind her desk and makes her way toward me. She clears her throat.

When I acknowledge her awkward presence, she says, "Mrs. Johnston would like to see you in her office."

Damnit. Guess Mitch didn't handle it. "She does?"

"She does," says Mrs. Rolland, like a parent who's failed to raise a child to socially constructed standards.

I leave the room after packing up my things, just as the other students begin entering. Harsh eyes follow my exit, casting judgement. It's probably paranoia, but I can't shake the feeling.

The whole world is turning against me.

I make it to the counselor's office without passing anyone who witnessed my violent outburst. An audible exhale escapes in relief.

The receptionist is on the phone and waves permission to venture on. I knock on a wooden door. *I hate this door.*

"Mr. Talavan," the counselor says.

"Mrs. Johnston. No offense, but it isn't a pleasure to see you again."

Her lip twitches. "And yet, here we are."

I take a seat. "Here we are."

"Do you know why you're here?" she asks once we're seated.

"I'm guessing it isn't because of my charming personality." I have no idea where the sudden boldness hails from. Everything about me seems different, ever since that damn dog came back into my life. My emotions, my personality, everything has become a sliding scale, a violent wave, altering course at a moment's notice.

She's surprised and taken aback by my abruptness. "Hmm, very well," she says, recovering quickly. "No formal complaint has been filed, but word has reached this office regarding the fight you were involved in yesterday."

I picture throwing Mrs. Johnston out the window.

"You have nothing to say?"

I can only make it worse, I think. *Don't admit to anything.* So, I remain quiet, steady.

"Okay, Mr. Talavan. Here it is, then. Due to past behavior, and the tragic loss of your mother, it has been decided to allow you two options. Your father is aware, but he wanted you to decide your own fate. You can either be suspended from school or attend mandatory counseling sessions with a professional. You will be required to go twice a week until he deems otherwise. You will be allowed to attend school during this time, but if you skip even one session, you will be expelled. Do you understand your options?"

Thanks, Dad. "I told you that this has nothing to do with my mother."

"It may not. But I believe it does. The school would like a professional to decide upon the matter."

"But no formal complaint has been filed. How can you threaten to suspend me? How can you dictate mandatory counseling? This threat sounds like a lawsuit waiting to happen."

I probably deserve worse than what's being offered, but I don't care. I can't fight a dream. The beast, its yellow eyes, seeing them in dreams and hallucinations, it's a lot to process. My reactions are foreign, different, and I no longer recognize myself. The transformation is unstoppable

"We'll find someone to verify the fight if we need to. We're giving you a chance to get ahead of this. If you agree to see a counselor then you won't be suspended, which *will* happen if you pass on the offer."

This blows. "What about baseball?"

"Baseball," she says under her breath. "There's a lot more at stake right now than baseball, Mr. Talavan. However, your coach is currently unaware of your actions. That will change If you refuse counseling. You'll be suspended not only from school but also the baseball season."

"Not much of a choice."

"No. No, it isn't."

Do I even care anymore? "When do I start?" *I guess I do.*

"Tomorrow."

13
THANATOS

SUSAN

With steady hands outstretched, shoulder high, coiled confidently around hard metal, I take a deep breath and exhale, softly squeezing the trigger as my body rests. The recoil is minimal, more experience and strength on my part than weakness with the weapon, but Matilda strikes powerfully, and I smile as adrenaline surges.

Every aspect of the shot is intoxicating. The sound of the discharge, the slight hum of the expelled shell, and the smell of gunpowder are familiar and comforting sensations that bring deep, soul-reviving satisfaction.

I peer down at the target then quickly return to the sight. Another long, deep breath. I double-tap the trigger, then empty the clip—no longer softly pulling at the trigger.

Still in the Terre Haute area, I have discovered nothing of relevance regarding the name Max Reynolds, or where he's fled. Everything I know about the killer supports that he's long gone. Despite the current roadblock, I remain steadfast in the belief he was here. That he killed those two girls. The fact one of the names on my illegally obtained list was used in a town where two murders occurred, both of whom fit within the killer's profile, is too much to be dismissed as mere coincidence.

It helps that the feeling, that mute voice within, encourages such thoughts.

My confidence, the perceived authenticity in the list of names grows with each passing day. It's as if Max never existed, which means I'm on the right path and there is no advantage in pursuing another case in that black book. I'm as close as I'm going to get, but I need a lucky break to close the gap.

I need to hear from Joyce.

I've been banging my head against a wall for days, the stalled investigation producing maddening boredom. Eventually, I had enough and decided to clear my head with a trip to a shooting range, where such frustrations can be expelled through putting holes in a paper target.

With a flip of a switch, the target retracts via a system of clips and wires. The shooting range has seen better days, having transformed into a dilapidated establishment fit for hillbillies who like to get drunk, make a bonfire, and shoot blindly into the dark while hollering like rabid dogs. Relatedly, the target system is slow. Nearly two minutes for the target to traverse thirty yards.

I empty the clip rather quickly, hit the switch again, and eject the magazine while I wait. I steal a glance to the right. Barren metal walls flaunt an orange hue of rust. The floor likely uncleaned in the past decade.

Suppose it's better than nothing. I eye the banks to my left and right, watching others in amusement. *At least I don't have to retrieve the target myself while dodging the piss poor shooting of those around me.*

The target finally stalls, and I smile. I unclip the paper and turn it sideways, the overhead light shines through numerous holes the size of one's thumb.

Someone at my back whistles, ending the moment of appreciation. I turn and discover an overweight, unshaved man wearing a stained, flannel shirt standing a short distance away. A crooked smile displays a handful of rotten teeth in an otherwise empty mouth.

The man does nothing to hide the fact he's looking at everything but my face. "That's some good shooting, honey."

Before I'm able to respond, a forewarning voice answers for me. "Mark, I don't think you want to offend a woman who can shoot like that."

The man, who is apparently named Mark, frowns and heads the opposite direction without another word. I watch him go with interest but then turn and, to my surprise, find a well-built, decent-looking man that seems both humble and confident.

The contrast between the two men, within such proximity, is almost overbearing.

About my age. Perhaps a little older. Maybe thirty?

"Not bad," he says, nodding toward the target. "Do you shoot better when angry or at peace?" he asks with a tilt of his head, as if contemplating his own response to the question.

"Why do you ask?"

"Forgive my bluntness, but I couldn't help but watch. He points toward the target. "All head and chest, not a single stray bullet. You've either had training or are a very talented amateur. Either way, it's impressive."

His eyes are piercing, focused, locked upon my own. Usually an uncomfortable boldness. Here, now, with him, there is something soothing, even desirable, about his gaze.

"Anger focuses my mind. Peace can cause complacency."

"Hmm. Interesting philosophy. Anger can also cause brashness and a lack of patience."

"It can. But with enough practice, you can control it."

"And you've had a lot of practice?"

"Years."

I take note of his height as he steps closer. "Do you shoot?" I ask quickly.

There's a pull at the corner of his lip. "Occasionally."

My brow furrows at his playfulness, his smirk morphs into a wide, but controlled smile.

"This is my place," he says in answer to my silent question. "It isn't much, I know, but not much of a white-collar society around here. The real money is in the gun store, and no one around here complains about the conditions of where they can shoot. They're simply happy to have a place they can go when they tire of their cornfields and woods."

I can't explain what's happening, or why it's happening, but with each word from his lips I want more. And it isn't conversation I crave.

"It suits my tastes," I say, looking around the room. Suddenly, it isn't so bad. *Wake up. It's a shit hole.*

"And what other tastes do you have? Aside from being one the best markswoman I've ever seen?"

"Drinking."

"Ah," he says with a quick and sincere laugh. "A woman I can finally relate to. Anger, drinking, and shooting. Nothing bad has ever come of that combination." He holds my gaze for a moment before saying, "You're different, intriguing."

As are you, I think while my rebellious eyes drift over his form.

A hand is extended. "I'm David, by the way."

I take it. *Firm, but not overpowering.* "Susan."

"If you're interested, my backroom has whiskey."

I want to say yes, to be reckless, to act my age, but I can't. There are more important things to do than spend the night with a stranger, although a very attractive one.

"That is a generous offer, especially being whiskey, but I will have to decline." I hate my response. Something sour rolling across my tongue, but it feels right.

David feigns a dagger to the heart but keeps that smile. "I hope I didn't overstep. I wouldn't want to lose a customer because of my personal interests."

A desire to stay, to take back my comment and accept the invitation, itches everywhere within, but it's a reverberation, swallowed up by a sense of duty. The events of my past aid in the suppression. Memories of a different time layer themselves in defense of David.

Disaster is sure to follow.

I doubt I'll ever feel something for another, an intimate connection, to the extent it matters. It's the result of something I buried deep, long ago, a scar that has only partially healed, harmless unless provoked by that innate longing for another's company.

"Not at all. I'm flattered, really. It's just...it isn't a good time."

David pulls a card from his wallet and hands it over. "In case the time ever becomes right."

I take the card. The front displays a terrible logo and the name of the gun store.

"Back," he directs.

I flip it over.

"It's my cell," he says as I read the handwritten digits.

I frown. "How many of these do you have readily available? Can't imagine you pass out your personal number to every customer."

He takes the card, scribbles something on it, and hands it back. I can't help but smile at the heart.

"One of a kind," he says.

"Uh-huh," I answer with more happiness than I intend.

"Until that time, I'll settle for having you here at the range.

It's been a while since I've seen someone *almost* as good as I am."

He winks and I respond with a huff.

Perhaps, when this is all over, I'll return. For now, David is and would be a distraction. I need to leave to clear my head. To set my mind right for what's to come.

I pocket the card and extend a hand. "Hopefully, someday, we will find out who is better. Good luck with the store."

David nods, shakes my hand, and is speechless as I turn to leave.

I exit the range and pass through a dimly light and dank hallway with rooms to either side, eventually making it to the store floor where I move quickly out the exit and into the Mustang.

Back at the motel, I relax a few minutes before showering as the sun sets. Wrapped in a robe, I pace a small runway left of the television, a glass of whiskey in hand. I sip at the amber liquid and contemplate my next steps, as I've done every night since connecting this town to the name Max Reynolds.

Despite that monstrous breakthrough, I've failed to build upon the momentum. There is nothing to suggest where Max is holed up, what he looks like, or where he might have run off to. In the absence of any evidence, every move is a stab in the dark, so I've chosen to stay put until something more concrete comes along.

I hate waiting. A need to act claws against flesh, desperate to be set free. Progress is achieved through action, but I have no clue what tree to shake.

I ultimately settle and turn toward the wall. An oversized map of the United States sprawls atop dull colored paint, pinned at the corners. The morbid project birthed from boredom, and possibly a self-destructive nature. Eyes squint in determination, but also in fear and failure. What's displayed anterior is my burden, my life's purpose. A purpose I never requested. It wasn't thrust upon me by anyone, unless I count the extra sense as something unnatural bestowed upon me by a higher power, but I will see it through. I will see it finished. No matter what the hunt does to me.

I stare at the thumb tacks sprinkled throughout the East Coast and Midwest. The mere sight of what I'm up against causes both mental and physical pain.

It's chaotic. Through the mess of color, I find a small pattern, which is frustratingly too macro to be of any significant value. The tacks flow southwest, more west than south the past few months, but the spread is too random to predetermine the location of the next murder. The miles between murders I've identified are different each time, west, north, south, north, and ultimately westward.

West. Will you strike again in Indiana? Will you move on to Illinois or Kentucky? One mistake, that's all I need.

Staring until my vision blurs, I take a mental count of the varying colors. For cases where the body, or bodies, was found and the evidence fits within the unique and selective profile of the killer, a red tack is used. Yellow is deployed for cases where the body was discovered but certain evidence is lacking, meaning I'm less confident of who carried out the murder. Where the body is still missing, but I found the case potentially relevant, a white tack is used. Lastly, green is used for missing persons that caught my attention but I've yet to decide upon.

A head shake refocuses the map, and I can't help but think I'm insane. There are so many thumb tacks, too many to be realistic. It's impossible for someone to kill this many people without anyone taking notice.

He's so young to have committed so many murders. Maybe he's older than I think? Older than the profile suggests. Are there others? Has an evil pastime passed from father to son?

"How can one man be responsible for so much death? How can one person be so evil?" I think aloud. I'm not the best of humanity, I know that, and God knows I've committed my share of sins, but this is something different. This is evil in the purest sense of the term.

Red tacks litter the eastern part of the United States, 43 to be precise. The remainder sum to 167, for a total of 210 murders. Not every tack is the result of an action taken by the man I hunt. My stomach threatens rebellion anyway. I force myself to understand the number, both individually and in total. The overwhelming number of cases is a trap, hard to contemplate, a mind quick to numb itself in disbelief. A single murder, committed for no other reason than to satisfy a twisted pleasure or need, is considered horrific. What emotion can be felt for 210 suspected murders? The answer, in my experience, is shock, then a tendency to forget. The human mind incapable of understanding, or unwilling to confront, this level of evil.

I've spent years researching that human flaw. I've read hundreds of books on the subject, some of which provide theories, but they all fall short in my mind. It seems as if science and psychology fail to provide a genetic truth within each of us. I've given up on attempting to understand, vowing to fight against the instinct with sheer willpower.

So much death. So much horror.

Thanatos, I think while chills run down a straightened spine. In college, I took a class on Greek mythology for fun. There, I learned that Thanatos was a minor god, the personification of death, often portrayed as a youthful figure. The mythology held he was spoken of but rarely seen, making him mysterious and somewhat unknown. The comparison is unnerving. The man I'm hunting is known to very few—likely just myself—most likely a younger male who brought death to those marked.

Thanatos, I repeat over and over in my mind. Goosebumps flee across raised skin as I imagine what the Greek god looks like. The man I'm hunting is worse, a darker and more twisted visage played upon my imagination. Thanatos had a purpose in a society that found death to be an essential aspect of immortal life. This man, Max, or whatever name he has assumed, killed for pleasure or satisfaction. There is no beauty in the lives taken by his own hand, only sadness and pain born out of horrific and selfish action.

After two more glasses of whiskey, and a wave of dark thoughts, I become restless, and reckless. Feeling brazen, I decide to pick up the phone and dial a familiar number.

"What do you want?" Comes a sharp voice.

"I've hit a brick wall."

I have enough time to consider the consequences of this call before she responds. "Maybe because there is nowhere else to go."

"Let's not do this. Not now."

"Why did you call, then? Are you drunk? You're slurring."

Don't you judge me. You have no idea what I've gone through, or what I'm dealing with. "I've had a few. It helps clear my head."

"You and I both know it does the opposite."

Now who's holding something over the other. "It focuses me on the task at hand, which is what I need right now."

"Fine. What do you want?"

I sigh, knowing our relationship would never heal. Not after forcing my old friend's hand on more than one occasion. "Have any of the names flagged?"

"No. I would've called if one did."

"I needed to be sure. Can you look into something else for me?"

"You're all out of favors to leverage against me."

"Think of it as keeping me out of trouble. I saw a news report on a murder in Ohio the other day. I looked through a couple of databases but couldn't find any details. You have more resources. Can you tell me if there are any suspects?"

"You're a pain in the ass."

"I know," I answer with guilt, but there is no other option.

A clicking sound draws my attention, and I press the phone closer against tingling skin. The sound is muffled, but it sounds like fingers at a keyboard. "Joyce, you still there?"

"Yeah," Joyce answers, sounding annoyed. "Give me the name."

"Of the murder victim?"

"Yes. I'm pulling it up now. I really don't feel like talking to you more than necessary."

Ouch. You're being overly dramatic about this, Joyce. I give the name and wait.

A minute or two later, Joyce clears her throat. "The boyfriend is being held in custody, and...the murder weapon was found in his car. The district attorney has a solid case, so there is no need for you to go to Ohio." More hesitation. "You should come home."

That's very damning evidence. "Thank you," I say, ignoring the last comment.

"I'll call you if one of the names triggers. Try to stay out of trouble until then."

"You know me too well, and you would call bullshit if I promised that." Joyce may have been a thousand miles away, but I swear I feel Joyce smile before hanging up.

Maybe not so damaged.

14
A SAVIOR

JACOBY

I've been staring at an expressionless white wall long enough to have zoned out. In the veil of absent-mindedness, my deceitful eyes play tricks on me. The wall ripples as if a shaken blanket, then melts away like hot plastic. The world returns to normal when someone coughs.

The waiting room isn't much to look at. Four bland walls display less than a handful of frames, and cheap wood, decades old, encloses failed attempts at abstract art.

A small and even cheaper looking table stands uneven near the center of the room, displaying outdated magazines. Even the chairs look and feel cut-rate. They are quite uncomfortable in a business dedicated to making people feel comfortable.

It's also too quiet, and empty, except for my father and myself. There is one caveat to the peaceful and calm environment, and it comes at the pounding of a keyboard by an overzealous receptionist seated across from us. It reminds me of the scene in *Meet the Parents*, where the airline agent, with no one else in the terminal, takes several minutes to frantically type out who knows what before addressing Ben Stiller's character.

Although the sound causes involuntary twitching, I quietly laugh as I recall the scene.

I looked to my father, who is perusing through one of the worn magazines. Neither of us have said anything since the car ride. There wasn't much discussion there either. James attempted to make small talk on numerous occasions, each of which I answered with either a huff or grunt—a yes or no answer without speaking in any discernible language.

The incoherent mumbles were all I could muster. Not only did the mere thought of talking seem exhausting, but I also had no idea what to say. Each attempt at conversation felt forced, and I didn't have the energy, or willpower, to take part in it.

The thick, brown door on the left opens and the pen-wielding charlatan bounces confidently toward us. "Mr. Talavan," he says with too much excitement, extending a hand toward my father.

James takes John's hand and simply says, "John." It's their second meeting, and I sense my father's awkwardness, despite John's attempt at charm. "Please. Call me James."

A hand is then thrust my direction, which I take after a grunt from my father.

"You're off to a good start," my psychiatrist says with a smile. "Two sessions in a row, and on time for both. Most make it to their first session but many fail to attend their second, which ends up not going well for them."

"Thanks for the warning, but I wouldn't miss it for the world," I say sardonically.

Another grunt from my father.

To my father's credit, he's taken this whole thing well. Upon discovering my involvement in a fight, he didn't yell or scream or carry on about how I'm failing as a son. He simply explained the school had called and told him about the incident, and how the incident, combined with my other outbursts, resulted in a shared belief that I need to see a shrink. He also admitted to knowing about the offer before the counselor graciously presented it to me, which he made no argument over.

Although James wasn't overly upset, he apparently agreed with the school's position because here we are, at my second session with a man who thinks he has all the answers.

I've laughed mockingly at this charade for days. John, or my father, or anyone else for that matter, will never understand what's happening to me. The hallucinations, the dreams, are otherworldly, something our earthly science can't explain.

"See you in an hour," my father says, inelegantly patting my arm.

"Yeah, sure," I grumble.

John sidesteps and points toward his office with an open palm.

I know where I'm going, you smug bastard. The door closes behind us and I plop onto the couch, the same one I found a few days prior, just as John's happy ass finds the same chair across from me.

Despite no noticeable improvement since our last session, I feel better. At least, less along the rabbit hole. I'll never admit John's hand in the progress. Rather, I credit the mindset change as my own journey in mental toughness, consequent from my own willpower.

We stare at one another. I randomly spasm while John twirls his glasses, occasionally biting at the ends. The whole situation remains foreign. I don't know what to expect or how to act. I find it troubling John, during our first session, so easily kindled a desire to lay bare my troubles. I fear what he may magically pull from my mind the longer we sit across from one another.

"So," I finally say, "who goes first? Do I start, or do you? These situations always confuse me."

John's face twitches, just a little. A light bulb flickers where he didn't know one exists. "Do you always use humor and sarcasm to hide your anxiety? Your fear?"

"My fear? Who said I was afraid?"

"We're all afraid of something."

I lean into the couch and cross my arms. "What the hell does this have to do with anything? I hated the silence, so I asked a question."

"Fear has a lot to do with everything. Jacoby," he says encouragingly, "fear of silence is a symptom of something. It isn't the root."

"You think my fear of something else has led to a distaste of silence?"

"I think something in your past has led to you becoming anxious in moments of silence."

"This is ridiculous, and silence has nothing to do with what's going on."

"Then tell me what's going on. What's on your mind, what are you thinking, what are you feeling?"

"I think that is too many questions to ask someone you accused of being anxious, Doc," I say with a sly smirk.

John shrugs, saying, "You can handle it."

That's a ballsy answer. "Well, apparently I'm a confused teenager, so go ahead and tell me what you're thinking."

That elicits a very small sigh, almost too small to notice. "To be honest, from what we discussed last time, I still believe you fear dealing with the loss of your mother. Your father told me that you never truly grieved."

"Screw you. I grieved for my mother. I cried for my mother."

"Crying for a day does not constitute as grieving."

"And my perceived failure to grieve, which you say is because I didn't cry enough, has led to the projection of the dog, the beast...for whatever reason you can't explain. Blah, blah, blah."

"And is probably what caused you to strike another student," he says with accusing eyes, which peer over the golden brim of his overly expensive glasses.

What? I think, shaking my head back and forth. "You're all over the place today, John. That was because *that* student was being a dick. And there is something...just off about him."

"Dick or not," *Did he just say dick?* "could you see yourself hitting another person, for any reason, a year ago?"

The question catches me off guard, and I take a moment to seriously consider myself a year ago. I've never been in a fight before, which gives John's point some validity. If I'm honest with myself, my nature isn't a violent one. Sure, there are circumstances where I could be driven to violence; like in defense of a loved one, but I wouldn't have hit Michael a year ago. Not for what he did.

Despite the revelation, I'm not going to admit John is right, so I settle on, "I'm not sure."

"Well, that's a start."

Arrogant prick.

"Does it feel like your temper is spiraling?" he asks after a moment.

My jaw tightens as John seemingly reads my mind. I look at my hands, avoiding an answer.

"Jacoby, I'm not here to judge, just to talk. Give honesty a chance and see how it feels. It might help."

Honesty. "Fine. Yes. I feel like everything is spiraling, not just my temper. My life is a mess. Everything is a mess. I have no control anymore, of anything. Things just keep happening and the person responding is no longer me. You happy?"

John leans back into his chair and scribbles about the finely stitched notepad, murmuring something indiscernible.

That's it. Taking notes will fix everything. "What's your prescription, Doc? What do your notes tell you?"

"The notes are to ensure our sessions are progressing. Don't read into it. I'm not as young as I used to be," he chuckles, "and my memory isn't as good as it once was. The notes help me to remember." When I say nothing, John moves to the edge of his chair. "Okay. Here it is. I think you fear dealing with the loss of your mother."

"You already said that. And now it's really starting to piss me off. Repeating it over and over won't persuade me it's true."

"I know I already said that, and I stand behind that analysis. But I need you to listen to me. It's not a fault, Jacoby. It's human nature to shy away from issues that hurt us. The mind has defenses, which are sometimes deployed without us even knowing. What separates healthy minds from unhealthy ones is a person's ability to become aware of their mind's activities, then to overcome them. To master oneself, I suppose you could say."

"That's ridiculous. We haven't even really talked about her. She left a while ago now. Why wouldn't I have turned this way before, if that was the root cause of all my problems?"

"It wasn't that long ago, and an event could have triggered these emotions, Jacoby. It happens all the time. We bury something so deep that we can only see the surface. Then, something comes along and unearths it entirely. The shock of seeing something whole, that we have trained ourselves to only see partially, can be very overwhelming at first."

"You have answers for everything, don't you? What the hell could you know about my life? We've had two sessions, and you think you've got me figured out. You don't know the half of it."

"I'm trying to understand *all* of it, but you won't let me," John responds sternly, but also calmly. The guy really can't be shaken. "If you want to be difficult," he continues, "that's your choice. I will only ask one thing."

"Oh yeah? That's it, one thing?"

John nods. "In our first session, you said the dog seemed to be getting closer, right?"

"I did."

"In both your dreams and the hallucinations? And is that still the case?"

"It has been a while since I hallucinated, but yes. And yes."

"I want you to confront the dog...the next time it appears. It will be difficult in your dream, but I'm guessing that so long as you are dreaming about the dog, it will most likely manifest itself in reality. When it does, stand your ground and confront it."

"Then what?"

John shrugs. "Who knows, but the answer to that question might surprise you. You may overcome it, it may disappear for good, or it may even have something to teach you. Something will happen, I promise you, but you won't know until you try. And what harm can come from trying?"

"I completely lose my mind."

John smirks, then smiles. "This will pass, Jacoby."

The session ends thirty minutes later. My father is waiting for me outside the office, looking at the same magazine as before.

John's hand is upon my shoulder as we pass into the waiting area, a passing from one captive to another, who each fear I'll become lost or run away absent a leash.

"We'll see you next week, Jacoby," John says, turning toward the overzealous receptionist, who's somehow still typing as if her life depends upon it.

Does she ice those fingers at night? "Can't wait," I mumble in response.

The car ride back begins as awkwardly and silently as the drive in.

"So, how did it go?" my father asks as we pull into the driveway.

Despite my desire to run to my room and forever live like a hermit, I decide my father deserves some sort of response, since he's been relatively understanding. "He said you told him that I never grieved for Mom. I figured he would tell you all about our sessions."

"Not at all. Unless you become a threat to yourself, or others."

"Huh," I grumble as I hang up my coat. *Society and its disclaimers.* I pause with hands clinging to the hanger, then turn and face a man who is truly concerned. A father who truly cares.

After a sigh, I say, "It went okay."

"Do you want to talk about it?"

"Not really." James' face falls into sadness and defeat. I cave. "Not yet," I say warmly. "I just need some time." It's every bit of compassion I'm able to muster.

A skeptical smile slips through downtrodden features. "Whenever you need to talk, or whenever you're ready, I'll be here."

"Thanks, Dad. I'm going to get some homework done."

"Alright. Dinner in an hour."

"Sounds good."

Jocelyn's door is open, so I knock on the frame. My sister, who is working at a desk to the left, turns with a blank stare, a thick textbook sprawls out before her.

"Hey," I say.

"Hey, golden glove," she says with a smirk.

"Very funny. What's up?" I ask, moving toward the bed.

She turns to face me, smirk vanishing like smoke. "Just finishing up some homework. How are you doing?"

She knows more than most, it's been that way for years; the product of a level of trust gained through what we've endured together. I've shared details about my torments that others will never know, even my therapist.

"I'm okay," I answer tiredly.

Her eyes slither. "People at school are talking a lot. You may not have gotten into trouble, at least in the traditional sense, but everyone knows."

Awesome. "About my freak-outs, or the fight?"

"Both," she answers, eyes falling upon the carpet as if embarrassed. *Are you worried? Ashamed?*

"I guess there's nothing I can do about that at this point. I'm sorry you have to hear about it. To be the sister of someone at the center of gossip. Someone that everyone thinks is crazy."

"That's okay. I'm not mad at you or embarrassed of you. I just want to throat punch those who bring it up."

I fail to contain a laugh. My mood brightens when Jocelyn laughs as well. "Please don't do that. Dad might actually lose it with two fighters in the family."

"True," she says as our ruckus subsides. "I'm sorry you're going through...whatever it is you're going through."

"I'll be okay. The Doc has some ideas, and although he's an arrogant ass, he might be onto something. And I haven't hallucinated in a while. It's just the dreams."

"People are saying this has something to do with Mom."

I rub at dry eyes. I know she means nothing by the comment, but I'm tired of hearing the same thing. "I don't think it does," I manage to say calmly, peacefully.

"Okay," is all she offers. I hear the doubt in her voice, and it makes me question my own opinion on the matter.

Her fidgeting increases, and our eye contact diminishes completely. "I hear you sometimes," she says slowly, quietly, encroaching on something intimate. "You don't scream, it's more like quick coughs, like you're choking, suffocating, or something like that."

"My dreams?"

She nods.

They are worse than they sound. A chill runs down my spine as I think about the dream, then the beast. "Well, at least I don't scream," I say, forcing a smile. "That wouldn't be very manly."

I expect a witty response, but she remains silent.

I stand and give her shoulder a pat. "I got some homework of my own to do," I say, nodding towards the book atop her desk. "I'll see you at dinner."

"Hey," she says before I'm able to shut the door.

"Yeah?"

"You should hang out with some friends. It helps me to get my mind off things."

My initial response isn't an agreement. But, as I think about it, the idea makes sense.

"You might be right." I head toward my own room, pulling a phone from my pocket and sending a text to Mitch. I ask if he wants to go see a movie. It's Friday night, and I haven't been out much since this whole thing started.

By the time I make it to my room, Mitch has replied. He and Megan are hanging out but don't have any plans. I don't feel like being the third wheel, but my sister is right, I need to get out. I agree to pick them up from Mitch's house in an hour.

I find my father in the kitchen and tell him the plan, who seems overly happy that I'm going out for the night. After apologizing for missing dinner, I shower and change and am out the door with a few minutes to spare.

"What's up, man?" Mitch asks as he fumbles into the car, claiming shotgun while Megan crawls into the back seat.

"Hey, bud" I reply, bumping knuckles. "Hey, Megan," I say, looking back.

"Hi. Thanks for the ride."

"My pleasure. Thanks for letting me tag along and ruin date night for you guys."

Mitch strikes my arm. "Nonsense. We weren't doing anything special, and we had no plans. It's nice to get out."

I notice the empathetic smile that passes between Mitch and Megan, as if they've jointly decided to do whatever it takes to support me through my struggles, which are apparently known to everyone at school.

I'm not looking forward to school on Monday.

"Well, I appreciate it. There hasn't been a lot to do. Baseball is slow going and I haven't heard back from Erika on yearbook stuff in a while."

"I'm sorry about Erika," Megan says after a few seconds of silence.

Mitch throws a stern look her direction, then quickly looks at me in horror and surprise, as if getting caught with his hand in the cookie jar.

"What do you mean?" I ask nervously. *Did she get hurt? Is she okay?*

"Umm..." Mitch hums.

"Is she okay?" I ask.

"Yeah, she's fine."

"Then what?"

"Well...come to find out...she and Michael are dating. Well...at least it seems to be that way." My two friends look worryingly at one another, then to me. "Sorry, man."

I nod, taking off toward the theater, inwardly attempting to process the news. After the fight and the chaos that followed, I forgot to ask anyone whether it was true—what Michael said about going out with Erika. I buried the comment deep, afraid to discover the answer, which now strikes me to the core. I'm too angry, too confused, to outwardly express my emotions, so I drive, never remarking on the subject.

Halfway to the theater we come upon a red light at an intersection for a major highway that runs east and west. The sun is gone, and dense clouds obscure the moon's light. Streetlamps, businesses, and headlights are all that bring existence to the world around us.

After the car stalls, Mitch turns up the volume to the radio. Some new pop hit is playing, which doesn't interest me. It sounds more like something an amateur, epileptic artist put together through a soundboard than actual music.

I'm about to give Mitch a tough time for his taste in music when an odd feeling washes over me. It's different from what I've felt in the past. Eerie but also comforting, familiar but less horrifying. The mixed emotions are hard to process, and I stare at Mitch as he tries to understand what my gut is telling me.

"Jacoby," I hear someone say.

My eyes refocus and Mitch is staring at me with a half-amused, half-annoyed look.

"What?" I ask.

"Light's green, man. People are honking," he says quickly, looking through the back glass.

"Sorry," I say. I move to let off the break, but my foot stays where it is, pressed firmly against the pedal. There, in front of the car, not twenty feet away, standing in the middle of the intersection, is the beast.

"What the hell?" I hiss out.

The dog stands at an angle. Its head is raised, and those vibrant, otherworldly yellow eyes meet my own. There are no snarls, no barks, not even a slight movement. It simply stares as if chiseled rock; its fur slick, combed through with something shiny.

Mitch says something, but I'm not listening. Megan pats my shoulder, which I ignore. I stare in bewilderment as the dog steps. I'm transfixed by the slowly moving figure, but I recall the conversation with John. I want to do as instructed, but confronting my torment in the middle of the road is a terrible idea. Too many eyes, and too many moving vehicles.

Instead, I decide to run the dog over, thinking I might figuratively kill something not real by crushing it. However, just as I let off the brake, a semi-truck barrels through the intersection—clearly running a red light—and the dog disappears.

"Holy shit," Mitch blurts out. "Dude, that semi would've

killed us. Screw you man," he yells from the seat, middle finger chasing after the semi.

"Okay, okay," Megan says while attempting to suppress Mitch's gesture.

The semi passes safely in front of us, but Mitch is right. The timing was perfect, and our car would have been demolished if the beast hadn't stayed my foot.

The dog saved our lives, I quickly realize, going from torment to savior in a matter of seconds.

That was good timing, for once. I once again consider John's suggestion about confronting the beast. And because it had just saved my life, I begin to seriously consider facing off with the animal.

It could have been coincidence, fortuitous timing that lacks a deeper meaning. But John's suggestion, the difference in what I felt prior to this manifestation, and the fact I could have just died, is too much to ignore. Perhaps my subconscious is telling me something, and maybe it's time I start listening instead of running.

"Is everyone alright?" I ask, inching into the intersection.

"Yeah," answers Megan.

"Uh-huh," agrees Mitch, head on a swivel for anything else that might kill us.

"Alright. Well, let's go see a movie," I say with a quick and nervous laugh.

Courage amasses ahead of the day I'll come face-to-face with those insatiable eyes.

15
SAINTS AND SINNERS

Susan

I ignore curious and measuring eyes that swirl brazenly around me. I've held the attention of men most my life, so the lingering gazes do little to unsettle my nerves. I've never thought of myself as overly attractive, but men, and sometimes women, have done their best to persuade me otherwise. They fawn over my dark hair, my seemingly always tanned skin and toned physique. Compliments I discard because I'm not that kind of girl. Not like those who seek power and influence through physical attraction. I prefer legitimate power, a lasting power that's earned through dedication and skill.

Despite my appearance, men flee upon discovering what lies beneath. My unusual behavior, temper, and unique hobbies act as a fire hose against any potential spark. I'm told I possess a threatening personality. The most cited reasons being my dedication to work, physical assertiveness, independence, and aforementioned temper. Usually more than one attribute is referenced.

I sport black, tight, malleable pants that draw attention from undisciplined eyes. A gray top reveals toned shoulders and a sculpted back, holding tight against my hip line. I could have worn something different. Something more conservative, but the workout is infinitely more comfortable with clothes designed for such movement.

Sweat flows uninterrupted, pooling atop a cushioned floor. There is freedom in letting oneself go, to allow sweat and blood to run unhindered. I'm in the zone, relentlessly giving a punching bag hell; employing a mixture of fist, arm, and leg strikes at various points as I rotate around the bag with confident and practiced footwork.

A few days have passed since my conversation with Joyce. I know she'll call if something triggers, but idly waiting permits dark thoughts. I needed something to keep the shadows at bay. By sheer happenstance, I discovered this gym and resorted to excessive physical exercise over a desire to drink and sulk. It isn't the greatest of self-improvements, but it's a start, and I take pride in the decision.

I've called the gym—appropriately named The Dredge—home for the past few days, spending most mornings lifting, running, and kickboxing. The equipment isn't great, probably decades old, and the air smells of a high school football locker room, but it's perfect.

My body is pushed beyond what's healthy because the alternatives exponentially decrease one's lifespan.

Eventually, when arms fail to lift and legs tremble, my body demands a halt by nearly shutting down. I find my bag atop a bench along the western wall and use a towel to dry.

With the towel draped over head and eyes, I'm blind to what's happening around me, but sounds of metal colliding with metal, grunts of both men and women as they struggle through repetitions, and gloves pounding against bags fill the small room in a cacophony of eclectic rhythm. It's beautiful, and the music of hard work will lull me to sleep if I allow it.

After a few minutes, when my heart rate has normalized, I rise from the bench, remove the gloves, shoulder the bag, and leave the gym in a solemn exit.

I pull off the road and into a gravel parking lot of an old-school looking diner. A red neon sign, with a quarter of the bulbs burnt out, is displayed across a tin roof.

"Hey, Ken," I say, taking a seat at the counter. Harry's Diner looks the same on the inside as the outside, which isn't a good thing.

Ken, a greasy, overweight, middle-aged man with dirty brown hair, smiles at me from beyond the counter. "Hey, Susan. The usual?"

"Yes, please."

Ken's smile blossoms as he flies to the back with my order, pouring a cup of coffee before doing so. I've stopped at this run-down diner for lunch every day after discovering the gym. I have no idea why it caught my attention, but I'm thankful I took the risk. To my surprise, the food proved delicious and the staff friendly, but not overbearing or intrusive. It didn't take long for an outsider, who repeatedly visits a less than busy establishment, to become familiar with the small and homely staff.

Ken returns a few minutes later and we talk a little while I sip at the coffee. It's lighthearted conversation, like talking to a well-liked uncle, but mostly small talk. Time passes quickly, and before I know it, my order is bagged and placed in front of me. I thank both Ken and the cooks before heading out the door.

It's a short drive back to the motel, close enough that steam billows as I dive into the bag. I grab a beer from the fridge with a mouthful of fries. Despite being a hot mess, food and beer are needed more than a shower.

Climbing atop the bed, I reminisce over the past few months. I may have promised Joyce I'd stay put, but that doesn't mean I'll stay idle, so I grab my computer and begin searching through several databases, looking for anything relevant to the hunt. I find nothing. Same old shit, different day. I'm losing ground after being so close. The hope I've amassed slowing fading away.

Halfway through my meal and in need of another beer, the cell phone rings. "What?" I yell in the phone's general direction. I nearly spit my food out when I read Joyce's name. I quickly reach for it, greasy hands fumble the device in a rare display of clumsiness. "Come on." I mumble out.

I manage to grab the phone, swallow, and answer. "Joyce?" A fry sticks at the back of my throat. Even I don't understand what comes out of my mouth.

"Susan?" Joyce asks.

I take a big, dry gulp, looking angrily at the empty beer bottle, then collect myself. "Yeah. Sorry, I'm eating."

"Alright. Well...umm...a name flagged a bit ago. One of the names on your list."

My heart races and, for the briefest of moments, I don't know what to say. I've waited so long for this moment, and now that it's here I'm paralyzed by a whole legion of emotions.

"You still there?" Joyce asks.

"Yeah. Yes, yes!" I yell. "What state? What name?"

"Slow down," chides Joyce. "It could be nothing, a coincidence, but I promised to let you know when one flagged. So, here I am," she says lowly and with contempt.

The anticipation kills me. I want to scream at Joyce, to quit holding back information I've spent countless hours, days, weeks, even months in search of. But our relationship is strained, so I drum up a reserve of patience I didn't know existed.

Without being consciously aware, I begin biting at unpainted nails. Something I haven't done since childhood.

"Erikson flagged in Indiana," Joyce finally says. "In a small town called Harrison."

An overactive mind races through the illegally acquired list, taking note of the full name, and then I pull up a map of Indiana. Harrison isn't plastered anywhere with a dot, so I pound the keyboard. The search result is nearly immediate.

"How? Why?" I ask while plotting the quickest path to the small town.

"Why was the name flagged?" Joyce asks.

"Yes," I answer in annoyance, still playing with which roads to take.

"Non-functioning taillight."

My mind rolls, and I almost laugh out loud. *After all this time, a burned-out bulb gave him away.*

"Joyce, listen to me. I need you to call in the cavalry. I'm talking everyone. This guy won't stay around long if he was pulled over by the police. Harrison is only a few hours away, and we have a real chance of catching this bastard." I'm standing now, pacing the length of the room.

"Susan," comes a motherly tone, "you know I can't do that." There was no hint of regret, or sorrow, only a non-emotional response of an unwillingness to help.

"What the hell do you mean? The name I gave you flagged. This is the killer. This is the guy. This is a man who has killed so many people, so many girls, and he won't stop. But we can stop him before he kills again. We can stop all this death." I've ventured into hysteria, voice rising to a near shout.

Why can't anyone else see it? Sure, I've been acting on a gut feeling for months, but the evidence is piling up. The painting has focused, clearer than ever before. All doubt about this investigation, and my sanity, falls away like a dissolvable film. My resolve, my confidence in this case, is now rock solid, and nothing is going to stop me.

Certain aspects of the case remain unexplainable, but the

outside of the puzzle is complete. Each detail linked, anchored at the corners. The rest will come more quickly. The path is true, and there is work to be done.

"*One* of the names you gave me flagged," Joyce says condescendingly. "I looked it up, there are dozens of matching names in the area. It could mean nothing that this one flagged."

"Mean nothing? Joyce, don't do this to me. That town is too close to be a coincidence. I may be on leave from the FBI, but I'm still FBI, just like you. That has to count for something. You are still in good standing; you could persuade them—"

"Voluntary leave," Joyce clarifies.

"Joyce. You know I didn't have choice. *They* didn't give me a choice."

"Right now, you can come back. A little groveling, a lot of apologies, and they will reinstate you."

"I can't. You know me. You know I can't." I let loose a lingering sigh. "Please try to persuade them."

"I will do no such thing," Joyce says matter-of-factly. "I'm in good standing because I didn't follow you down this rabbit hole. There isn't enough evidence for me to go to our superiors, let alone for those superiors to allocate resources for this wild goose chase. I would be laughed out of the building."

"You're making a big mistake," I say warningly, a hint of desperation mixed in.

Right before the phone clicks, Joyce quickly says, "Goodbye, Susan." Then there is silence.

"Shit," I yell, throwing the empty beer bottle across the room, shattering into dozens of pieces as it strikes the far wall.

On my knees, breathing heavily, I slowly began to settle, and once again find my resolve. A peace washes over me, a warm blanket of comfort, as if fate descended against a backdrop of an orchestra, showing its face and bestowing a promise of fulfillment in my greatest desire.

It's just me. It was always going to be just me, I think as I stand, spine straight with steady breathing, fingers curling into tight fists. My eyes open slowly, after envisioning the future, seeing the end of this hunt.

I'm coming for you, Thanatos. I'm going to kill a god.

I quickly pack my things and throw on a coat. After checking out of the motel, I slam the Mustang's accelerator to the floorboard, barreling my way toward Harrison with reckless abandon.

16

BRAVERY AND REBUKE

JACOBY

I move slowly down the assembly line, frowning at the day's offering. I'm aware of the unattractive expression but powerless to overcome it. I liken my predicament to Botox, and concede my will to unresponsive muscles, at least until I'm free of this overly fluorescent room.

The sense of dread and misery comes by way of captivity, or participation within a serfdom society. I march quietly in a lengthy line of soulless prisoners. What stretches out before me, and behind, is a chain-gang of youth who are tormented by having to repeat the same, monotonous actions daily.

Disapproving eyes peruse the day's options, my appetite diminishing the longer I stare. I dare a look beyond the mounds of grub, at those working behind the cold metal of shiny stands and square containers, and observe an environment of joy and pride, as if they had constructed a meal worthy of men and women clad in gold, adorned with sigils of superiority.

How can they be happy with life? I think in confusion and

disgust. The false happiness—which I'm sure is the case—a condition set forth in their contract. The school demanding smiles as students come and go in exchange for a paycheck. It's the only explanation, because no one in their right mind would find this job delightful.

With something that looks like a mashup of stuffing and oddly shaped sausage piled upon my tray, I lethargically exit the lunch-line and emerge into the comfortably lit atrium. I look over the mass of students, noting the political structure of the school by who sat with whom, until I find a group I mildly identify with.

An intense debate over last night's televised singing competition is underway as I take a seat at one of the cafeteria's many round tables.

"She ended well but the beginning was terrible," Megan is saying to anyone who will listen. "It was like she forgot the lyrics and mumbled until she found them."

Some murmur agreement while others roll their eyes and make counterarguments. The most popular defense comes from referencing the original song, which apparently begins soft but builds into something of a crescendo. I'm not familiar with the song, so I have nothing to offer on the matter, which doesn't bother me.

Somebody to my left mumbles. Melissa would rather talk about some love reality show, but no one hears her heart's desire.

The table is full, and consists of Megan, Mitch, Mark, Melissa, Jeff, and Jenny. Jeff and Jenny practically sit atop one another. I scan the room, looking for the teacher on duty. I can't imagine such comfort will last long.

Alexis is nowhere to be found, a normality since Jeff was caught cheating with Jenny. It's still a sour subject, which everyone has dealt with by ignoring it all together. The practice infuriates me. I think less of my friends as a result.

Alexis avoids the group whenever Jeff and Jenny decide to grace the rest of us with their presence. Merely seeing either one of them puts me in an irritable mood, but I keep my opinions to myself, despite my newfound temper. I consider the false kindness my decent act of the day, passing along a smile rather than a slap to the face.

I've always enjoyed having Alexis around, so her sudden departure is tough to swallow, especially considering the *why* of the situation. She is kind and caring, perhaps too innocent, and ignorant as a result, but she is a good person, which I find a rare quality these days.

A thought tickles at the back of my mind. I bravely look around the room until the itch is scratched. I find Michael and Erika near the outskirts. Michael leans in, hand upon Erika's back, as he whispers something. She laughs. That beautiful laugh. He pulls back. I dive into my meal as he notices my stare.

"What are you talking about?" Jenny fumes. The question directed to those who don't agree with her position about last night's performance. "I've heard the original before. She changed the whole song, and it wasn't for the better. Now, Dominic...that boy can sing."

Food from Mark's mouth splatters the table. "He's the worst. He sounds like a girl. You can't understand a word he's saying." After a deep breath, he quickly adds, "You only like him because he's a pretty-boy, and he can dance."

Jeff doesn't seem bothered by the comment. He's engrossed with something on his phone, which I scowl over. Our world has become one of reels, threads, posts, reposts, and quick videos—nothing of substance or importance. All the information in the world a click away, but everyone wastes their time over cat videos, guys getting hit in the nuts, or young adults performing rather risqué acts. It disgusts me.

No wonder we're all depressed.

"It's called a falsetto. And, well," Jenny says with a wink, "his looks certainly don't hurt."

I've been silently sitting at the table for at least two minutes when Mark looks my way. "What's up, J.J.?"

"Mark."

A few grunts and smiles are thrown my way from the others, but everyone quickly returns to their food. The larger debate fades against my acknowledged presence, with an occasional side conversation breaking out over individual preferences or lingering opinions about the voice competition. The atmosphere dense, passion neutered. I consider finding an excuse to leave, to allow joy to return to those around me.

I focus on the food until I catch a fraction of a conversation to my right. I find Jenny, who's speaking with Jeff.

". . .he was put on leave while the investigation takes place," she finishes.

"Who was put on leave?"

Jenny and Jeff turned toward me, to one another, then finally back to me. Neither look overly pleased with my interjection. I'm not the first to blink in a long pause. Jenny sighs and relents by answering, "Mr. Porter."

"The substitute filling in for Mrs. Lawson?"

"That's the one," says Jeff. "Apparently," he continues, leaning my way after a quick glance toward Jenny, "he likes high school girls. Rumor is, he's been with a few students, but someone apparently wasn't having it and turned him in."

"This shit happens way too much," huffs out Jenny.

Jeff turns, shock in his voice. "Didn't you say he was very attractive?"

Jenny answers with a shrug and a sly smile. "Well, yeah. But he has to be over thirty, way too old for a relationship with a high school girl to be considered even remotely okay. Then, to continuously make advances toward a girl who indicated she wasn't interested," she shakes her head, "just isn't right."

I collapse into the back of my chair, somewhat bemused and thrown by Jenny's comments. If anyone would have been in favor of teacher-student relationships, I would have bet my life that the adventurous and promiscuous Jenny would be at the top of the list.

My mind turns to Mr. Porter, who's only been at the school a few months, filling in for Mrs. Lawson while she's on maternity leave. I never had him as a teacher, but I've heard rumors, most of which were dismissed because any discussion of Mr. Porter—especially when coming from girls—always began with how attractive the guy is.

Still, if true, it's wrong. The world seems to continually gravitate toward the worst of humanity. New cases of spousal abuse, infidelity, inappropriate sexual conduct, and so on, flood the media every day. I wonder if the world is going mad, or if people are more courageous, with more platforms, in the reporting of such things—things that have taken place since the beginning of time.

When the lunch bell rings, I distractedly head toward a wall of trash and recycle cans, emptying my tray and returning it to one of the baskets located throughout the cafeteria. I turn down the eastern hallway and see Michael and Erika crossing through an intersection up ahead. I freeze then turn sideways, but I can't divert my eyes as they move quickly to the left and disappear.

Piece of shit, asshole. I wait a minute before continuing, ensuring I won't catch them on the way to my next class.

I round the corner and nearly collide with someone. It's an ungraceful act, but I somehow manage to dive right and avoid an unintentional tackle.

"Hey, bud," says Michael.

I gain my footing and look around. I don't see Erika, but others, who I assume know about our previous fight, slow as they pass, casting excited and anticipatory glances toward us.

Michael is stone-cold. Eyes piercing, unwavering, no matter how much attention the two of us garner. I can't find it in myself to respond. I tell myself it's because I hate the guy, that I have nothing nice to say, but it's due to surprise and awkwardness, an encounter I unrealistically hoped to avoid for the remainder of my high school career. I should have been more prepared for this.

"You're not avoiding me, are you? What sort of guy punches another guy in the face and then hides like a coward?"

I'm only partially listening, distracted by the mark I've left. Purple fades into yellow and puffy skin around Michael's left eye. A moment of satisfaction spreads like wildfire as I trace the outline of the bruise with my own eyes.

Michael points to where my eyes have fallen. "Yeah. Still wearing your cheap shot. Does that make you feel great? Powerful? Do you feel like a badass?"

You are something else. You're lucky they pulled me off you. I smile, imagining what another handful of punches would've done to that smug face.

"Still nothing to say? Just going to smile like an asshole?"

This can't go on forever. I take a dry gulp, consider how close I was to being expelled, my future down the toilet. I swallow my pride, my anger. "It *was* a cheap shot. I'm sorry."

"He speaks," Michael says rather loudly, turning to those who've braved gathering, then squares up with me. "I get it."

"What?"

"Why you did it. I would've been pissed too. I take your job, then take your girl. Well, she wasn't ever really yours. That has to be infuriating."

How did you know? The suppressed anger threatening to vomit. Fists clinch, body coiling in preparation for a fight. *You can't. I can't*, I tell myself repeatedly. A battle between mind and body. *My baseball career will be over.* I retreat, breathe. Fingers straighten. "I'm sorry. I said it was a cheap shot. Can we move on?"

"There is no moving past this. But, I'm not here to threaten you. No. I just want you to know, no matter how many punches you throw, it won't change the fact that Erika chose me over you, and that I'm going to be the starting shortstop."

"Don't be an asshole. You got Erika, good for you. You don't have my job yet. You're going to have to pry it from my dead hands."

Michael's cold and stern facade cracks into something devious, a devilish smile. "It may just come to that." He closes the distance. I scold myself for flinching. His smile grows at my discomfort. He leans uncomfortably close. "Don't worry, I won't take her for too long. You can have her back...when I'm done with her. I have to warn you, she might not be the same though."

What the hell does that mean? I envision shattering his face, laughing as bone and cartilage snap, blood pouring from various wounds. Instead, I stand there like a frightened child. I blankly stare ahead as Michael slithers off to the left, whistling the X-Files theme song.

The rest of the day passes quickly enough, and I find a sliver of happiness in that Mitch and I are supposed to hit after school. It's my first time practicing since the fight, and I feel out of shape. I need a workout to get back into the swing of things.

My phone vibrates on the way to hit. I read the text quickly. Chris had contacted Erika, asking us to come over to review a draft of the website.

The sight of her name sends me spiraling down a beautiful but treacherous cave. My heart flutters while teeth grind between a clenched jaw. Those passions die upon a crumbling bridge as I reread the short message, which is concise. I feel her distance as I read each word. The cold void between us comprised of disappointment and disinterest.

I attempt to reply in kind, stating I'll pick her up after batting practice. I receive a one-word acknowledgment a few seconds later, so I text my father to let him know I'll be home later than planned.

I spend about an hour with Mitch before packing up my things. I find a somewhat clean shirt in my bag and change into it as Mitch retracts the cages. I send Erika another text when I get into my car, letting her know I'm on the way. Another one-word acknowledgement.

What did I do? Nothing. I replay hitting Michael at practice. I shake my head. *I did nothing. She's the one who went and started dating an asshole.*

For an unknown reason, I steal a glance out the window before turning the key. My heart painfully skips a beat. There was no feeling, neither good nor bad, or eerie sixth sense. Nothing in warning. But there it is. The black dog isn't more than thirty feet from my car, and the shock of its stealthy appearance makes it impossible to breathe.

Shit, I finally manage. The word a thought, but I'll take it after both body and mind had slipped into a state of comatose. The paralyzing fear doesn't last long. A mysterious calm engulfs every concern. The outside world blossoms like a flower. The colors are dull, but warmth replaces a cold, persistent darkness. Without giving it much thought, I open the car door and venture into the unexplainable.

A light snow blows from the southwest. The parking lot is nearly empty, so the wind marches unhindered, kissing my cheeks with frozen lips. A faint glow from hidden rays cast the world into an odd twilight. I confidently step away from the car, leaving the door ajar.

I decide to take John's advice and approach the beast, but

that doesn't mean I'm stupid. The last incident involving the beast and this parking lot is a fresh memory. There will be no fumbling of keys this time.

It's not real. Repeating it over and over again fails to negate a distant, pulsating thought; that despite being a hallucination, the beast transcends dimensions. Physical harm a very real possibility.

"Been a while," I whisper.

The incident with the semi relatively fresh, but the beast came and went with haste. Before that, I hadn't seen those eyes for weeks. I'm unsure if my newfound sense of courage stems from the fact I've seen less of the beast, or if John is actually good at his job.

You did save my life. The beast's appearance stayed my foot, therefore saving my life. I would be a pancake in a coffin somewhere otherwise.

I slowly inhale, exhale, stepping toward the beast.

Yellow and unblinking eyes watch with bored interest. A recently fed and lazy lion discovering a mouse off in the distance. The dog is on all four legs, but relaxed, almost tired. On my third step, the dog shudders, squaring itself toward my approach. The head drops, eyes rise to meet my own.

There's a hitch in my step when the beast responds. I stop on a dime, raising hands slowly into the air, showing my palms as if to say I come in peace.

I hope I don't go in pieces, I think, absolutely befuddled why an old action flick comes to mind at such an intense moment.

I can't help but scan the parking lot, a full circle verifies I'm alone. There have been enough witnesses to these types of encounters. I find the dog again; afraid it might have charged during the spin.

It's still there. Same spot, same posture.

"Hey boy," I say awkwardly. *Is it even a boy?* I'm certainly not going to attempt that discovery.

The dog doesn't respond.

"I really am losing it," I say aloud, but to myself. "I'm talking with an imaginary dog, and I'm expecting a response. Uh, I'm Jacoby. You've been haunting me for a while. Just wondering if there is an end in sight?" I ask with a shaky voice.

Another step elicits a response.

Slow and steady.

Another step. The dog's tongue falls from its mouth. *Soon.*

"Soon? Is that you in my head? What do you want?"

A moment later, as if seeing a squirrel, the dog turns and runs off.

"Huh," I hum out, straightening myself, watching the beast disappear into a thick wood.

Although more confident than before, tense muscles uncoil in near euphoria. I stand a minute, watching the place where the dog had disappeared, half-expecting the beast to come barging back. Nothing happens. No sounds, no eerie feelings.

I turn and plop into the driver seat, quickly rotating the key and cranking the heat. I consider heading after the dog. I stare beyond the window, contemplating. I decide chasing after a hallucination isn't a pragmatic approach. I'll find it again when my mind decides it's time. No reason to chase after smoke when your mind is the fire. Instead, I put the car into drive and head for Erika's house.

The car is put into park atop the long driveway as I hope, pray, Erika will venture out on her own. After a minute, with no activity at the front door, I sigh and shut off the engine, painfully working my way out of the vehicle. I look longingly at the vehicle as an icy wind finds exposed flesh. I steel my mind and head for the red-colored double-door.

A small, shivering pep-talk occurs before numbly striking

the doorbell. A few seconds later, Erika's father jubilantly swings open the door.

"Jacoby," he says, extending a hand.

I take the hand and try to return the smile. "Mr. Jones."

"Come on in," he encourages, retreating into the house.

I pound boots against concrete, snow splattering across the porch. "Thanks."

Mr. Jones stops at the bottom of a spiraling staircase. "Erika," he hollers upward. "Jacoby is here."

We wait a few seconds in silence before Erika crests the peak.

"Ready?" she asks distractedly, avoiding eye contact.

"Yep," I reply, defeated, failing to hide how much her coldness disturbs me.

"Alright." She turns back toward her father. "I'll be back in a couple of hours," she says, hugging her father.

We cross into the freezer-like outdoors in silence. Erika doesn't protest when I open the passenger side door, but unlike the past, she doesn't show any sort of gratitude.

Awesome. Great times ahead.

The car ride itself fails to bridge the gap between us. I have no idea what to say to the girl of my dreams. A girl who is dating a guy I've punched. I can only imagine what the two of them have said about me since the fight. So, we sit in silence, a few words here or there around the weather and yearbook website. We avoid the topic of school and Michael like it's the plague.

I nearly cry in relief when we make it to Chris' house. We quickly disembark the car, shaking off the foul smell that haunts us, both seeming to prefer the cold air over cold conversation. Erika doesn't give me a chance to open the passenger side door. She's off toward the house before I've pocketed the keys.

"Good evening," Chris says with that same welcoming charm I remember from our first encounter.

"Hey, Chris," Erika replies, an excited voice laboring through a swallowing cold.

I don't want to admit the cause as anything other than the weather.

"Come on in and get warm. It's freezing outside," he says, genuinely concerned.

I follow Erika into the house, and I shrug off the chill as I transition into the warmth and comfort of the house.

"Can I get you two something to drink? Coffee? Water?"

"Coffee for me," I reply.

"Do you have decaf?" Asks Erika.

"I do. Regular for Jacoby and decaf for Erika. Coming right up. Black, right?" Chris asks.

He remembers. Impressive. "Yes, please, and thank you."

"My pleasure," he says quickly, already heading for the kitchen.

Chris returns a few minutes later with three cups, handing both Erika and I our respective requests.

Once everyone is seated, Erika breaks the silence. "So, how does it look?"

Chris flaunts a childish grin. Innocent but confident. "That is for you to decide. I took some liberties in giving it a little flash. If it's excessive, then feel free to tell me that. This is your project. I'm just the tool to see it made. I can change anything easily enough, you just need to be vocal about what you like and dislike."

Chris abruptly stands and ventures to a table along the opposite wall. Laptop retrieved, he places it on the coffee table. After a few clicks, he turns the computer so Erika and I see the screen. I notice our school colors first. I've always hated our mascot, but Chris has somehow designed a bad ass sparrow.

Chris returns to his own chair. "Apologies it took a little

longer than expected. Go ahead and poke around. You can't hurt anything, it's in preview mode, so mess around with it for a minute and let me know what you think."

Erika reaches for the laptop and starts clicking various links, each of which send her to a different page populated with headers and titles. "This is amazing," she says quietly, distractedly, marveling at the screen. "And no need to apologize. This is very much appreciated."

I'm straining left to see. Everything is blurry from this angle, but I'm able to make out the gist. It's impressive. The functionality looks simple enough, which is what we wanted, but the graphics are elegant. Simple but professional. Fun but classy. It's high-quality work, and although expected from someone who builds websites for major corporations, I hadn't expected Chris to spend much time on a free, high school project.

"I love it," I say, straightening my neck with a crack.

Chris' childish grin returns. "Wonderful. Erika, what do you think?"

"I agree. This is more than I think either of us could have imagined asking for."

"I'm happy to hear that. Anything you want changed or added?"

Erika's eyes roam left and right, scanning quickly, contemplating the question. "I don't think so. Jacoby, anything you noticed?"

"Nope. We'll have to play with it. Add some photos and text and see what we can do. We might have a better understanding once we start populating the meat of the website."

"Fair enough," Chris replies after taking a sip of his still steaming coffee. He stands and works his way beside Erika, outstretching his hand, which holds a slip of paper. "Here is the website's address and the administrative password to make changes."

"Thank you," she says, taking the paper. Were her cheeks flushed from the warmth of the house and decaf coffee? *Probably not,* I answer to myself.

Chris is still an attractive guy, and I find myself liking him more with each conversation. I imagine Erika feels the same with a slight twist. It's infuriating and laughable all at the same time. Erika is dating an asshole who, for some reason, has it out for me, while also being attracted to an older man I can't help wanting to become.

Life sucks.

We finish our coffee over some non-website related conversation, then we say our goodbyes. Chris requires a promise to reach out if, and when, we discover something we want changed with the website.

A part of me wants to stay, to avoid another awkward car ride back to Erika's house. I mentally prepare for disappointment, deciding to focus on a discussion of the website and Erika's plan on how to best use the tool to reach the student body, or at least entertain those who purchase a yearbook this year.

Erika, however, is the first to speak. "We should write an article about the website. Give students a heads up on what they can get with a yearbook purchase."

"Not a bad idea," I reply. "It might be a good way to spread the word before the website goes live. We can use that article as a marketing tool."

"Exactly. And I know Chris wants to stay anonymous, but I want to give him some credit in the article."

"Are you sure? He seemed pretty adamant about wanting this to be a silent contribution. He might be unhappy."

"Don't be ridiculous," she says with a belittling tone. "Only a decent guy would do something like this for free and not want credit for it. It isn't truly a donation if you ask for something in return...like getting credit for the work. He will appreciate that we recognized that."

"Alright."

Erika sends a reserved, sideways smile my way, deep in thought as she turns to peer out her window. "It will be a nice surprise. I got his full name from a document on a table next to the couch, so we can do this right and maybe get him an award, or some more work."

I think about Chris' business. "I think he said something earlier about having a full workload. But I can't imagine a community award would hurt."

She nods but says nothing.

The entire conversation is lifeless. I'm nothing more than a sounding board for ideas. I'm here to listen, valuable as long as I remain quiet. I brave a glance, eying her longingly and with pain, knowing I've missed my chance to be with her. A dark, insurmountable chasm lays open between us.

She is, and will forever be, out of reach. I see how we got here, but that doesn't mean I understand it fully. Michael is at fault. He's an asshole who pushed too far. Who he is doesn't align with someone Erika would be with. The only explanation is Michael is someone different with her, and that scares me.

Sitting mere inches apart, we might as well have been talking on the phone while on different planets.

Come on. You don't know until you try.

A shutter ripples, a stampede in pursuit of a shaky breath. I glance toward the passenger seat. *Out with it.* "He egged me on."

She turns, surprised. "What?"

I look everywhere but at her. "Michael. He said some things."

"I don't want to talk about this." She returns to her window, crossing both arms and legs.

She needs to know. She should know. "I just want you to know. I didn't do it for no reason."

Turning with clenched fists, she says, "It. You mean hit him, right?"

I nod. "He said things about me. He said things about you."

She runs a hand over her face. "He told me you would say this. That it was his fault. That you would claim things that weren't true."

"It was his fault!" My leg twitches, knuckles whitening as my grip on the steering wheel tightens.

I feel her cold stare. "Who is going to be the shortstop this year?" she asks. Accusation laced into the question.

I manage to look her in the eye. "That hasn't been decided."

"That's why you hit him, right? He's threatening your position. Don't you put this on me. I had nothing to do with it."

"Erika. That isn't what happened."

"I thought I knew you. I don't, and I'm done talking about this. From now on, we only talk about yearbook."

"Erika..."

"I said enough!" she screams, a glistening tear falls from the corner of her eye.

I retreat into myself, and we say nothing the rest of the way.

17
A WINDING PATH

Susan

I frown while coasting into Harrison. *What is it with small towns?*

I'm by no means a city girl, but it's exhausting jumping to and from towns where Dollar General stands as the main attraction. There is no sign, no banner, or any other form of identification indicating I've arrived at my destination. Only the GPS gives away that information.

The sky is overcast, a gray canvas reaching as far as the eye can see. Limbs of tall but barren trees sway wildly against an eastern wind. Everything a shade darker under nature's gloomy visage.

Downtown, a haphazard assembly of three-story buildings, sprouts less than a handful of stoplights.

Barren fields and depressing animal farms with worn fences encircle the limited number of structures. They branch out in eternity, collapsing against the horizon and rising sun.

The police station is easy to find. There's a main road running through the mass of collapsing buildings, the station nestled near the town's center. It's the only building with a sign, and worn letters off its deteriorating brick side reveal a diverse heritage. Two squad cars from the 00s-era are parked out front.

No point in wasting time. I whip into one of the open parking spaces next to a squad car and kill the engine. Outside the car, I violently battle my collar into submission, desperate for warmth. I enter the station as a cowbell rings overhead. *Where the hell am I?*

A receptionist with stringy hair chews angrily at a wad of gum mashed between overly white teeth. She looks up at me with curious eyes, some mindless game playing on the phone nestled between thin hands, which angrily chirps at her distraction.

"How may I help you?" she asks, repetitive chirps luring twitching eyes downward where thumbs swipe with practiced precision.

What a hick town. "I'm looking for the sheriff."

"Well...we don't have one of those at the moment."

"What?"

The receptionist curses as her phone screams dreadful sounds of demise. My heart rate quickens. I picture myself pinning this woman, by the neck, against the far wall. To hear her gurgle for help, attention no longer slave to a damn game. Her complete disregard of duty, and blatant lack of respect, needs addressed.

Cost versus benefit. I need information. The lesson unimportant compared to saving a life. After a deep, calming breath, I reach over the desk and smoothly pull the phone from the woman's hands.

"Who the hell do you think you are?" the receptionist yells, standing with a very pointed finger. I notice long, painted nails. I wonder how quickly my knife could remove them at the cuticle.

I flash my FBI badge, expecting immediate obedience. To

my surprise, the woman chomps loudly at her gum as she leans over the edge of the desk, crossing into my personal space. A low-cut top reveals way too much flesh. The receptionist's forehead wrinkles as small eyes squint.

After taking a step backward, I realize she's likely never seen a federal badge. Why would she? This is a small town where nothing of significance ever happens.

After a few seconds, a failing light bulb miraculously stabilizes for several seconds.

"Is that real?" the receptionist asks, a lazy finger pointing toward the badge. A bemused but rebellious smirk replaces the one of confusion.

Unbelievable. I don't have time for this shit. "Yes. It's real. So are my handcuffs and weapon." The smugness evaporates. "What's your name?" I ask.

"Marci."

"Okay, Marci. You said there is no sheriff?"

"That's right. Sheriff Nevins died of a heart attack a few months back. Apparently, the village bicycle, that would be Janice, was too much for the old geezer. Town hasn't gotten around to replacing him yet. Saving a little money, I suppose."

"Wonderful. Is there someone in charge?"

Marci blushes. "Brody is in the back. He's filling in."

I wait for more, but I am once again disappointed. "Can you get him, please?"

"Yeah. Sure. Sorry," Marci says quickly, working her way free of the desk and disappearing through a set of old western-looking doors that swing from rusted hinges.

The station is nothing like the hundreds of others I've seen during my time in law enforcement. The small entrance plays home to the receptionist, her desk, a jug of ancient water, and three dusted-over chairs along the far wall. The whole place smells of musk and wet wood.

The swinging doors are east of the desk and offset by

several feet, nestled between an infected wall with something foul and alien spreading unencumbered. Marci pushes open the two doors like a cowgirl walking into a saloon, the hinges moaning in protest, granting a brief glimpse of what lies beyond. A young but stocky man catches my eye, gone as fast as he'd appeared.

Cracked wood and cheap glass once again block my view.

Marci emerges a few moments later, the young cop following her with an unattractive swagger. "This is deputy... acting Sheriff Brody Teller," she corrects when the young man grunts in protest. The scolding glance sends poor Marcie fumbling over herself.

The *acting* sheriff's hands rest atop wide hips, elbows flared, with a well-fed gut threatening to snap a cheap and shiny belt that struggles to stay whole. His small mouth bulges on the left, and a few flakes of black are crusted upon chapped lips. A mostly empty soda bottle swings from his left hand.

Brody chews tobacco. It's a nasty habit, something one of my very short-lived ex-boyfriends had enjoyed. Years ago, I had the misfortune of mistakenly taking a sip of a beer I thought my own, only to discover it was Jim's spit bottle. The realization resulted in a very nasty trip to the restroom, and when Jim failed to quit, I left him. There were likely other foundation problems, but the chewing is what I focus upon.

Brody looks me over with a bored expression. "What can I help you with, miss?"

I watch as Brody adds volume to the soda bottle. How people respond to a federal badge has always amused me. Some found religion, others became territorial, while the rest sought to impress. Brody seems the territorial type, eager to dismiss me as nothing more than a nuisance passing through his small kingdom.

"I need information about someone recently pulled over in this town. And I need it quickly." I look around the room with little hope. "I'm guessing, hoping, that you have some sort of file system, or database."

"Marci here says you flashed an FBI badge. May I see it?"

Territorial it is. "Sure." I, deciding this small gesture might save time in the long run, pull forth the badge and hold it eye-level. I overextend and wave it crassly mere inches from Brody's face. My impatient temper getting the best of me.

"Satisfied?" I ask, dramatically holstering the badge.

He's about to argue when something shifts. "Come on back," he grumbles.

Brody is first through the doors and makes no attempt at being a gentleman. He most likely hopes I'll wander face-first into the glass as they swing back. This man is turning out to be a real delight.

We emerge into a sparse but large space with a handful of desks littered with unorganized paperwork. Another door is at the end of the far wall, and I see the silhouette of several metal cages through marred and unwashed glass.

Brody leads me to a desk along the western wall and points toward a low chair off to the side. *I'm not a perp.* I'll let him have this moment of power, but he'll learn soon enough what I'm capable of.

"What was the name?"

"Erikson."

"And what would a federal agent want with a guy in Harrison, Indiana?" he asks as swollen fingers type, arrogant eyes devoted to his computer in a rebellious dismissal of my presence.

"No offense, but that's of no concern to you."

That gets his attention. "This is my town. So, if I say it's a concern, then it is."

"Listen, Brody. I'm sure, given that you're not actually the sheriff, more like a steward playing at sheriff, that you have to be an asshole to keep your temporary power. But with me, that's not a good plan. You'll give me what I'm requesting, without question, or I'll call my superiors, and we'll make sure you never find work in law enforcement again. We have a very wide influence, so if you cooperate, we might be able to help you get the sheriff title legitimately."

"No one gives a shit about our little town, especially feds. Why should I believe that you'll help me in return?"

"You can believe it, or not. Frankly, I don't care. I can make your life hell either way. I'm offering something I don't have to, to get something I need...to move this conversation along. If you spit on that offer one more time, you'll find out exactly who you're talking to and what I'm capable of. I will call in some of my buddies, forcibly remove you and your entire staff, slander your name across the state media, and get the information I want with a smile on my face."

Awestruck at the threat, and taken aback by the audacity of my words, drool nearly falls from his mouth. I can't tell if he is scared or aroused. I don't care which it is, as long as I get my information. It's probably the first time anyone has stood against him in this hick town. He stares with a gaping mouth, mind scrambling for a response. He convulses several times, about to say something in return but never able to put words to those thoughts. In the end, his eyes revert to the screen, and his fingers type once more.

Brody clears his throat a few minutes later. "Erikson. Doesn't live in Harrison. Looks like he was pulled over for a non-functioning taillight."

"I knew that already. Tell me what he looks like!"

Brody strains a blood vessel over the question, pulling at his eyebrow. "Umm...this says I was the one who pulled him over, but I can't exactly recall."

Not exactly what the answer I'm expecting. "What do you mean, you can't recall!?" This is it. This is my moment. Brody has seen Thanatos' face. The face of a god responsible for so much death. "It wasn't that long ago. This is important. Think real hard," I command, a warning in my voice.

Think very, very hard. Come on.

Brody shifts uncomfortably. "I'm sorry. I think he had dark hair. Maybe."

"Maybe? What the hell does that mean?" My gut churns. I might be sick with anger.

"I'm sorry. I, for some reason, can't recall."

I'm fuming at the mouth. "Are you hiding something from me? You have to remember! Think again. I don't expect there are a lot of traffic stops in Harrison."

Brody seemingly tries but fails. That's when the sense tickles at my mind. A desk drawer is ajar, and I barely make out a half-empty liquor bottle. Looking at Brody, I see what lies beneath. There is pain, maybe even trauma. Something eats at the man's core, driving him to drink and partake in other unhealthy habits. A high-functioning alcoholic, my mind replays the event. I watch as Brody approaches a vehicle. It's dark, late at night. Brody appears fine, walking straight, but his mind is elsewhere, fractured from an empty whisky bottle in the passenger seat.

The sense demands understanding, grace. His story is not unlike my own. I want the opposite. I've come this far, talking to a man who has seen his face. This should be the last clue I need. I want to beat the memory out of him. To open his brain and dig until I find the face of Thanatos.

In the end, I cater to the sense, which has served me well thus far. "Shit. Okay. How about make and model of the car?"

Brody stares at the screen. "It says...2018 Chevy Silverado."

"You don't recall that either?"

"Now that you mention it, not really." Embarrassment, maybe shame, engulf the man. This isn't the first time something like this has happened. He wants to improve, to get help, but something dark anchors him. I see Brody's future, which is short. I want to help but there isn't time, and I don't have the expertise for something like that. Admittedly, expertise suited for my own life.

"Fine. How about an address."

"Okay. Umm...looks like we ran an address for Brighton." Brody's movement slower than before.

The town doesn't ring a bell. "Brighton?"

"Yep. Closest big city. Well, bigger city. It's about forty-five minutes from here. Got a few booming manufacturing plants. Growing population. An asshole for a sheriff."

There you are, Brody. "Thanks for the summary. What's the address?"

Brody writes it down on a piece of paper and hands it over.

I stand and head for the nearest exit without saying anything more to the troubled, self-imposed, ad hoc sheriff.

"You're going to make the sheriff thing happen, right? I did as you asked."

I turn with a very sad smile. "I'm going to get right on that. Don't worry."

Brody watches me intensely, wheels turning. He apparently sides with hope. "Thanks."

Part of me feels sorry for the man. A larger part bathed in anger. I can't forgive him, no matter his torment.

Back in the Mustang, I plug the address into the phone's GPS and take off; smoke from screeching, burning tires flare in the rearview mirror. Brighton is to the northwest.

A swell of dark clouds is on the horizon, but I give it little thought. Whether chance or omen, the sky's foreboding mood does nothing to quiet my spirit.

I have become steel—the embodiment of determination.

This is my chance to end the cycle of death. To stop the god of death. I will not cower. No, I will see this through.

The rain intensifies, but I push through and arrive in Brighton an hour after departing Harrison.

I want nothing more than to go charging in with Matilda ablaze, but I still know very little about my prey. Despite the burning desire to put a handful of holes into Thanatos, I steel my mind toward a stakeout. I know myself well enough to realize I can't endure that type of boredom on an uncomfortably hungry stomach; so, before heading to the address Brody provided, I order something resembling beef at a busy fast-food restaurant.

I park the Mustang along a choppy curb catty-corner to a worn, four-story apartment building that sports ancient air-conditioners outside flayed windows. I'm not surprised. A serial killer like Thanatos would keep a low profile, and taking up residence in a low-income apartment building with a high turnover rate is an intelligent move toward that goal.

I remove a hamburger from a soggy paper bag in the passenger seat and take a bite, eyes forward, appraising the apartment building. A swig of whiskey helps wash down the processed meat. I see Brody's face in the bottle's reflection. *Is that what's to become of me?*

Another swig chases away the dreadful thought.

An army of diverse emotions descend in storm. This is the climax of my hunt; the epitome of every discomforting decision, action, and circumstance I've endured these past months.

I've been to hell and back in search of this man. The world had been against me, but I've overcome the critics—those who called me crazy, banishing me to the fringes of society.

They will see soon enough.

The world will know what I've done, that I was right. Thanatos will be pulled from the shadows and bathed in light, on display for the world to see.

For all the struggles, the frustrations of repeated failures to save lives, the depressing nights and trails of empty whiskey bottles, the gap is closing. It's surreal, more nerve-wracking than I could have imagined, but also less satisfying.

No words can describe the numbness within. Perhaps a stronger sense of accomplishment, a self-satisfying excitement, will come after I put a bullet in Erikson's brain.

The adjacent streets are in opposition to my overactive mind. A few disheveled humans, and wild dogs, come and go but nothing, and no one, stands out.

I'm in the car for hours, mind pondering the lengthy timeline that's led to this moment. I consider what I know about the man I call Thanatos, and what I don't know. Through practical reasoning—more likely impatience—I decide the stakeout is a waste of time. I have no idea what I'm looking for. Thanks to Brody's alcoholism and piss-poor memory, which still boggles my mind. What are the odds? Add it to the list of unexplainable phenomena during this investigation.

I had applied an amateur profile, a natural but untrained gift, that successfully uncovered behavioral patterns critical in my pursuit. However, the limited profile, and convoluted timeline of the murders, means I know nothing of Erikson's appearance. Anyone who sees his face in passing will think nothing of him, and those who have realized what he is are no longer alive.

He is a ghost, moving through life without drawing attention to himself. Unforgettable enough to spontaneously move on to a different town without anyone connecting the departure to a recent murder.

I leave the car at the curb and head for the building. I stand next to the entrance and light a cigarillo, propping a foot against the decaying brick. A resident exits after a few takes, and I toss over half the barrel, sliding through the door before it closes.

Two flights of stairs later, I emerge into a small hallway with apartments to either side. There's barely enough room for two people to walk side-by-side.

The air is thick and stinks of unwashed clothes and water damage. I expected Erikson to keep a low profile, but the state of the building doesn't fit the profile. Erikson is neat, tidy. He couldn't have carried out so many murders, without being caught, if he wasn't orderly and detail oriented. Something isn't right.

It's cold, but I push the discomfort from my mind and plunge forward in confident strides. Apartment 2D is at the end of the hall and on the left.

My heart races, and the familiar sensation of adrenaline washes through me like a tidal wave. I pause a moment to calm my mind, swallowing several deep breaths before squaring up with a rotted door frame. Loose and discolored gold markers stand at an angle near the top of the door.

I unholster Matilda and look back the way I'd come. If this goes sideways, I couldn't live with collateral damage. Not again. There's also a chance I'm going to kick in the door, which I don't want anyone to notice until I've had a chance to look around the apartment.

In my mind, there's a thousand different ways this can play out, almost all of which end violently.

That's been the plan all along.

This is the man responsible for an amount of death very few people can fathom. A man who has ruined too many families to satisfy a twisted pleasure. He is the embodiment of a type of evil forgotten to history, washed out through science and skepticism.

I ready myself to die for the cause. I am at peace with the possibility. This, despite months of internal opposition, is my life's purpose. All roads have led here. If my purpose ends here, then so be it. I'm ready.

I ignore the creeping skepticism laying siege to my mind. A voice tells me this is too easy, that this isn't the end. After a shrug, and another breath, I knock and stand to the side, placing a finger over the peephole.

Nothing.

No movement. No sound. Only silence. A television blares from an apartment down the hallway. The bass from a stereo system rumbles beneath my feet.

I lean against the door and knock again. Still nothing, except deep moans from old and warped wood.

I take a step back and wait several minutes before holstering Matilda, turning to leave. A troubled mind dives deeper into thought with each step. I need to decide what I'm going to do before I reach the bottom of the stairs. I return to the main level and nearly complete a full-circle before finding the appropriate door.

I knock.

There is cursing and yelling, then labored movement. The door swings open and I nearly laugh. The man behind the door epitomizes this forsaken building, a human manifestation of the despair I feel. He is half-bald, with stray and wild hair protruding at the sides. He wears a stained robe with a stretched, white shirt underneath and mismatched shorts that halt well above the knees. Slippers with holes cover half the man's feet.

"What do you want?"

I show him my badge, and he catches a cough in his burgeoning throat. I count at least a dozen health code infractions, with many more lurking, waiting to be discovered during a thorough investigation.

"What's your name?" I ask quickly. I've found blitzing to be the most effective tactic in situations like these.

"Johnny."

"Johnny. Are you the superintendent?"

He gives a shy but frantic nod. Johnny is likely considering his options—desperate for a practical solution that keeps him out of jail. "Yes. What can I do for you?" Tone very different than his initial welcome.

"I'm looking for the man in 2D."

His eyes fly wide. There is something about that room, or its occupant, that causes a squirm.

"Why?"

"That isn't important. What can you tell me about the person who lives there?"

"I can't give out personal information. Not without a warrant. Do you have a warrant?"

A simple raise of an eyebrow crumbles the man. "Okay. How about I go around and start talking with your tenants? I'll be sure to ask them about the conditions of their living, your performance as the superintendent, and ask if they have seen anything...unlawful take place during their stay here."

"Okay. Okay. I'll give you want you want. You'll leave me be if I do?"

"Yes. I don't give a shit about this damned place. Just give me what I ask for, then I'll be gone. Forever."

"No one lives in 2D."

"What? It's unoccupied."

"Not necessarily," Johnny says, shamefully.

"What the hell does that mean? No games, Johnny. I don't have time for them."

"Fine. A couple of months ago I got an envelope with a wad of cash and a note. I was to hold an apartment, apartment 2D, for someone named Erikson for six months with no questions asked, and, in return, I would get enough money to cover the rent for two years."

"Do you still have that envelope, or the letter?"

"No. It was a few months ago. Probably thrown out a day later."

Shit. That would have been too easy. "You never met the guy?"

"No. It came by mail. No return address. I've never seen anyone go in or out of 2D."

"Have you been inside the apartment since you received the envelope?"

"The envelope said not to, but my curiosity got the better of me."

Please tell me you found something interesting. "And?"

"Nothing." *Shit. You could have missed something.* "The room is completely empty. Looks exactly the same as when I cleared everything out after Mrs. Hinton passed away."

"Damnit!" *It was a safety net in case someone got too close. There'll be nothing in that room. Smart bastard.*

I pull out a card and shove it into Johnny's hand. "If anyone ever comes to that room, visits, or so much looks at it too long, I want you to call me. If you receive another envelope, I want you to call me. Anything related to 2D, you call me. Understand?"

"Yeah. Sure," he says, shaking. Johnny is nervous and curious. There's a chance he makes a call to someone other than myself, but I'm confident the threat of investigation is enough to hold his tongue.

"Never say anything of this conversation. No matter what. Do you understand that as well? Otherwise, I'll be back here with a SWAT team and raze this place to the ground."

"I do."

"Good. Have yourself a wonderful day, Johnny." I consider asking for a key to apartment 2D but decide against it. Instead, I turn on a dime and leave.

It's risky enough that I stood outside the apartment for so long. Forcibly entering the apartment could potentially collapse my element of surprise. There is no need to add unnecessary risk. Every bit of evidence suggests nothing of value is stowed away in the apartment. A serial killer as intelligent as Thanatos wouldn't leave evidence lying around in an apartment he didn't live in, let alone never visited.

There are too many unknowns. A camera could be hidden somewhere within. If that's the case, entering the apartment would give me away. If my intentions are discovered, Erikson would either hunt me down or pack up and move on.

It's too great of a risk for almost no chance of reward. Too many lives are at stake to make a mistake now.

I leave without knowing what to do next. This was supposed to be my big break. The chance I've dreamed of and begged for, only to discover another dead end.

The road may have collapsed, but my destination has alternative routes. It must. Despite my anger and frustration, I believe that. I know that. My extra sense blares it in declaration, urging me forward. It moves within me, clawing against the darkness, desperately supportive, persuasive in a coming victory.

Thanatos is close, I can feel it. I pray the vicinity comes with benefit, revealing a path before another murder takes place.

18

THE BEAST WITHIN

JACOBY

The classroom is dark and uncomfortable. The air is warm, but I shiver. My body temperature drops quickly and without explanation.

I look quickly around the room. The setting reminds me of a gothic-styled cult classic movie. There is something unreal about the situation, but I can't place my finger on what's causing the unsettledness.

A faint light seeps through open windows to the left, the source somewhere overhead and out of sight.

I'm sitting at a desk, a pen of some sort in my right hand, but there is nothing to write on.

A moment of panic sets in. The classroom is empty, then it isn't. Students slowly materialize in the desks around me, appearing out of thin air and acting as if they've been there all along. It's irksome, strange, and should be horrifying, but I merely shrug at the instantaneous change.

Something is off. Very off.

Voices float over otherworldly waves that sway through the very air I breathe. My classmates talk in hushed conversations.

My eyes dart left, out through a bay of windows as antsy hands fidget. I strain but fail to discover the source of light. I beg for discernment, to know which path leads to the light. The longer I stay within the classroom the more I fear something terrible.

Erika's voice rises above the others. She is here, behind me, talking with another student. I go to say something, but no words came out. Erika's head bobs left, and I see hands interlocked.

It's Michael, and when he notices me, he smiles unnaturally wide.

I want to yell, to scream at them both, but my words have no voice, no volume. My mouth moves in silence, and I'm ignored. My head becomes heavy, weary of frustration, and I rest it upon open palms. I don't know what to do. There are too many things happening, too many unexplainable events to understand or comprehend. This reality is foreign and miserable.

I'm about to stand, to try something else—perhaps overturn a desk—when I feel something unfamiliar beneath my skin. The feeling slowly transitions into a muted discomfort. I scratch at my forearm, then my legs, as if thousands of burrowed insects are about to explode from flesh. Suddenly, the disconcerting itch is gone, replaced by a coolness; the sensation begins near my neck and methodically works its way down both arms. An unstoppable force that eventually assumes full control.

A soft breath falls against my neck. Every discomfort is forgotten as I shiver deeply. My bladder begs for release. Someone, or something, is beside me, mere inches from where I sit. There is a low rumble, a hungry stomach, a growl. Another breath, foul in stench, rolls across my face.

The room falls silent. Everyone turns and stares. My classmates wear blank faces. Their eyes shift, in unison, from me to whatever, whoever, is beside me. I've never been more horrified.

I press my eyelids shut. *This has to be a dream. Wake up. Wake up. Please, wake up.* Nothing happens. The breathing continues, the beat of my own heart slows, matching the one that torments me. I don't want to look, but there is nowhere to go.

I will my eyes open and slowly turn. Inch by inch, I take in more of the room. Something black creeps into my periphery. I instinctively close my eyes, but my body continues to rotate. I stop when I feel the breath upon my forehead.

Just do it.

Yellow. That's what I see first. Yellow eyes, focused and wanting, meet my own. No more than six inches away stands the beast that haunts my existence. Teeth are barred, but it makes no sound. It stares at me as if I'm its next meal, but it never moves. A strong body shakes at each breath, tongue occasionally lapping against the back of its unnaturally white teeth.

We stare at one another for what seems hours. Then, without warning, the beast's mouth widens and into the abyss I fall.

I awake in a room darker than that of my dream, but I find comfort and power in the unknown as I look out over the bed. Not even the translucent rays of a hidden moon can be found through the unseen windows to the left. My breathing steadies and there is a sense of calm in the air that surprises me.

The dream begun horrifically, but something changed at the end. I recall the eerie and unnatural occurrences of the dream, how it felt to have the beast's breath upon my neck. My skin crawls as I scratch at my throat. I relive the moment the beast opened its mouth. I should shutter in fear, but I don't. The darkness there is comforting, a forgotten home, a missing piece of myself. Strength replaces confusion, and, for the first time in years, I feel at peace.

Something within me has changed. What that is, however, I haven't the slightest idea.

"Then you woke up?" John asks. His face flat, revealing nothing in terms of an opinion.

"Yep."

"You were scared at first, then confident as the dream collapsed?"

"That's what I said." John looks disappointed, unappreciative of my impatient and sarcastic tone. "Sorry," I say. "I'm trying. I tried to confront the dog in the parking lot, then I wanted to in the dream, but I woke up before I could. I got lost...froze up when I looked into the dog's mouth."

"I believe that you're trying, Jacoby. And you have come a long way. It sounds like you simply woke up when you looked into the beast's mouth, not that you froze up."

"Maybe. Is this normal? I mean, is what I'm going through... has it happened to anyone else?"

John slips a sideways laugh. "Jacoby, I'm not going to lie to you. This is one of the most interesting cases I have ever been a part of. Specifically, I've never heard of something like this. However, projecting a manifestation is not uncommon. So, to answer your question, yes and no."

"Glad to be your entertainment for the day, Doc."

"Don't be dramatic."

Don't be an asshole. "I don't think that's something you should say to a patient. Aren't you supposed to be understanding? Supportive?"

"I behave differently with each patient. You can take the direction without spiraling. I believe it is even beneficial in your situation. Besides, there is good news."

Lucky me. "Oh, yeah? And what would that be?"

"I think you're close to moving past this."

"How so?"

John peruses his notes. "Keep trying to confront the dog. I believe you two will face-off soon enough. I can't say for sure, but it seems like the projection allowed you a look into itself, its purpose...when it opened its mouth."

"Its purpose? As in *why* my mind created this projection?"

"Precisely. Understanding is the first step in acceptance, then you will be able to overcome it."

"And you think this will all end, once we *face-off*?"

"I do. One way or another. Don't lose your resolve. It's imperative you stay determined to confront this dog. If you waiver, I fear any progress you have made would be lost."

"Easy enough for you to say. You don't have a mad beast haunting you at random. I'll admit, things seem better, at least not as terrifying, but I'm sure that could change in an instant."

"We all have our demons, Jacoby. Some more seen than others."

"Very philosophical, Doc."

"I have read a lot of Plato," he says with a wink. "Our time is up, Mr. Talavan. Before you leave, I'm going to ask that you call me when you...and this dog both stand your ground. This might occur before our next session, and I don't want you to wait. Please, call me immediately after this happens so everything is fresh in your mind. Can you do that?"

"Yeah, sure." *Want a hamburger while I'm at it?*

"Thank you. I'll see you in a few days."

I leave feeling better about my insanity, despite a lingering sense of internal turmoil. It helps I'm not handed off from shrink to father. I take it as supporting evidence of my improvement.

Outside, I think about where to go next. I haven't much to do and nothing of any importance comes to mind. Erika hasn't reached out regarding the website, and team practices are nonexistent at this time of year. Not that I'm in the mood to practice, alone or with teammates.

I need some time alone. To think without interruption. So, I take off without much thought as to where I'll end up.

After a few minutes of driving around aimlessly, a small park emerges on the right, and I veer toward one of its empty parking lots. The air is frigid, so there aren't many people out wandering through the gardens, or children playing atop plastic constructs scattered across several acres of land. It's a barren landscape, and I smile at the vastness.

I throw on a heavier coat stashed in the trunk, buried under several layers of baseball equipment, and find a bench at the back of the park. I'm in a mood to be dramatic, sitting alone on a bench in the cold, contemplating the meaning of life and what I've endured, seems appropriate.

I think of my mother and, for the first time since this all began, consider how her death might be feeding into the manifestation of the beast. It seems absurd, but life is full of absurdities. Who am I to complain? There are far worse things one could endure in this life.

Maybe.

I'm mentally unstable and haunted daily by something that isn't real, but I admit to feeling different, maybe even improved. My mind is clearer, my energy reignited, and the world appears brighter than before. I'm also alive.

My attention falls upon the dog, and I play out every encounter, every dream, hoping to recall anything I might have missed. It all seems clear, and nothing of importance, nothing new, comes to me.

A slight shiver runs across my chest as a gust of wind sweeps in from the left. The shiver deepens as I recall those yellow eyes. Those eyes still terrify me, and the unnatural smile more suited for human than animal. I thank God, out loud, that

I haven't seen that smile lately, either in dream or manifestation.

It's time to stop the fear. To replace it with something more productive. I'm determined to see this through, to see it done and over with. Part of me still wishes there is something epic or meaningful about what's happening, but as I piece together the events, I relent to the common opinion that I'm simply *unsettled* in the mind. There is nothing I can do about it now, except purge it from myself.

I need to face my torment.

A chill runs throughout my body. It's a familiar shiver not caused by weather or anything else related to the environment.

I shudder, then take a deep breath before standing. *I guess this is as good a time as any.*

I walk around the bench and turn west with eyes wide and hands shaking. The feeling holds true. Thirty feet away stands the beast. It's grown since the last time it manifested. Slightly taller, thicker build. This isn't a dream. It's a manifestation, and it's time to end this.

After a glance around the park, ensuring I'm alone, I say, "Hey."

The dog does nothing, seemingly impervious to the elements—its fur lies flat as a strong wind speeds to the northeast.

"Uh…yeah…this is crazy. I'm crazy. Listen, are you going to do anything? What do you want?"

Nothing. No movement. Anger rises. Impatience takes hold and itches at the corners of my brain. I am tired of these games. I want something, anything, to happen. Although things have improved, I desperately want to put this whole thing behind me. To move on in life, to focus on baseball, girls, college, and life beyond.

I want a sense of normality.

"What the hell do you want?" I yell. Calm and resolve

return after several heavy breaths. This beast is me, at least a part of me, and outbursts will serve no productive purpose.

I remove my hands from their respective pockets and hold them steady at chest level. My breath floats in the air after each exhale. "I'm ready. Whatever your purpose, I'm ready. I accept you. Whatever it is you want, tell me, or come take it."

Finally, a response. The beast's head drops, eyes affixed to my own. Those yellow, unnatural, and eerie eyes draw closer, body lagging. Then, my torment smiles. The same smile I remember from the dream.

"You can't scare me anymore, you bastard." I trail off, confidence wavering. *But that is still messed up.*

It is time.

"Is that you in my head?" I ask.

Yes.

"I guess that makes sense. I'm still insane, but yeah, makes sense."

Are you ready? The beast asks.

My resolve strengthens. "Yes. This ends now."

The dog steps, then another. The movements are slow, a predator stalking its prey. The standoff has ended. Something is happening, but I have no idea what this ending looks like.

I spread my arms wide and laugh. "Come on!" I yell once more, not in an outburst but as a declaration, an acceptance of what is happening.

The dog breaks into a sprint. Its smile grows with each leap. I embrace the chaos, the madness. I expand my mind and body to accept myself, my fate.

"That's it," I continue to laugh. "Come on, you bastard!"

The dog a mere few feet away now. I dig my feet into the earth and lean into the coming impact. I yell as loud as I can, something from deep within unleashes, shatters, bursting into a thousand pieces. What comes out of my mouth is as much a growl as it is a scream. I dissolve at the molecular level, then fire and electricity painfully stitch me into something new.

Life slows, an eternity passes between every second, as I watch the beast leap and strike. There is no impact, and I topple forward in anticipation of the collision.

I rise, dusting snow from my jeans, shaking my head while completing a full circle. The dog is nowhere to be found. The beast had passed through me like a ghost. I feel odd, sick maybe. I collapse and vomit. I stand upon shaking legs after several violent heaves. I can't help but run hands over my body, searching. Something sticky clings beneath flesh, attached to muscle, organ, coursing through my body with each heartbeat.

Teeth grind as I kick at a pile of snow. I hadn't expected the heavens to open up, or to hear the blare of trumpets, but I had hoped for something more than getting sick and feeling sticky.

I shouldn't be surprised. It isn't real. This whole thing isn't real. Luckily, no one had watched the past few minutes unfold. If they had, I'm sure a swift call to the police would have transpired, claiming someone had escaped an insane asylum.

The dog is my imagination. Part of me, sure, but not real. It's a manifestation of what's probably a failure to grieve my mother's death.

Is it gone? Is this over? These are questions running through my mind, and I have no idea how to answer any of them. I know someone who might.

I dial a number with shaking and clumsy fingers. It rings several times before a friendly receptionist answers. I hear busy hands against a distraught keyboard. "Right Mind Associates, how may I help you today?"

"Yes. Hi. Can I please speak to John?"

"John is currently unavailable. Is this an emergency?"

"Yes, it's an emergency."

"Sir, are you a danger to yourself or anyone else at the moment?"

"What? No. I'm not looking to kill myself or anyone else, if that's what you're asking?"

"Good. I'm sure your call is very important, so can I have your name and the issue you are having?"

"That doesn't mean this isn't an emergency. Just because someone isn't about to die."

"I understand that, sir. Please, remain calm."

"Holy shit, lady. Look, tell him it's Jacoby Talavan. He told me to call him. He will know how important this call is."

There's a brief pause. The phone silent. I'm about to hang up and redial when I hear, "Please hold."

"Thank you," I say, pacing a small section of the park.

Less than a minute later a burst of static comes across the line. "Jacoby, it's John. What's wrong?"

"Nothing really, Doc. At least, I don't think it's wrong. We had our standoff."

"Really? Already?"

I replay the events in my head. "Yep. Just a few minutes ago."

"Wonderful. Can you come back in?"

"Now?"

"Yes. I'll cancel my lunch appointment," offers John. "I want to work this through while it's fresh in your mind."

"I'll be there in about 10 minutes."

"That will work. See you soon, Jacoby."

19
THE CHOSEN

SUSAN

Nothing has changed, for better or worse, since my visit to the apartment complex. No call from Johnny. No lead miraculously appearing in terms of Erikson's whereabouts. My computer is silent, indicating no violent activity related to Erikson's profile. I hold my breath. It won't be long until that changes. I need something to change.

The absence of a murder, or even a missing person case, within the vicinity of Brighton causes doubt. I question whether I've gone astray. *Did I lean too far into a lead? Am I completely off course?* He will strike soon, if he hasn't already.

Joyce hasn't called, and I've repeatedly suppressed a burning desire to reach out to my friend. I tell myself, despite the growing animosity between us, that Joyce will call if anything triggers regarding Erikson, or any of the other names on the list.

I grab my laptop and black notebook and head out the door, hoping food will distract an overworked mind from my repeated failures. I'm trapped in a nightmare, watching events unfold but unable to change the course of history. Girls are dead, and more will die if I continue to fail.

A few hours later, with a greasy double-cheeseburger and Diet Coke rumbling somewhere within my stomach, I've worked through every database at my disposal. I find nothing.

On one end, I'm relieved I haven't missed anything. On the other, I'm exhausted from the mental and physical demands of this hunt and frustrated there isn't a lead to unearth.

I depart the diner and notice a hipster-looking sign that hangs from a post mounted to a sleek building. The word *HeBrews* is burned into wood and outlined in white. An inscription at the bottom of the sign indicates it's a Christian coffee shop and bookstore.

For some unknown reason, my feet take me to the front of the building, where I reluctantly enter. A set of doors open into a rather spacious room. Bookcases filled with coffee bags and machines are to the left and lead to a metal staircase that ascends to an active social area above.

I follow a string of hanging lights as guilt floods my soul. This isn't a church, but, in my mind, it might as well be.

My curse—the voice in my head drawn to evil—has led to numerous unhealthy habits. Habits inconsistent, even rebellious, toward the teachings I remember from my youth.

Despite what most surmise when examining my life, and contrary to certain lifestyle choices, I believe in God. How could I not? I'm drawn to evil, the worst of its kind. No one sees or feels the things that I have without believing in evil as a supernatural force. It's powerful, capable of influencing men, women, and even children into horrific acts. These experiences, the encounters with unexplainable madness, have led me to believe in an opposing force. You cannot believe in one without the other. There has to be a God, otherwise the evil I've faced is uncontested, free to flow into every fiber of life and consume the world.

I have touched so much evil, but I've also experienced the good. I think of Joyce, the Asian man I helped earlier, my father.

Although I believe, I've rarely given it much thought. When I have considered the spiritual realm, I find myself angry with God. Angry for allowing me to see what others could not. For giving me the ability to see evil, the spiritual battles raging all around us, while everyone else remains mercifully ignorant. Angry that He does nothing to stop it, to protect the good from those who would do evil, other than give me the torment, the burden, of stopping it.

It's unfair. I'm just one woman, and the burden to stop a single serial killer is too much, let alone save the world.

I've often wondered if there were more like me in the world. The answer likely a mystery until after my deathless death.

Yes, ours is a strained relationship, why I rarely gave religion, Him, much thought. It's been a long time since I've truly prayed. Not since that day many years ago, and since that day, I've done things, thought things, said things that I'll eventually give an account of.

The fear of having to pay the piper someday has yet to yield drastic changes within my life. Anger burns brighter than fear. I consider sharing an eternal cell with Thanatos. The thought results in a deep reflection. *Maybe. Once this is over.*

There is an inherent understanding, a self-realization, that I'm rough around the edges, more so as the years have passed, consumed by a purpose I don't want. I believe the extra sense is meant to be a gift from God, as it's drawn to the vilest of humanity, not the good. Although it often feels more a curse than a gift, I had often, in my younger years, considered handing it over to Him. That I should give into the sense and surrender to a higher purpose. For some reason, most likely a result of past experiences, I've chosen anger and resistance, battling a power that overtakes me at every turn.

I've always done as the voice suggests, but I do it with scorn more often than not, even if it saves my life and the life of someone else. Maybe, one day, my mindset will change. Something will have to give, one way or another, for that transformation to take root. Killing Erikson would be a good start. My mind has bent, another straw will break it. The pull between selfish self-destruction and serving whatever gift has been bestowed upon me can't last forever.

"Welcome to HeBrews, what can I get for you?" asks a spritely teenage girl from behind a long, wooden counter.

"Can I get a medium caramel macchiato?"

"Absolutely. Any whipped cream?"

"No, thank you. Just the coffee."

"Not a problem. If you want to take a seat, I'll bring it out to you when it's ready."

"Thank you." I pay the young girl, who wears a wide and genuine smile, before turning to find a seat.

I settle upon a small table facing high windows that look out into a busy street. It's late afternoon, but the sun still throws warm rays upon vibrant pedestrians wearing heavy coats. Lovers hold hands and young friends rush carelessly down sidewalks, kicking up dusts of snow. The atmosphere is happy and contagious, and for just a moment, I forget about my troubles—lost within the peaceful moment.

"Here you are," comes a soft voice.

The young barista interrupts my daydream of another life with a steaming cup of coffee in hand. Although thankful for the coffee, the words summon every aspect of the hunt to the forefront of my mind, and I feel my mood sour. The barista places the coffee on the table and heads back toward the counter.

I yell, "Thank you," in case the young girl mistook my demeanor. She turns and waves before disappearing into a curtained back room.

Nearly an hour passes before I pack up my items and leave the cafe. Back in the motel, I collapse upon the bed and release a slew of moans and curses, some out of exhaustion, the rest in frustration. I roll over onto my back and sit up, leaning heavily upon the rickety headboard. After sitting in silence for several minutes, I withdraw my laptop.

Why the hell not? I think, bringing the computer screen to life. I pull up a public search engine and type in Erikson's full name. I've tried everything else. I don't expect to find anything from a generic search for a man who doesn't exist to the rest of the world, but it can't hurt.

My fingers work quickly, scrolling to the bottom of the screen. Nothing of importance is noted. I select page two and nonchalantly scroll again. I reach the bottom of the page when my heart suddenly flutters, a breath catching in my throat. I trust my gut and scroll upward, looking more closely at the headings and descriptions.

A link toward the middle of the screen catches my eye. The title of the page, something about Brighton High School and its upcoming yearbook, is nothing to be excited about, but everything changes as I read over the summary.

There, near the end, is the name I'm looking for.

Muscles everywhere tense, building, strengthening. A fingernail taps repeatedly against the computer. Finally, it's too much. I jump from the bed and let loose months of frustrations. Twirling, I collapse upon the bed, finding the article.

Doubt, that familiar friend, returns in haste. *This is too easy.*

After everything I've been through, all the avenues I've been down to find this guy, it seems impossible a simple internet search will be Erikson's undoing.

My breathing is heavy, palms slick with sweat. I read the article quickly, scanning for the name. I vaguely process what I'm reading, but I get the gist.

Brighton High School is attempting to create some sort of

online yearbook, and the article is a marketing campaign for the product. It isn't until the end of the article that I find what I'm looking for. The last paragraph is a dedication, a copyright of some sort, which thanks the man responsible for the development of the website.

It's a thank you to the killer, Chris Erikson.

I have found Thanatos.

After staring angrily, shockingly, at the name for a moment, I scroll back to the top of the article, another bit of influence tugging at my scrambled brain. I find a picture of a young girl, the author of the article.

Erika Jones, I read quietly as I look over the picture. "You're a brunette," I repeat aloud, the statement growing in importance each time it's said.

The hunt, the evidence, the victims, everything relevant to the man I call Thanatos, plays out in my mind like an out-of-control-movie reel. It all adds up. It has to be this way. My line of thinking becomes clearer with each passing second.

It's you, I think, looking at the picture. *You're next.*

I jolt from bed and frantically don a few layers of clothes, holstering Matilda and yanking free my phone. I'm halfway out the door when I call Joyce.

"Susan, I don't have anything—"

"Listen to me, Joyce. I don't need your shit right now. What I need is for you to look up a name and give me an address."

"What's wrong?"

"I found him, Joyce. And I know who his next victim is."

"Susan," comes a motherly tone. "How can you be sure?"

"I just am. Trust me." *Please, just trust me.*

"I can't. This is insane. You're on a wild goose chase. There is no mass murderer. No serial killer running rampant across the country. You need to come home. You need to see someone, Susan."

I want to scream and curse and reach through the phone to

punch Joyce in her smug, all-knowing face. Somehow, I manage to reason that any of those actions is counterproductive. The last impossible.

"I'll make you a deal," I say instead.

"What might that be?"

"You give me the address, and if it turns out to be nothing, if I am wrong on this, I'll come home, and you can send me to whoever you like to get help for this obsession of mine."

There's a strenuous pause. A girl's life hangs in the balance, and her fate comes down to my ability to persuade a disgruntled friend to help me one more time.

Joyce clucks her tongue. "You're serious. You will promise me that?"

For shit's sake. We don't have time for this. "Yes. I promise, Joyce. This is it. All or nothing."

More silence, which reaches sinisterly into eternity. "What's the name?"

Thank you. Thank you. "Thank you! Erika Jones. Brighton, Indiana is city of residence."

"Give me a minute." I hear the phone fall against something hard.

It's five minutes before my friend returns. "Susan, you still there?"

"Yep. Still here." *This is taking too long. The girl is next, Joyce.*

"I want you to promise me, one more time, that you will end this chase if this turns out to be a dead lead. Promise me this is it, and then I'll give you the address."

"I promise, Joyce. I promise that this is it."

There is a sigh, but I know my friend will relent. This is her chance to bring me home. This is her chance to end this, just as the address will be my chance to end this madness. Everything is coming to an end.

"2241 Markle Street."

I have you, you bastard. "Thank you, Joyce. I'll call you later."

"You better."

I break every traffic rule I know on my way to the Jones' home. About a mile away, I slow the car and collect my thoughts. Barreling into a family's driveway I don't know and rushing wildly to the door will certainly put them at unease. I can't afford the turmoil that's likely to cause. Adding complications to an already complicated situation will collapse any momentary advantage I possess. These next few moments need to go as smoothly as possible in order to go as quickly as possible.

I haven't planned this conversation in its entirety, whether with the parents or the daughter. I figure I've made it this far with wit and charm, so this last little bit can come together on the fly.

The house is magnificent, large and aesthetically pleasing. Tall, black lamp posts run the length of the driveway. I slowly run the car halfway up to the house before turning off the ignition. The hour is late, and I'm sure, via the headlights and roar of the Mustang, the Jones' know of my arrival.

A response comes after one ring of the doorbell.

"Yes?" Mr. Jones' asks with prying and curious eyes.

"Mr. Jones?"

"Who is it, dear?" comes a female voice somewhere behind the door.

"Not sure yet," he answers. "Yes. I'm Mr. Jones. How can I help you?"

I flash my federal badge and quickly return it to my coat pocket. The father's eyes remain weary, but his demeanor hints at trust. Mrs. Jones is now beside her husband, arriving just in time to see the badge.

"What is it? Is it our daughter? Is she okay?"

"Why do you ask that?"

"It's not our daughter," she says in a whisper, more to herself than anyone.

I take a deep breath. "There is no reason for alarm. As far as I know, everyone is okay. But I am curious as to why you asked about your daughter. Erika, correct?"

"Yes, that's our daughter," says the father. He looks to his wife. "She was supposed to be home two hours ago, and she won't answer her phone. We thought she was just running late. She said she was hanging out with some friends, but they said they hadn't seen her all night when we called. We then called the local police station, asking about any accidents, but they said there hasn't been any tonight. Then, you showed up. It just has us worried."

"As I said, there is no need to be alarmed. As far as I know, your daughter is okay. However, I am here to speak with her. I need to ask her a few questions about something she may have seen, unbeknownst to her, relevant to a person of interest in a case I'm investigating."

Mrs. Jones steps out into the cold with a raised voice. "Could this have something, anything to do with her being late tonight. Did this person of interest take her?"

I can't blame her.

"Absolutely not," I answer confidently. I hate lying, but I don't see another choice. "This person of interest is far away from here by now. Which means these questions need to be asked in a timely manner. Can you try calling her once again?"

Mrs. Jones wipes a tear from her eye. "Of course. Let me find my phone."

"No need. Here," I say, extending her own phone, "use mine."

"Thank you," she says, taking it and dialing without question. She holds it to her ear for a minute before sighing and handing it back. She shakes her head.

"That's okay. I will work with the local police, and we'll find her. I'm sure she just lost track of time and is in a basement somewhere with some friends."

The father gives a shy smile. "Thank you."

"I'll be in touch." With that, the door closes and I'm heading back to the car. I make a call of my own.

"Are you coming home?"

"Not yet," I answer sternly.

"Why are you calling, then?"

"The girl, Erika, is missing. It may be nothing. The parents said she should have been home two hours ago, and they can't reach her. She could be with a boyfriend or simply lost track of time, but I need to find her to be sure. Can you run an open trace on her cell?"

I hear the grinding of teeth. The tension between us almost unbearable, a rope about to snap.

"This is it. You hear me? I'm done after this. No more favors. I'll ignore every one of your calls until you come home. Do you understand?"

"Yes." *This will be it. One way or another. Just one last favor.*

"What's the number?"

"Hold on. I'll send it to your phone." I back out of the call and pull up the history. I find the number the parents had dialed and send it to Joyce's phone. "Just sent it."

"Got it," says my once upon a time friend. "Hold on."

I turn to the key to the Mustang and begin backing out of the driveway. I turn the car west and take off slowly.

"Still there?"

"Yeah," I answer.

"Just sent the trace to your GPS. It will stay active as long as the girl's phone is on."

"Thank you," I pause, choking back an emotion I thought lost to the sands of time. "I'm sorry, Joyce. I'm sorry to put you through all of this."

"Don't you say that. Don't be dramatic. Don't act like this is a goodbye. This will turn out to be nothing. You come home."

"I will. One way or another."

"Be safe, Susan."

"You too, Joyce." I want to say more, but I can't afford additional emotions right now. I need a clear head.

I can't explain my confidence, I have no real reason for it, no true evidence, but I somehow know tonight is the night this ends. I will either kill a god or fall victim to one.

The voice inside my head works hard to bolster that confidence. What worries me is the lack of clarity on whether the confidence is one of victory or death. Time will tell.

20
IN THE FLESH

JACOBY

I can't recall the last time I felt this good. There's a lingering sense of chaos, of strangeness, a tingling residue of the eerie feeling that came after the dog had passed through me, but it has faded into the recesses of my mind, hardly noticeable. There has been no dream, no manifestations since the day in the park, and I've been able to sleep soundly for the first time in a long time. I've never been more thankful for anything in my life.

Aside from having lost my mother, enduring judgmental gazes from students aware of my bewildering and violent outbursts, and the girl of my dreams dating my arch enemy, life is great.

I'm back to dealing with struggles suited for a teenager's life.

I'm deliberating how happy I should be when my phone vibrates. I roll onto my side and read the text message. My heart skips a beat when I see it's from Erika.

Michael and I broke up. Need to see you ASAP.

All the anger I've felt toward Erika and Michael the past few weeks falls away with those few words. I sit up in bed and think a moment before typing out my response. I write over a dozen sentences, then edit and delete each one until I finally settle upon something simple: *where?*

A few seconds later the phone vibrates again.

Sparrow's Woods.

It's the woods adjacent to the school on its eastern side. There is a path that leads from the parking lot to a small gazebo and decent-sized creek. It's a place where, when students feel rebellious during after-school hours, young couples will go to make-out. I can't help but imagine what that's like with Erika. Imagining her lips on mine, our bodies flush, produces a smile and quickened heart rate.

A wrecking ball crashes into my gut as reality sets in and ruins a moment of euphoria. Doubt and skepticism replace happy thoughts. I have no idea why Erika wants to see me. Nothing in her message indicates she's thrown off all feelings for Michael and wants to fall hopelessly into my own arms.

I do some math and reply that I'll be there in thirty minutes. I quickly change into clean, warmer clothes, style my hair, brush my teeth, and practically jump the entirety of the stairs.

My father and sister are in the living room, watching something that sounds like a romantic comedy.

The things fathers do for daughters, I think while briefly looking at the screen.

"Need to head out for a bit. Be back in a few hours."

I'm at the door before my father has a chance to respond. "Whoa. Hold up. Where are you off to?" he asks, rising from the couch like his pants are on fire.

"A couple of friends are getting together."

"On a weeknight? It's really late, Jacoby. Whose house are you going to?"

I consider lying then think better of it. "It's not a bunch of friends getting together. It's one friend, who is struggling through something right now. I'm going to see what I could do to help." It isn't a lie. I withhold details my father doesn't need to know, and that I don't want to explain.

The explanation visibly throws my father. "Okay," he finally says. "Text or call me if you can't be back by eleven."

"I can do that," I promise, closing the door behind me before anything else is said.

The sun had set over an hour ago, and the world outside is frigid and dark. A steady wind crashes against my coat, stinging at my ears, but I hardly notice. Excitement and anticipation flow through me in great waves, staving off whatever merciless conditions nature throws at me.

Tonight could be the night I've thought about for so long, imagined and dreamed about for years, or it could be the worst —possibly the greatest letdown of my life. I'm a realist, hoping for the best but planning for the worst. That mindset is the reason my excitement comes in waves, crashing against solid rock built upon a foundation that Erika's text could mean anything.

What I want to believe and what I should prepare for plays tug-of-war inside my mind.

I arrive on school grounds ten minutes later and park my car next to Erika's. It isn't running and the inside is dark. I look through the window to ensure she isn't inside.

I turn to the woods. The night plays host to a full moon, which throws a murky light upon the landscape, partially revealing some things while the rest remains hidden in darkness.

I pull out my phone and send Erika a text with shaking hands: *where are you?*

She responds a moment later. *Near the gazebo.*

A smile pulls at his mouth, but I quickly suppress it.

Walking up to Erika, hours after a breakup, with a smile fit for Disney World, doesn't seem like a good plan.

Instead, I force a somber face and take off along a dirt path that weaves through the woods for a few-hundred feet until it opens into a small clearing. With only the false light of the moon and my phone's flashlight as a guide, I make an awful ruckus with each step, piercing the silent night with a sharp blade. Twigs and leaves buckle under my feet to a point a deaf rockstar will have heard my approach.

A smooth entry lost to nature, but at least Erika won't startle.

The path snakes at the end and gives way to manmade, circular clearing that houses a worn, white gazebo with a brown top. The construct is unkempt, but the rugged appearance gives it a charming look, romantic in a way. The small and tamed stream that flows thirty feet beyond the gazebo moves at a leisurely pace, only a slight hint of the water's existence can be heard through a modest wind.

I approach the gazebo slowly, with neck craned and eyes strained, peering into the dark space enclosed by open railing. Benches of chipped wood are within, but the shadows are too heavy to see where she sits.

"Erika, you there?" I ask lightly.

She doesn't respond. "Erika. It's me, Jacoby. You there?" This time a bit louder, but I'm still afraid to disturb the night.

Still nothing. No answer. No sound other than nature and the beasts that call darkness home.

I complete a full circle. "Erika, you here?"

I step toward the gazebo. Something snaps behind me. Then, I feel it. A presence, but I turn too late.

Something strikes my head and the dim light of the moon collapses into complete darkness. I feel myself falling as my consciousness surrenders to nothingness.

There is a distant sound, faint and foreign, like someone yawning. I see black. Every effort to open my eyes is suppressed by something invisible. I don't feel much, my body numb and as useless as my vision.

The strange sound persists.

My right arm begins to tingle. The sensation spreads throughout my body. I flex both fingers and toes as my body awakes. I roll onto my side and groan as the numbness surrenders to searing pain. I recall being struck. I want to touch the tender spot, but I discover restricted hands.

I attempt to stand but fail. Darkness fades into a hazy world. My vision returns slowly. I find my hands first, then my feet. Both are bound by rope.

I fail to recognize what I manage to see. I must have been drug here from wherever I fell unconscious. I shake my head back and forth, nearly throwing up in the process, but my vision improves. That's when the horror sets in.

She's here, just a few feet away. Several lanterns stand between us. Erika is also bound, resting atop shaking knees, body convulsing. Some type of cloth shoved into her mouth and hangs loosely from bloodied lips. She's gasping, attempting to yell, but her voice is faint and incoherent.

I stare into scared and tortured eyes. Those eyes widen, looking somewhere else, frantically falling upon something toward the tree line. Erika attempts to retreat, but her position awards her no opportunity.

I follow her eyes, and I find a man standing not a dozen feet from us, his back to the tree line. I've experienced no greater terror in life. The moon grants a silhouette of the man, who holds his right arm outstretched, a steady hand circling, holding a knife that glistens.

The man sways to the right, head tilting in unison. "Welcome back," he says neutrally, a bored confidence falling over each word.

"Who are you? What do you want?" I ask, frantically attempting to free myself of the smooth, and seemingly padded rope that binds my hands and feet. Despite several physical improvements, I remain slightly disoriented, unable to comprehend or fully understand what's transpiring.

"I didn't want you, Jacoby. I rarely kill boys." He sniffs the air. "Your Essence is special, and it's new. It's dangerous to confront someone as powerful as you, but I don't think you know what you have. Good for me, not so good for you.

"Her's," the figure says, leisurely pointing to Erika, "smells of cinnamon. Not nearly as powerful as you, but much sweeter. I find male's meat distasteful, no matter how strong the Essence. But I may have to make an exception for you. The power I'll consume from you is intoxicating to consider." The voice is familiar, but I can't place it.

What the fuck? "What the fuck," I repeat aloud. *Meat? Essence? He's going to eat me?*

"She had to keep you involved, to the point you knew too much about me. It's her fault, not mine. I couldn't risk it. You had to be dealt with. I'm sorry that it will end this way for you."

Killed a boy before? Killed. My mind fractures. I find myself considering which is worse. To die or to be eaten. "What are you talking about? I don't know who you are. Please, let us go." I look to Erika, whose head is downcast. Her body shakes uncontrollably. "Please." I'm begging now. Not just for me but also for Erika. This can't be happening. This isn't real. This type of thing doesn't happen.

This is a horror story told in movies or books, not in reality.

"As for the *who* I am," he steps closer, removing a dark hood.

The face is familiar. It isn't the charming and happy face I've seen before, but I recognized its form. Gone is the warmth from his eyes, replaced by something twisted and evil. There is a darkness in those eyes that has no definition. His skin has paled, revealing a hint of blue veins beneath.

I look to Erika in confusion, then back to our tormentor. "Chris? What the hell, man? Is this a joke?"

"Oh, Jacoby. Innocent and ignorant Jacoby. No, this is no joke," he says with sincerity. "I'm sorry to tell you that. I meant what I said. You seem like a good kid, but you were in the wrong place at the wrong time. Interested in the wrong girl."

"That—"

"Ah, ah," he interrupts before I continue. "Don't even try to argue. I knew you were in love with her the moment you came into my house. We've spent some time together, her and I, before you arrived. She feels the same way. You just took too long, my friend."

"Help," I yell.

Chris is fast, unnaturally so. An open palm strikes my face, silencing the cry of help. The slap knocks me several feet to the side. An impossible strike. A metallic taste forms quickly, then my mouth is wrenched open and stuffed with cloth. I'm sure my cheek bone is fractured. I feel the fabric gaining weight, soaking up saliva and blood.

"Now, why would you go and do something stupid like that?" he asks, standing. He runs a free hand through disheveled hair. "I can't blame you, I suppose. In my experience, a silent shock comes first. It takes people time to understand what's happening, to comprehend the threat. Pleas and cries of help come once they realize they are helpless in a very bad situation.

"I would know. There have been hundreds, over decades of time."

He looks me over with a strange expression, with eyes that pierce. I see his mind at work. "The cloth would have been needed for what is to come anyway." Chris steps back and looks from me to Erika, then back again.

I have a hundred questions, with enough pleas to match, but everything comes out muffled against the cloth.

What's coming next? What did he mean? Why is this happening?

Chris extends the knife, looking down the blade as if a sight were fixed atop. Odd carvings are etched along slivers of gold. There is a jewel in the hilt that sparkles abnormally. Chris's face devoid of emotion as he inspects the blade. This is just another day to him. Something he's done over and over again. A hobby continued more out of habit than jubilation.

I struggle against the ropes and gag. I'm not the only one. I find Erika, who struggles in all the same ways. She no longer shakes uncontrollably. She's fighting. I catch glimpses of her face from time to time. The dim light plays off the steady stream of tears rolling down her face, glistening like stars. Falling stars. Bright lights burning their life away as they rush to their demise.

Chris draws closer, and my entire body convulses. Chris' movements are smooth and confident, his mind settled upon what comes next.

"Shh," purrs the web developer, a man we've spent hours with. "This is going to hurt. There will be pain, but I promise you'll be dead when I begin to consume your flesh." He sniffs once more. "Your Essence is nearly repulsive, but it oozes with power." Chris licks his lips as blue veins enlarge and his already pale skin intensifies.

No. Please no, I think, scream, as the blade approaches. Chris, suddenly and without hesitation, thrusts the knife into my shoulder. I scream, louder than I thought possible, but the cloth acts as a silencer. Only Chris and Erika hear my cries of agony.

The knife appears as quickly as it had disappeared. I find

the wound with wide eyes and heavy breaths. Blood seeps into both shirt and coat. Chris tilts his head and gazes upon the gore. The jewel shines brighter. Chris licks the air then brings the blade toward his mouth and chants something. A red-orange mist spills from the jewel, and Chris laps it up. He shutters and spits.

The world stills, quiets for just a moment. A calm before the storm. Chris' skin transforms, turning nearly translucent. Blue veins sparkle, spread, grow, while eyes somehow darken. I see no white, the whole eye turns black.

Chris shivers. His form increases in size. He lets out a scream from hell that's so low that it sounds like thunder. "I hate this," he says after regaining a semblance of himself. "So powerful, but so disgusting," he says to me while looking to Erika. "I want no more from you, but I can't stop. I've never felt anything like what you have inside. The things you could do if you knew. If they had gotten to you before I. You don't deserve this, not like her. But it has to be this way."

I'm unable to look away from my damaged shoulder. My clothes conceal the incision, but my mind has no problem visualizing what it looks like.

This can't be happening. He just stabbed me. The shock, the sudden violence, holds the pain at bay, for the moment.

Chris says something, jerking me from my thoughts.

"...she broke up with this Michael guy and then texted you," Chris is mumbling to himself, as if playing out a scenario. "You," he continues, pointing to me, "became upset when you discovered that she only called you here to talk as a friend. Upset that you two never dated, and were never going to date, became enraged and attacked her. However, Erika is strong and athletic, and a fight ensued. Both of you will bleed out from the wounds you gave one another.

"You will die first. I will eat you first. Yes. I am so very hungry after a small taste of what you have to offer. I will make her watch you suffer. Her suffering will enhance the taste. Her Essence. This is all her fault anyway, and she deserves to suffer more."

What did you do to him? I think as I find Erika.

"I hate that you have to die," Chris continues to himself, "but she told me about your mind, how everyone at school thinks you're crazy. Everyone will believe you finally snapped. They will blame you."

Chris turns and finds me. "It's nothing personal, but she must be made to suffer. She loves you, deep down, and it will destroy her to watch you being tortured, then die, then consumed. Pity I can only take a little. Can't be too careful these days." His mind goes somewhere in the distance. "Things were much simpler in the past."

Chris unzips my coat. I find my shoulder and blood-soaked shirt. The knife comes again, this time at my side, slicing instead of stabbing.

The pain is immense. Tears and screams flow uncontrollably. I hear Erika, distant but audible, still muted against her own cloth. She's somehow inching closer, using her entire body to crawl toward me, her pleas like a flood against her gag. She falls to her side, the restraints pulling her back to the earth like possessed vines.

"Isn't that adorable," Chris chides. "Coming to save the day, are we?" He goes to her, standing above her as she slowly rolls and crawls along dirt and grass.

Chris grabs her by the hair. With neck arched, he strikes her face. There is a gasp and gurgling. Chris, somehow larger, stronger, than before he did whatever that was with the knife, manages to knock Erika unconscious with a flick of his wrist.

Chris looks down upon the limp form. "Damnit."

My blood boils. My own pain forgotten. Fear turns to anger.

I'll kill you! I scream. First in my head then aloud. *I'm going to kill you.* Reality sets in as I consider my situation. I begin to sob as I realize I have no power here.

I decide to die fighting. I struggle against the restraints. I turn and pull and struggle but there is no give, not an inch of relief. Tears return in droves when I realize I'm helpless to save myself, helpless to save her.

We are going to die here.

Chris turns, a sly and devilish smile on his face. "Look what she made me do. I guess you and I will have to play a while until she wakes up." He's beginning to enjoy this. It's the first sign of emotion. A twisted pleasure, a satisfaction from someone else's pain.

I straighten and still. I mumble calmly, forming an incoherent sentence.

Chris eyes me skeptically. "I will let you speak, if you promise not to scream. Deal?"

I shake my head in agreement.

The cloth is removed. I cough several times, spitting blood, looking at both my shoulder and side. I've lost quite a lot of blood. "Why? Why her? What did she do to you?"

"That is a very long story. But, at a high level, the Essence within her gives someone like me life. An extended life. Her death begets my immortality. Now, her, specifically. She is like the others. She is like the *one*. They are all the same. The world is better without girls like her. They will only hurt and prey upon good boys, good men. Like you. Like me." He places his free hand over his throat, his skin pale once again, squeezing against his own flesh, deep in thought. "They will cause pain. She would thrive upon the pain of others if it wasn't for me."

You're insane. "She has a good heart. She hasn't done anything to you. You can stop this. You can let her go. Let us go. Please, let us go. Take me but let her go."

"Very noble, Jacoby. But that won't do. It simply won't do. She must die, and you must as well because she brought you into my house. You saw my face, knew of my involvement in her life. Bad timing is all it was." He fiddles with the knife. "Well... fortuitous as well. For me. To find someone as powerful as you, and for you to have no idea how to wield the Essence you possess. Quite fortuitous."

The cloth is forced back into my mouth, then Chris drops to a knee, the knife once again hovering inches from my flesh. "This one will hurt."

The knife disappears inside the left side of my abdomen. I shake, pain assuming command of my entire body. It hurts, beyond what words, what screams, can describe, but my mind collapses.

There is too much to process.

The knife comes free, blood following after the blade. My mind dizzies, the world spins like a fair ride. Something within nudges. Something stirs. It's comforting. I think it death welcoming me. That the reaper has come to collect my soul.

I beg for it. Beg for the end. The torture, the torment, it's too much. I welcome the darkness with open arms and pray that Erika will somehow find a quick end.

Not yet, a familiar voice echoes across my darkening mind. I ignore it, too tired to consider its meaning.

My mind falls upon Erika. She doesn't deserve this. I can't leave her here with him. I barricade what life remains and fight like hell against the coming tide of winged beings that seek to usher me into the world beyond.

A determination to live, to save another, fills my spirit. *Yes,* the voice says. *But not yet. She is coming.* I recognize the voice, the feeling. I felt it before when I accepted my torment.

The beast. The dog.

I smile, somehow understanding, discovering what lies within. The puzzle comes together as I completely become one with myself.

Yes, the voice purrs.

Chris is consuming the mist from his knife when a gunshot rings out. Chris doesn't react, eyes finding my own. I have no idea where he is struck, but I see the blood spatter. He smiles. Standing a moment later, he turns toward the tree line. He then drops to a knee.

She's here, the voice of the beast says in triumph. *It's nearly time.*

21

STRANGE THINGS

Susan

I stumble through the woods, flashlight in hand, until I hear distant voices. The GPS was accurate up to a point but seems to have grown confused the deeper into the woods I go. *Technology.* I turn the flashlight off and listen intently. I move quickly when the screams begin.

I come to a clearing and stop along the tree line, careful to remain hidden from sight. I find three individuals huddled about twenty feet into the clearing, a few lanterns giving away their position. A man dressed in black hovers over a boy. A girl, Erika, lays unconscious beside them.

I found you. I watch intently, working through my next course of action when I hear a muffled scream. My prey, Thanatos, Chris Erikson, is between my line of sight and the boy. I work Matilda free. I want to move, to act, but that feeling within draws my eye to the right. I quietly work toward the pull, Matilda drawn, eyes never straying from Chris.

I settle in after a handful of paces. I see both Chris and the boy. Chris wields a knife. I watch as he draws it toward his nose.

Something within nudges. I check my angles. I won't hit the boy. I step out into the clearing, aim, and take the shot.

The sound echoes throughout the clearing and into woods beyond. The shot is true. I see the blood splatter. I hold my breath. *It can't have been that easy.* My body desires celebration while something else issues a warning.

Light from lanterns play tricks. It must be a trick. A red-orange mist jettisons with the blood splatter. It lingers in the air around Chris before disappearing back into his body.

I watch as nothing happens. Chris doesn't move, doesn't speak. Finally, he rises and turns. I see the man I've hunted for so long. I've closed some distance. Maybe ten feet separate us. It's impossible not to stare in awe. He isn't human. I stare into pitch-black eyes and enlarged blue veins that spread over pale skin like a distraught spider web. He's larger than I imagined. His clothes are a size too small. He smiles and Matilda shakes. I sigh in relief when he drops to a knee.

It'll be over soon, I think, watching blood fall into a pool beneath him.

Matilda begins to fall when Chris stands. I watch, impossibly, as the red-orange mist reappears, swirls, stitching, healing until the chest wound disappears.

"What the hell?" I hear myself ask. I receive a smile in response.

I empty my clip. Stepping forward after each round. Chris takes the first few rounds with ease. The next couple put him to the ground. I stand over the man with one bullet left. I aim and put one straight through his skull. I stand in silence, watching. Nothing happens. I breathe heavy.

I hear muffling behind me. I turn and find the boy. I see several stab wounds and a similar red-orange mist rising from pools of his own blood. *This is getting weird.* I run to him and remove his gag.

"Thank you," he says through gritted teeth.

"You're welcome. Let's get these off." I pull my knife and cut through the rope binding his hands and feet. I sit him up. "You've lost a lot of blood. I need to get you and Erika out of here." He nods, then stills. I watch his eyes widen, looking somewhere over my shoulder.

I stand and turn. Chris is upright with mist swirling all about him. He laughs low. Wounds heal as bullets crawl from holes. The last to fall is the round I put in his skull.

"Who are you?" he asks.

I fail to find words. I put enough rounds in the man to stop an elephant. This isn't possible.

"Who are you?" he asks, louder, demanding an answer.

I clear my throat and shift my weight. "Someone who has been searching for you a long time."

He looks at me long and hard until black eyes widen. "You're the woman from my dreams. I should have known it meant something."

I'm speechless. I have nothing to say in response. Too much has happened in a short time. He should be dead. Instead, he's alive and spouting on about dreams. I recall my own dream of him, but I don't have the capacity to analyze what it means.

He notes my confusion. "Doesn't matter. You've stumbled into something you cannot explain." He sniffs the air. "Your Essence is strong, nearly as strong as the boy's. You've learned to use it more than he has. Still immature, however. With more time and training you could have had a chance. As it stands, you'll die here."

Something tells me he isn't wrong. *Shit. Shit. Shit.* I look to the boy. He's struggling to remain conscious, not born with enough hands to press against his various wounds. He'll die if I don't get him to a doctor. I find Erika. Her chest rises and falls. She's alive, but I have no idea what state she's in.

Chris licks his lips. Blue veins enlarge and his skin pales further. "Savory. You'll be sweet to taste. A meal for the ages.

It'll be years before I need to feed again. Thanks to you and the boy."

I find the tree line. I could make it, but I can't leave the kids to die here. I steel myself and raise my knife.

"Good girl. A fight makes it so much better." He handles his own knife, which glistens. The mist swirls around the blade. A jewel on the hilt the focal point.

I move first. Never one to wait. I skip left, right, then directly at Chris. I go for his chest and find air. He moves unnaturally fast. He whistles. I turn and find him behind me. I swing for his head. He ducks below the thrust and returns with a right hook to my side. I'm launched a couple feet to the side and hear bone crack.

I fall to my knees, hand at my side. He has impossible strength. I've taken my share of punches but never anything like that. I had twisted at the last moment and avoided the brunt of the punch. It was still enough to feel like I got hit by a train.

I stand on wobbly knees. Knife raised. He comes fast. I parry his first thrust but can't connect with the second as something sharp bites at my shoulder. I never saw the blade penetrate flesh. I swing once more. My knife hand catches in a vice grip and my left leg is kicked out from under me. I fall upon my right knee, wrist still bound.

"Too bad you never learned to heal yourself. I had hoped for more."

I throw a punch with my free hand, which bounces off solid muscle. I doubt he even notices.

I'm driven to the ground from a slap to the face. I hit hard, spitting blood and what I'm sure is a broken tooth. I rise to hands and knees, sure I have a concussion.

"You have fight though; I'll give you that."

I manage to stand through labored breaths. My knife lies upon the ground. He lets me pick up, twirling his own as if an extension of himself. He's about to end it when I hear, "Chris."

Chris slaps the knife from my hand. I fall to my knees once again as he turns toward the boy.

"A little fight in you as well," he says. "Good."

The boy stands, smiling. He must have broken, or he's on the verge of death. It doesn't make sense. *Why are you smiling?*

I watch as an already bizarre situation turns into something I'll never be able to explain. The boy steps toward Chris, arms wide, as a void opens within his chest. Maybe a few inches wide at first, it quickly morphs into over a foot in diameter. In it, I see eyes that will haunt me the rest of life. There is a deep, thundering growl from the great beyond. Behind the yellow eyes I see a form lurking. It emerges from the boy's chest one leg at a time, landing quietly upon the ground. A black beast with white fur beneath the chin.

The thing that birthed through a human's chest resembles a dog, but something is different. The form isn't quite right, and it moves with heightened intelligence.

"What the literal fuck," Chris stammers out.

The dog snarls, then pounces. Chris is driven to the ground as teeth find flesh. He screams out in pain. Red-orange mist escapes from the wound, flowing into the dog. The dog grows. Not much, but muscle visibly builds. Chris reacts, slicing at the beast. He finds a leg. The dog howls but again finds flesh, quickly consuming the mist that escapes.

The song and dance continues for what seems eternity. An unholy beast and Thanatos locked into an epic battle of traded blows. I watch as Chris slows. His wounds take longer to recover as the dog grows stronger. I think the battle over when the dog latches onto Chris' throat, but Chris manages to grab the beast by the tail and lifts, thrusting his dagger into its underside. The beast's hold on Chris' throat loosens and is then thrown several feet. Chris claws at his own throat, which I manage to connect with his victims and find fitting, in attempt to stop the flow of blood and mist.

Chris screams. Angry. He lets loose a war cry.

I find the dog struggling to stand. A whimper turns into a war cry of its own. Mist engulfs the beast, bringing life and strength.

My eyes dart back to Chris. I notice empty hands. I look around and find his knife upon the ground.

Chris charges the beast, who also lunges. They collide in a chorus of scream and growl. I muster what might I have left and dive for the knife. Standing, I steady myself and plunge forward. The knife connects with flesh. I stumble backward, dizzy, vision blurry. I see the knife buried to the hilt in Chris' throat. I reach and pull it free, blood chasing after the blade. The beast takes a chunk from Chris' throat, who then falls.

Chris lays alive, but in silence. He looks between us three. "How did you find me?" he asks through gurgles of blood.

"Taillight. Then she," I say, pointing to Erika, "put your name online."

A laugh. "I was just passing through. Thought Brighton was far enough away." Every word is labored. No mist rises to heal his wounds. His eyes fall upon Erika. "I had to have her."

I watch the girl for a moment, relishing a moment of victory. "You got me instead," I say, watching Erika's chest rise and fall.

"You can't kill me. I am legion. You have no idea what will come for you." His words lack conviction. A fact once, maybe, that's become unclear with the passing of time, or an action.

"What are you?"

"Part of something ancient. Others will come."

"Who?"

"They will consume you. All of you. Mine will be a deathless death."

Chris begins to mutter something foreign. The mist responds, seeping from the blade.

Hell no. "Prove it." I plunge the knife into his skull. His body goes limp. I find the beast standing beside me, watching. The boy has drawn closer as well, still applying pressure to his wounds, but he seems to have miraculously recovered enough strength to avoid death. The three of us watch Chris for several minutes. He never rises.

"Susan."

The boy turns to face me. "Jacoby," he says with an outstretched hand.

I take the hand, his grip weak. I nod toward the dog. "He have a name?"

"You can see him?"

I nod. I should be surprised by the question, but I'm not. I imagine it will take a lot to surprise me after tonight.

The boy stares at the beast. "You know, I have no idea. I'll let you know if he tells me sometime." His breathing labors and skin pales.

"He talks to you?"

He shrugs. "Something like that."

The beast breaks the silence with a howl. I turn and watch as it disappears into the boy's chest—the endless, black void.

I simply stare and shake my head. I find Erika, stare at Chris' corpse, and then watch the black void weave itself shut. I catch the boy as he passes out. "What the hell just happened?"

22
THE DEBRIEF

SUSAN

"For the record, please state your full name."

I look around the room with scorn. I hadn't expected a hero's welcome, but being treated like a criminal seems unfair. I faced the supernatural, side-by-side with a beast that resides within the chest of a high school kid and defeated the god of death. A god responsible for hundreds of murders.

Obviously, I have omitted details around the more supernatural elements of my encounter. I hope the kid has the same sense. I wanted to tell him to keep his mouth shut about certain things, but he never regained consciousness.

My career is in enough trouble. I don't need to compound my problems with claims that will see me institutionalized. I recall my initial interviews. I relive my altered, normalized statements given to several agents and agencies. I cringe. I had done my best to avoid any discussion of the supernatural but certain elements were simply too strange. My superiors have latched onto those unexplainable aspects.

This is procedure, common practice for an incident where an agent is involved. The problem is, there's no precedent for what I've been through, even the modified, more realistic version of events. The FBI doesn't know how to respond. There isn't a X-Files division buried in a basement they can summon, so they act in the only way they know how: by the book.

"Susan Frost McGraff. Are you going to fix my tooth anytime soon?" I smile, flaunting several chipped teeth. The slap from Chris Erikson, whatever he was, did a number on my pearly-whites.

"Thank you," replies the man sitting across from me, blatantly ignoring my concern over exposed bone.

I imagine my jagged, sharp teeth taking a sizable bite out the man's throat. He is a nobody. Someone sent to collect a report. Those who will decide my fate stand behind one-way glass to the right. I know this, and I won't give them the satisfaction of looking desperately upon my own reflection.

"Anything for you and the FBI," I say sarcastically.

The man in an inexpensive suit and large, round glasses ignores the comment, eyes downcast upon an organized pile of paper while soft hands wield a large pen that works quickly. I have no idea why he's writing.

"Ms. McGraff, explain the events surrounding your leave of absence from the FBI."

"Truthfully?"

"Please lean into the microphone. Accurately. Factually."

"Then there wouldn't be a need for your shorthand," I say with a smile. When that elicits silence, I repeat, "Accurately. Factually. Well, in that case—"

The only door to the room, a grey hunk of metal with no window, is thrown open and a man in a very expensive suit swiftly glides into the room.

The intruder looks around as if he owns the building. Quick, calculating eyes briefly pass through me, then fall more heavily upon the interrogator. "Excuse us," he says to the man across from me, who frantically searches the one-way glass. He clearly doesn't recognize the man issuing very direct orders.

Quinton, Special Agent-in-Charge of my old field office, appears outside the open door and nods. My former boss looks tired and beaten, probably fresh off losing a turf war with whomever stands beside me.

The interrogator quickly collects his things and is out the door, without so much as a glance toward either myself or the new boss. Two men, dressed similarly to the intruder, take up positions to either side of the room's only door.

I watch the man closely as he closes the door. He moves with purpose, no step or action wasted. After disconnecting the four cameras mounted to space's corners, he attaches a small device to the center of the one-way glass and takes up the now empty seat across from me.

Another device spontaneously appears in his hand, like the one against the glass, which he places at the center of the table. I can't help but lean forward, examining the foreign object. It's circular with a flat bottom. Completely black with scales that remind me of the Death Star. A red dot shines near the top. Having not the slightest clue what the device is, or what's happening, I turn my focus to the man across from me.

I open my mind, asking the voice within to give words to unseen details. No matter how hard I try, I hear, feel, nothing. I ascertain only what I'm able to see. His suit is solid black, as is the shirt underneath. He wears a white, thin tie with a gold tie clasp centered neatly chest high. I squint, focusing on the shiny object. The clasp is subtle, but I find a downward facing sword piercing a diamond. It looks expensive.

The mysterious intruder crosses his legs and interlinks long fingers. I stare a moment, his gaze piercing. "Ms. McGraff, I have a few questions I would like to ask you."

Brazen, smug bastard. "Is that so? Well, I have a few of my own. Like, who the hell are you...to start?"

He takes no offense at my opening bout. "Of course. My name is Adam, and I work for an independent organization that takes interest in cases such as this one."

"Like this one?"

"Yes. Cases of peculiar events, people, and actions. Cases that have unexplainable elements. In order for our conversation to be as productive as possible, please understand I'm aware this case involves unexplainable phenomena. You have not been honest in your statements. I understand why. Very few people will believe what actually happened. I will."

I eye the door, then the glass. "Where is Scully?"

Either Adam has never seen X-Files, or he doesn't find the joke amusing. He sits in silence.

I'm uncomfortable with the silence. A rare occurrence. "How's the boy?"

"Jacoby?"

"Yes. Jacoby. Who the hell else?"

"He is fine. Healing."

I wonder if Adam knows about the dog. The beast that lives inside Jacoby. Curiosity nearly gets the better of me, but I decide it's not my place. "Good. You must work for some very powerful people, to be able to walk in here and push aside the FBI, in their own building."

"Power is an interesting topic. One that I could discuss at length for hours, but that's not why I'm here."

I've never interacted with a shadow government organization before, but this is starting to feel like something out of a movie. I can't decide if I'm excited, nervous, or annoyed.

"Not at liberty to provide details? I assumed as much. Who are you, really? Does your organization have a name? What do you want with me?"

Adam suppresses a rebellious smirk. "Adam is what people

call me, but it's not my real name. Our organization has a name, but I'm not at liberty, as you just said, to reveal it to you. And, to answer your last question, we are interested in the man you killed...among other things. Specifically, how you found him."

His honesty, although vague, surprises me. Likely a practiced method to produce trust. I cling to distrust like my life depends on it, but something about Adam softens my resolve. It's hard to imagine someone accepting the supernatural elements of that night, but my gut tells me Adam will without question.

"However, before we get to that," he continues, "I'd like to know about you."

My favorite topic.

"Why should I tell you anything?"

Adam brushes invisible lint from his pant leg. "As you said, I possess enough power, influence, to direct the FBI within their own building. They stood by as I disconnected their cameras and commandeered one of their own agents in questioning. Do you think it's a good idea to be in opposition with someone like me?"

No shortage of confidence for you. This man is either full of shit or perhaps the most powerful person I've ever met. Years ago, I shook hands with the President. What I felt then is a fraction of what I feel now.

I'm considering my options when Adam clears his throat. "The FBI can't terminate your employment after saving two high school students. The fact you were on leave, even though self-imposed, which was related to this case, complicates matters further for them. It would be a public relations nightmare.

"The FBI will likely award your efforts, tout your accomplishment. In the end, however, they will find a way to bury you with a godforsaken assignment that removes you from the public eye. They can't have an unsettled agent hinting at the supernatural, and they don't like to be proven wrong. Your future here will be miserable. That's where I come in. I can assist with your future, or I can make it worse. That choice is now yours to make."

There is no threat in his voice. These are mere facts to him. I believe the words. Most people would retire after such a violent case, bury themselves in a hole in an attempt to forget the horror. Not me. I can't be resigned to a desk, away from the action. Not after what I've seen. I need answers, and the boredom would kill me.

The voice within applauds. "Fair enough. I find it odd that I just killed something inhuman, but you want to start with me. But who am I to judge? What do you want to know?"

"Let's start with Andrew."

The old scar. "Fuck you. Off limits. Anything else but that."

Adam considers the importance, the relevance, of the question against his desired goal. A moment passes before he responds, "Fine. Tell me about the first person you killed."

I sigh. I should have expected that horror as a follow-up question, but I fail to hide my surprise. "What about it?"

"It was your action at the mall, correct?"

"It was."

Adam alternates legs. "Walk me through what happened."

The memory, the one I've attempted to bury so many times, unleashes violently across my mind. I hear the screams, feel the horror.

"Why?"

"We will get to that. For now, please walk me through what happened that day."

"Fine. I was a cop at the time. Early in my career. Recently graduated and off-duty. I was Christmas shopping."

Adam leans forward. "You were carrying a weapon?"

"Yes."

"Do you usually carry a weapon when off-duty?"

I consider the question and shake my head. "Not then. I do now, obviously."

"Obviously," he says with a smile. "Why, then, were you carrying a personal weapon that day?"

"I don't know."

"Are you confident you can't recall?"

He knows I'm lying. His question drips with disappointment. I can't look him in the eyes. He knows too much. *How do you know these things?* "I had a feeling."

"What's that like? The feeling."

"That day?"

Adam nods.

"It was like an itch in my brain. An itch I couldn't scratch. A voice that wouldn't stop until I did as it demanded."

"And it wanted you to carry your personal weapon."

"Yes."

Adam nods once more. "Good. What happened at the mall?"

I breathe. Hands begin to shake as I hear the screams. "I had just walked out of a store, into a crowd of people, when I heard gunshots. I was startled at first. It was chaos. People running, screaming. I was about to join them when that scratch, that voice, told me do something different."

"What did it tell you?"

"To pull my weapon and wade into the chaos."

"You listened?"

A tear slips from my eye. I wipe it away with a heavy heart. "I did."

"Then what?"

"There was so much chaos. People screaming. Gunshots. People running. Eventually the gunshots stopped. I continued to push my way through the crowd. I had no idea what I was looking for until the voice told me stop. I did. That's when I saw it."

Adam remains calm, poised, despite my unnatural claims of a past event. "What did you see?"

"Smoke."

"Smoke?"

"Yeah. Sort of. It was an aura of some sort. Colorful. Dark and ominous. I felt cold inside when I saw it. My instinct, that scratch, told me it was the killer. I don't know why, but I raised my weapon and fired without a second thought."

"Was it the first time you saw this...aura?"

That old scar. "No. The second time. Many years apart."

"Okay. Have you seen it since?"

"Nearly every day since the mall."

"I see. What happened after you shot the man with a disturbing aura?"

The question is absurd. No one in their right mind goes down this line of thinking. I begin to think I was wrong about the X-Files division. "The man I shot fell to the ground in a pile of blood. I saw the gun tucked into his jeans. I remember thanking God I was right." I stop there, unable to continue. My mind's defenses quick to fortress dark places.

"There was another casualty, correct?"

"Again, fuck you."

"You said anything else. I'd like to hear it from you on what happened."

"What happened!? Here it is. The bullet passed through the shooter and struck an eight-year-old girl in the chest. She died instantly while the bastard survived and is serving life in prison. He's alive while she is dead." Tears flow in force. I'm not quick enough to wipe them away before they rain upon the table. "I killed her."

"Thank you," Adam says. He waits a minute before uncrossing his legs. "What you don't know is that the shooter planned to leave the mall and force his way into a nearby school. Your actions saved many young lives."

"What?" That is new information.

Adam nods. "I'm sorry the girl was struck. What a weight to carry. However, no one knows, or will ever know, how much of an impact your actions made that day."

"Now, let's talk about your most recent kill."

An involuntary twitch escapes as I recall that night. *What did he mean that he was legion?*

"Chris Erikson," I say softly.

"Yes. That is one of the names he used. And his name isn't what he is. Was. Thanks to you."

"What he is?" I ask with heightened interest.

"Yes."

"Care to elaborate?"

"Nephilim."

I vaguely recall that word. I search deep into my past. "As in the Bible?"

"Most of us don't believe they are the same creature, but that is where the name comes from, yes."

"You're shitting me."

"I am not."

"What makes him a Nephilim? There are more?"

"There are many more. And what makes him Nephilim is that he feeds on the Essence of humans."

"I have so many questions, and this answering precisely what I ask is getting annoying."

"Ask."

"Essence?"

"Yes. Essence. Negligible for nearly everyone on Earth. For a very small percentage, Essence is high, powerful, manifesting in various forms.

"The Nephilim feed on Essence," he continues. "They consume it through pain, blood, and flesh. They do not die of age or disease as they continuously feed upon others' Essence."

I want to argue, but the explanation aligns with what I experienced that night. "Erikson had a knife."

"Ah. Yes. Consuming Essence is an unnatural phenomenon. It requires what you might call...sorcery."

My eyebrow furrows.

Adam chuckles. "All very alien, isn't it? Hard to argue when you've seen it, correct?"

My shoulders slump. "Yeah." This is madness. Essence, cannibalism, immortality, Nephilim.

"We can discuss the Nephilim, as an order, later. Time is short. Let's focus on the events the other night. This...Erikson."

"Do you also know of his other murders?" I ask.

"We do. We surmise that the death toll by his own hand is somewhere north of 200 souls. We hope to have a more precise number in the coming weeks."

So much death. "When were you aware of this? How do you know? I was put on leave from the FBI for believing those murders were tied together."

"We connected the dots several years ago. I'm sorry for your struggles at work, but we had no idea you existed, let alone you had identified this rather disobedient Nephilim."

"And you did nothing? There were so many murders you could have prevented. So many girls you could have saved."

"We were not as successful as you in tracking him down. This is not for lack of trying or effort on our part. We lost... agents in this pursuit. This is why you've become an interest of ours." There is pain in mentioning the loss of his own. "Our thanks for dispatching of him."

"He deserved longer suffering."

"Yes. He did. Walk me through the timeline. From when you first connected the dot to the moment Erikson died."

"You said time is short."

Adam pulls a phone from his pocket, types something, then returns his attention to me. "We now have an hour."

Who the hell is this guy? "You seem to have a pretty good idea of what happened."

"Astute," he applauds. "Our resources are vast. We've constructed a timeline of your activity via phone, internet, credit card, and witness data."

"What's the point then?"

Adam shifts, uncomfortable. "There are certain aspects that need clarity." He doesn't like not knowing.

I come forward with every detail. Every thought and action. Everything about the instinct within me. I start at the beginning and finish with Erikson's death, mouth uncomfortably dry by the time I've finished.

Adam slides a bottle of water across the table. I down nearly half the bottle in a single gulp.

"He wasn't wrong."

"Who?" I ask.

"Erikson. Your Essence is... evident."

"How?"

"I can sense it. Don't ask," he interrupts with raised hands. "Another topic for another day. We believe that voice within, the sense you call it, is drawn toward evil. Your heightened Essence is what allowed you to track down Erikson when so many others could not. You are alike very few in this world."

"Honored. So, what comes next?"

"We would like to make you an offer. Our organization could use someone of your rare talents."

I didn't see that coming, and I fail to hide a child-like smile. "What kind offer?"

Adam uncrosses his legs, smile gone, as he leans across the table with several documents in hand. "One where you can make a real difference in this bizarre world."

23
LUCIUS

JACOBY

Something beeps, softly, steadily, hypnotically. The repetitive sound, although soothing, lures heavy eyes open. I fail several times, each attempt to take in the world rebuked by an unseen force.

Determination eventually wins out. A sharp and cascading light rolls across the room in waves, a mass of different shades blur objects absent defined corners. White and gray fall atop one another, streaking here and there in organized chaos.

"Welcome back, Mr. Talavan," says a soft but firm voice. It's one I don't recognize.

Confusion grows in unison with consciousness. "Who's there?"

"My name is Adam. You are safe. There is no need to be alarmed."

"Are you the doctor?" I ask. "It hurts. My side."

Someone draws closer, fiddling with a pole beside me. My arm tingles, warmth spreading like a river as the pain eases.

"No. I am not your doctor. I am here to help, however." The

room falls silent for a moment before Adams add, "Perhaps a different type of doctor."

The room focuses. I find a large space with white-washed and smooth walls. Overly bright rays from artificial light conquers any hint of darkness. Past events lay siege to my mind. Chris, Erika, the fight, the beast, my mother's death weave together in a convoluted string of events. I gawk, looking nowhere in particular.

"Jacoby?" the soft voice asks, gently pulling me from my own mind.

I find something shiny in my periphery. I run my hand along the long, circular shaft. I lay on something soft and comfortable. *Hospital. I'm in a hospital.*

I grab at my chest, finding fabric and flesh. No hint of the darkness, or the beast.

I gasp for air, hyperventilating. The knife. Dark eyes. Death.

Calm, my head commands. The voice of the beast deep but soothing. My breathing levels as my heart no longer threatens to explode from my chest. I remember. I remember becoming one with the beast, permitting it to manifest in defense of myself, Erika, and the woman. Susan. I see her face. We are standing above Chris. Blood splattered everywhere. The beast is beside me. She asks about his name.

Do you have a name? I ask. No response.

"Jacoby." Adam sits across from me. Clad in a black suit with a white tie. He is middle aged with neatly styled hair. He looks like someone important. Wealthy. I look left and right. Half a dozen empty beds line the wall. We are alone.

"If you're not the doctor, then who are you?"

"Pertinent question. As I said, my name is Adam."

"Police?"

Adam looks himself over. "No. Not in the slightest."

Not police. Not a doctor. "What do you want?"

"To help. You have been through something...terrible. Terribly odd, maybe?" he encourages.

I no longer think of myself as insane. I know what's real, and what happened with Chris was real. Maybe. I test my mental capacity by asking, "Susan. How is she?"

Adam smiles. "I'm happy to say she is well. I met with her yesterday. Special lady. Very special, like you."

She's real. I sigh in relief. "How long have I been here?"

"Almost two days. You were in bad shape, but not as bad as you should have been. Doctors here likely want to write a paper on your miraculous recovery."

"I'm okay? I'll be okay?"

Adam smiles. "You are quite well. At your rate of recovery, the pain should subside in a couple of days. You will likely have several, faint scars."

I'm okay. I see Chris, Susan, the beast. "Erika! How about Erika?"

"Also fine," Adam answers. "She was released from the hospital this morning. I believe she is with her family."

"Good." I pick at a fingernail. "Where is my father? My sister?"

"They are here. Well...in a way. We need to discuss some items before they see you. They believe you are in critical care. A necessary lie, I'm afraid."

What? "You can't do that. I want to see them."

"In time, Jacoby. I promise."

Adam has a way about him that's hard to process. I should be frightened, but I'm not. He is direct but genuine. I accept that my family comes second in this moment. "Why can't I see them?"

"As I said, we have a few items to discuss before that's possible. You are not in trouble. You possess information that needs...addressed, related to your kidnapping."

The drugs battling ferocious waves of pain leave me limited

options. I'm unable to summon enough strength for a fight, and the thought of running churns my stomach. I nudge the beast within. He lies dormant, refusing to aid. I find the lack of response comforting. After all we've been through, I'm sure he'd rise if we faced a threat.

I consider our conversation so far. "What did you mean, terribly odd? And that I'm special?"

Adams shifts slightly in his chair, interlocking hands atop crossed legs. "I imagine you're afraid to tell me, or anyone for that matter, about what actually happened, correct?"

Is he baiting me?

Adam waits a moment before adding, "I don't blame you. Your past is complicated. So many people have questioned your mental state. I'm here to tell you that they were wrong. I know what transpired that night. How Chris Erikson held you hostage, hurt you, and how the beast saved your lives."

"How? How do you know that?"

"Time and effort, Mr. Talavan."

"You believe me? You believe that's actually what happened." I can't imagine anyone believing what transpired that night unless they saw it for themselves.

"I do. And believe it or not, I'm not the only person who believes you."

"How can I trust you? I don't know you. You could be setting me up. Looking for an insane answer to send me away."

"True. The thing you call the beast, it talks to you?"

I nod. "Not often, but yeah."

"Good. Would it help if he vouches for me?"

"Yes. Yes, it would."

Adam seems relieved. "Close your eyes, Mr. Talavan."

I do as asked without question. I should question more, hesitate to follow orders from a man I've just met, but I want answers. I fall victim to a distant hope that Adam can provide those answers. Something sharp slices through my mind. I squint in discomfort, a pressure building.

"Open your eyes," Adam commands.

I blink several times. "What the hell was that?"

"You want to know the beast's name, correct?"

"How do you know that?"

"I was in your mind."

"What the hell? You—"

"His name is Lucius," Adam reveals.

Yes, the beast hums.

Impossible. This man had just reached into my mind, did who knows what, and communicated with the beast within. "What do you want from me?"

"For us to help one another. How about I start by providing you some answers?"

"Answers are good."

24
COURT

Durian

We huddle around the largest, ancient and well-crafted table I've ever seen. The sight, smell, and elegance of the masterpiece never gets old. Its origin well documented. Commissioned by Lord Slavador following his great victory during the era of Blight, which was over 700 years ago. Dig far enough and you'll find several entries in our organization's financial report dedicated to the maintenance of the table.

It's ancient but preserved, like us. An anchor of tradition and order. The surface smooth but cold to the touch, welcoming but dangerous. Various colors roll in tides over one another and work their way toward rounded edges, immortalizing the significant battle that took place long ago.

Those around the table whisper quietly amongst one another. I sit in silence, listening, learning, adapting to the whims of the moment. A dozen or so lights fall from the dark ceiling, resting a few feet above the table, bringing life to the portrait of death, of victory, captured upon the wood.

The light expelled from the hanging lamps slave to the table's mural. Those who have made the pilgrimage retain their sacred mystery, shrouded in darkness. I see nothing but dark silhouettes, unless another member decides to lean out over the table. It's impossible to find the several dozen guards standing like statues around the room, armed with semi-automatic weapons and who knows what else hidden within jackets and rather risqué dresses.

A repetitive strike of steel stilettos shatters the silence. The newly arrived member enters from my right, a seductive scent luring unresponsive eyes toward a purposeful march.

An athletic frame, snug against a dress made of a material that shimmers, appears as she brushes up against the table. As the distance between us fades, I find long, auburn hair that flows in waves. A sharp and confident face is exposed last. There is no one more stunning, or deadlier, and I know a lot of women who fit into either category.

"Durian," she purrs without looking.

I say nothing as she passes. I find silence with Kate the safest route, derived from a rather unpleasant experience several years ago. Well, pleasant to start, terrifying after.

I turn back toward the table and find Raine's lazy but knowing eyes upon me, casting judgment. Old bitch misses nothing. *Just die already.*

Raine is something of a grandma to most of our members. More of a pain in the ass if you ask me. A seasoned warrior turned instructor, then adviser, after many years of service in the field. Her age and accomplishments allow her the opportunity to express her opinions without thought or repercussion. Something she exercises too frequently for my taste.

Kate hands several folders to Britton, Lord Governor of this political cesspool, who sits a handful of chairs down from me.

"Thank you, Kate," Britton says as he fingers through the pages.

Kate nods and retraces her steps, taking up her own seat several chairs to my right. The group falls into a familiar silence as we await an address from our fearless leader. I snort at the thought and receive several sideways looks. I know where the real power here sits, and so does everyone else, but we are an organization of rules and traditions.

Several minutes pass before each folder is reviewed and placed upon the table. A show. He would have been briefed hours ago in preparation. Durian eyes several members before stating, "Nephilim target 19414 is deceased."

The table erupts into an indiscernible amount of side conversations.

I lean back into my chair. Target 19414 was a topic of conversation for months, one of our top priorities since the frequency of his feedings had accelerated at an alarming rate. The target in question is, was, a ghost who evaded every attempt to track. A rather impressive feat with the level of technology and abnormal skill sets we possess. The target was a rogue, more dangerous than its disciplined counterparts within the Nephilim Order. Every agent dispatched to investigate has disappeared. I thought tonight's meeting was to discuss a tactical change after several losses, which would see a transition of dispatching agents to a deployment of Praetorians.

"How the hell did that happen? This council was not informed the target had been identified, tracked, or that resources were allocated to eliminate the threat." The question comes from the opposite side of the table. All eyes look to Janice, Chief of Government Relations, then back to Britton.

She put words to my own thoughts. I'm happy the bastard is dead, but I had been salivating at the opportunity to do the deed myself, directly or indirectly.

Our members fear a unilateral decision was made, and they

want answers. I know Britton too well. He doesn't have the spine to take matters into his own hands, which is why he was voted into the position. A puppet swayed by the whims of whomever holds power at the moment. And that power is currently wielded by a bloc of members who will likely say nothing tonight.

Janice is one of the younger members of the court, shrouded in a degree of mystery that's discomforting, even for an organization built upon secrecy. Skin as dark as the air that surrounds us, and straight, black hair descends seductively down a toned back. I've worked with her many times in the past, before her promotion. She is a force of nature, demonstrated through years of leading special operations against nests of Nephilim. A position with a historically limited lifespan. Someone not to be trifled with.

"This was not the work of this organization." More murmurs from the table. "Two individuals, who have been deemed a Spear and Shield," the table erupts into louder discussions, "identified, tracked, and eliminated the target," he finishes, voice rising above all others.

Maximus Wright, Director of Treasury, leans forward, a couple seats down from me. "The target was hunted down and killed by two that were not our own? How is that possible? Who are they?"

"No, they are not ours. As for how that is possible, and who they are, I turn the floor over to Adam," Britton states, gesturing across the table. "Adam."

"Thank you, Lord Governor." Adam stands in a ten-thousand-dollar suit and graces us with a stern look.

Pompous, emotionless prick. A man presumably content with his position. I have found nothing more dangerous than a man with no ambition who openly declares a passion for servitude.

"The two in question did not knowingly work together.

Instead, they were brought together through the actions of the target. The Spear had been hunting the target for years, while the Shield became involved when his classmate was targeted by the Nephilim." A practiced pause. "Both possess heightened Essence."

"Target 19414 is presumed to have killed several of our agents. How did they manage to eliminate the target?" Britton asks.

My eyes shift between the two men. Britton is steering this conversation. Perhaps spineless, but not completely ignorant or incapable.

Adam doesn't miss a beat. "Neither are trained in wielding what they possess. And neither understand Essence. They are not part of another organization. A Discerner will need to verify, but I believe they were able to eliminate the target for two reasons: their Essence, individually, is more heightened that that of the Guardian, and they are somehow connected."

A volley of questions fire from all sides. Words are dangerous. Everything said possesses a meaning within a meaning or is at least perceived as such. Power ebbs and flows upon each word as much as any action. What Adam said has implications. Hopeful, but potentially dangerous.

"Fucking blasphemy," cries a voice louder than the others. A shared thought because the ruckus fails to subside.

A cane strikes the floor. "Enough."

I was wrong in assuming they wouldn't speak. This is about to get interesting.

A tall, slim man with hollow cheeks and rather slick hair stands. "Adam. Lord Governor. To claim that one, let alone two, possess a power greater than the Guardian is a...bold statement," Dimitri Volvander states first to Adam, who quickly finds his chair. Dimitri then turns to Britton. "I assume you were informed prior to tonight's gathering?"

Britton nods.

"Then you permitted the statement without a Discerner's conclusion."

"I did," replies Britton.

"Why?"

"Adam, although not a Discerner, is rarely wrong on such matters. And I felt the importance of communicating a likelihood of such great importance merited an announcement. I'm seeking this court's approval to move with haste. To transport the Shield and Spear to Alkira, where a Discerner is waiting to levy a judgment so that we might act appropriately."

I trace Britton's logic and find that I support his decisions, but I have a lot of questions. I keep those to myself for now. We've all walked into a powder keg, and I don't feel like serving as the spark. Sparks, or fodder, don't survive the blast.

It's impossible to read Dimitri. He will not overtly challenge Britton tonight. Only time will reveal his verdict. Britton exhales when Dimitri sits.

"What of the claim they are connected? That's a new one."

I have no idea who asks the question. A rare lapse in concentration, but I'm overly stimulated with the conversation between Britton and Dimitri. A conversation I'd usually believe staged, but Dimitri seemed different. Perhaps even surprised, which means there has been a shift in power somewhere. How or why is something I'll have to uncover carefully. I'm sure Kate knows. I smile at the thought of reconnecting, then shiver at what would likely happen later.

Britton nods to Adam, who remains seated as he says, "Their crossing is likely to be viewed as chance. However, after interviewing both separately, I believe their Essence brought them together. Either would have likely been killed taking on the target themselves. But, together, their Essence overcame the Nephilim. The statistical likelihood of two with such power living in the same generation is improbable, but two of such power coming together at precisely the appropriate time to vanquish a Nephilim is...well, as damn close to impossible as you can get."

Britton steps in before an argument of theory breaks out. "An interesting analysis. One that we will have to explore once the Spear and Shield are secured."

We are missing the bigger picture. "Those of heightened Essence are not attracted to one another. Are we sure one isn't an Eater?" I ask. "Only Eaters are attracted to Essence, which would explain the connection." The table falls silent. I look to Adam. "Their Essence could be from recent consumption. Perhaps the Nephilim are in civil war? It's not unprecedented. We do believe this target was likely a rogue."

Someone loudly spits, some contain laughs as others curse.

"My apologies, Lord Governor," I say. "I forget how distasteful the term Eater is to some in this court. What a noble collection of sophisticated socialites to discard a term used by those who actually fight the demons. Allow me to correct myself. Nephilim."

That elicits several jeers, and curses. Raine smiles at me. Old bitch does have a sense of humor I can relate to.

Britton silences the table with raised hands. "You done?" he asks.

I nod.

"Adam," Britton encourages. "A valid consideration, no?"

"I'm confident a Discerner will verify their Essence is natural, not consumed."

"So, we are to take your word that neither are our mortal enemy? We are talking about sending them to Alkira for fuck's sake. A place where our enemy could do irreparable damage."

"Need I remind you, Durian, that I have conducted such... preliminary reviews in the past. Even yours if I remember correctly. I am not wrong."

"This is different. I'm unconvinced there isn't risk."

"Understandable," replies Britton. "We will dispatch Praetorians with their transport. Does that reduce the risk proportionally?"

I nod. "Transport them separately, several hours apart. A squad of Praetorians per transport. I'd like to tag along."

Britton isn't surprised. "The Praetorians are your charge, so that is your right to request. I approve as long as this court votes to move them into Alkira."

"And that they are transported separately," I state once more.

"Agreed," Britton answers.

"Hours apart."

"Yes," Britton agrees, exhausted from my interjections.

"Thank you, Lord Governor," I say with a nod.

"Adam," Britton says once again.

"Yes, Lord Governor."

"Before we vote, how do you suggest we proceed?"

Adam raps his knuckles across the table. "We will wipe Susan McGraff's profile from the FBI database, and all other databases. She will no longer exist. She has no social media presence, no family, and limited accomplices outside the FBI. The FBI will be informed that she was selected for a top-secret assignment, and to speak of her will result in imprisonment. We will most likely convey that she was killed during the special assignment in the months to come.

"Jacoby Talavan is currently recovering in a hospital. Once healthy, we will inform all appropriate parties he is being transported to a hospital that specializes in trauma rehabilitation. We are currently formulating a long-term absence strategy. Jacoby will either die by accident or suicide at the hospital.

"The termination of the Nephilim has already been resolved. We've coordinated with local and federal authorities to draft a press release that leaves no loose ends."

"Thank you, Adam," Britton states. "Thorough and logical,

as always. They have agreed to come willingly? Jacoby has accepted walking away from friends and family forever?"

"Susan agreed. Jacoby agreed to the transport, but we have not discussed the long-term plan. I feel it best to get him on-site before convincing him of the need for drastic action."

Britton turns to everyone. "The plan has been stated. The Shield and Spear are to be transported to Alkira under Praetorian guard." He looks to me, adding, "Separately. Several hours apart." He then turns towards everyone else. "There, a Discerner will determine their Essence origin and strength. If it is as Adam has presented, they will then face The Crucible. Objections?"

None are made.

I find Dimitri at the end of the table. He's saying something into the ear of The Shadow. I can't see The Shadow's face, but I imagine it's absent emotion.

I clear my throat, looking between Adam and Britton, saying to both, "I hope you're right. I'll be pissed if this transport turns into a food truck."

ABOUT THE AUTHOR

D.T. Pierce is an entrepreneur and hobbyist of sports cards, fitness, golf, reading, writing, and more if the day were longer. After a decade as a manufacturing professional, the seed that would become his writing career was planted while reading Red Rising, where his mind ventured into a dangerous place – the construction of his own, far-off worlds. Beautiful Torments, and the Torments series, is built upon his personal encounter with a mysterious dog.

He lives in Warsaw, Indiana with his wife and two children. Follow D.T. Pierce at dtpierce.com, or on Instagram and Facebook @dtpierceworld.

Made in United States
Troutdale, OR
10/25/2025

40714597R00173